Candice is a powerful executive with her whole life ahead of her. To take a break from the rigours of work, she sails to the orient alone as part of her dream vacation. Suddenly she is caught in an eerie and unnatural storm that shifts her in space and leaves her stranded in a bizarre land. She finds herself in a savage world where the two most rare and precious commodities are metal and human females.

Rescued from a primitive tribe by a team of salvagers, she is tightly bound and swiftly ravished. Candice discovers that the group intends to take her into one of the local towns for a swift auction at a very high price.

The rulers of the land intervene and confiscate her. They bring her to their huge Empire, where she enters their twisted palaces and finds a perverse culture dedicated to sexual servitude, bondage, and submission. The lords of the land have their expert slave trainers indoctrinate Candice, teaching her how to please them and how to take pleasure in her new caste as a debauched concubine. They employ techniques, acts, and positions that push the limits of pain and pleasure.

Candice excels at her lessons and soon becomes a valued possession, one that is vied for by the lords and envied by the other concubines. It is then that she learns the terrifying truth about their realm and how she came to be part of it.

Dragon Candy
Copyright © 2023 Talia Skye
ISBN: 978-1-4874-3583-7
Cover art by Martine Jardin

Published by eXtasy Books Inc

Look for us online at:
www.eXtasybooks.com

Dragon Candy
Dragon Candy 1

By

Talia Skye

CHAPTER ONE

The yacht swayed and the lullaby lap of ocean crests slapping against the hull began to rock Candice into a somnolent haze. The engines of the *Cassiopeia* chugged quietly to themselves, and it seemed that they were singing in time to the rhythmic motions.

Candice let her focus drift across the unblemished scene. The Pacific Ocean stretched to each horizon and no hint of land marred it. The raging orb of the sun reflected off waves and this forged great tracts of winking stars upon the uneven carpet of sapphire blue. No cloud perturbed the sky, and the air was warm from the caress of the sun.

The shade provided by the lounger's brightly patterned top warded off direct rays, but the reflection on the water provided more than enough golden light to tan her skin. Candice's body was completely naked, and her neck length bob of dark hair was woven up into a plait to keep it out of the way. There was not another human being within sight or sound, so she could happily work on a flawless tan.

The hours she'd spent networking in the company gyms had granted the side benefit of an elegant and sleek physique, one that was highly alluring to all eyes. However, Candice was a beast of business, and as such, she had little time for romance. She preferred the giddy high from destroying a rival, taking a company for a pittance, or brokering a multi-billion-pound deal. When compared to these passions, carnal pursuits such as coitus and masturbation seemed hollow and bland.

It was not as though she could not acquire a lover if she wished. Candice had icy blue eyes, smooth pale skin that contrasted her sable locks, and inviting lips that she often highlighted with vivid reds. The attractive set of her face was enhanced by the enticing curves and pert breasts that she often used to distract a rival or opponent. A sultry smile or sedate wiggle would sometimes throw them off guard and allow her to make the kill in their moment of hesitation.

Candice turned over, and with a sigh, she let herself sink into the cushions. She could ignore any control of the *Cassiopeia* because the sails were down and the automatic helm system was coping easily with the serene environment. This gave her all the time she required to relax.

The rigors of work were long gone. This vacation was well deserved and well earned, and Candice was relishing every blissful moment. Every pager, cell phone, fax, laptop, and organiser had been deserted before boarding. No one could reach her, and she could not be tempted into trying to reach them.

Lei's advice had been sound, and his providing of this specific route had ensured an easy and trouble-free voyage. She briefly wondered what he was up to right now, but then threw the thought away. This was a trip where she was to forget all about problems and responsibilities and simply drift upon the waters. All of the scheming and subterfuge was forgotten for the moment, and Candice drank in the silence and tranquil majesty. Soon the melody of the waves was steadily singing her into a shallow snooze.

A stark shift in the wind snatched her attention and caused her to lift her eyelids and scan the horizon in case a weather front was moving in. Only if the change were beyond the capacities of her computer pilot would she have to get up and do something, but all seemed well. The vault above was clear and peaceful, only the waters were different. They seemed to shimmer more wildly than usual, as though a ragged gust were chopping at the surface.

A piercing squeal poured from her radio. It made Candice squeak in shock and alarm from its sudden blaring intensity. The awful noise continued to rend the silence and pain her ears.

Clapping her palms to her head as protection, she jogged for the device to see what was wrong. Candice stopped dead in her tracks upon witnessing static electrical charge rolling along the surfaces of the boat.

The weaving crackling serpents of white light spat from all things metal and licked the surrounding deck. Current coursed along the guardrail and made the mast vanish amidst a maypole dance of crooked scintillating arcs.

Every hair on Candice's body stood to attention and her hairs rose even higher as the electrical storm continued to rage. The sight was both awe inspiring and terrifying.

Her inability to rationalise the source left her mortified and afraid, but also intrigued. The cloying stink of ozone assailed her nostrils and made her gag from the sheer ferocity as the charge tickled and then swamped her senses.

Candice strengthened her resolve with a hearty laugh, and as her fear passed, she became enthralled by the sight. Only the sudden tearing punch of a maelstrom gale drew her from the captivating phenomenon.

The tornado buffeted the craft with high velocity winds. They slapped her to the deck and started to push her along. Candice found herself heading overboard and into the seething mire of energy that raged without. It was a vortex of lightning that almost eclipsed any view of the ocean.

With a frantic cry, she cast an arm out and clamped her fingers about a railing. The gale still tore at her with forceful tugs, and Candice shrieked as electrical forks played along everything that was made of metal. The power wound like cyan snakes about mast and porthole, cable, chain, and railing. The dazzling tips bit along her arms and made her buck from their caustic attentions.

Candice fought the voltage and screamed into the howling hurricane. Suddenly, the roaring tune of the nightmare vanished as abruptly as it had come. A brief moment of free fall restored a less maniac breeze, and the boat landed on solid ground with a single crunching boom that completely shattered the hull.

The whiplash snap of the impact ripped her grip from its anchor, and a second later Candice slammed onto soil. The angry flare of pain down her entire right side forced the air from her lungs in a single croaking gasp.

With her sight flickering from the strike, she wheezed in uneven pants and fought the debilitating waves of pain and nausea brought about from the fall. Candice tried to rise, failed, and decided to lay still and recuperate awhile.

Candice restored her normal breathing, and the pounding ache in her flesh started to ebb slightly. She clutched her sore flank and scuttled aside before turning to survey the scene. She gave a sharp inhale when she saw just how absurd and impossible her relocation had proven.

Her boat now lay beached. It was lurching to one side and was semi-submerged in the dark brown crater its landing had punched. Crooked jigsaw splits and cracks leapt up across the hull from the lip of the pit and just from the damage she could see, her yacht was now a total wreck.

Despite all that had just happened, the first thing in her mind was the loss of her prized possession. It had taken her years to acquire *Cassiopeia*. Starting with a small boat, she had improved and upgraded it while she honed her sailing skills. Then she had sold that one for a significantly greater price before purchasing a larger boat in equal need of care. For eight years, she had continued this process, slowly gaining extra footage and space until she had achieved her ambition. *Cassiopeia* had satisfied her requirements of being capable of sailing across any ocean so she could at last fulfil her personal goal of reaching the Far East all by herself. It was a common sailing fantasy, and at the various marinas where it was circulated, her desire to follow it had steadily blossomed to obsessive standards. *Cassiopeia* was the last thing she had purchased before gaining her first vice presidency. It was the last thing she had ever needed to save for or struggle to afford.

Closing her eyes, she shook her head and tried to dispel what her mind told her clearly could or should not be. The boat was stranded, and despite her denial, the truth remained when she reassessed the situation.

Candice looked over her shoulder and found that she could no longer see the calm ocean. Instead, there were rolling plains that flowed to the horizons. The land was dry and parched, starved of water, and pockmarked with a few hardy desert bushes and grasses. No settlement or familiar landmark existed anywhere in sight. The air was still hot, but no cooling breeze washed over her, only a desiccating wind that was devoid of moisture. The tang of salt had also departed along with the sea.

Standing up with a little effort because of her stiff limbs, she dusted herself off and reached up to grab the guardrail. It took some effort, but she managed to haul her battered physique back onto the yacht.

Candice hooked a bare leg over the edge, rolled onto the deck, and immediately grimaced from the tumble upon her bruises. Nursing the throbbing contusions, she chose to limp below deck.

She gingerly rubbed her side and decided to move into the galley and check her stores. The need to undertake some sort of mundane task in the face of absurdity seemed paramount. Her mind was still reeling and denying acknowledgement of this clearly impossible occurrence. As far as her psyche was concerned, she had merely been shipwrecked. Further and deeper scrutiny of the situation was deliberately being ignored else she risk becoming hysterical.

Counting aloud in a strained parody of normality, she finally surmised that she had provisions enough to last her perhaps two weeks. Her journey had almost been complete and her arrival in Japan had been a few days away at most. The major port of Yokohama would give a fresh city in which to play, plus proximity to Tokyo so she could easily visit it should the whim take her.

The chances of supplementing her provisions from the lands without were slim. The terrain looked inhospitable and unforgiving of trespassers.

Returning towards the deck, she stopped at the radio and stared at it. She hoped that it would speak and ease her subdued angst. When nothing save static came from the instrument, she slowly reached out and turned the channel dial. She flicked from channel sixteen and moved through the myriad frequencies in search of life.

Hope filled her soul when she stumbled upon dialogue in the last backwater channels. Delighted, she listened in on the faint and unusually weak signal. It sounded like Japanese, but the dialect was strange and unfamiliar. Candice took the handset and entered the conversation. She hoped that they also spoke English, or at least some Japanese she was vaguely familiar with.

The two individuals became extremely agitated and the angry tones in their voices gave sudden cause for concern. When she addressed them in the fragmented Japanese she had been encouraged to learn for business dealings, the conversation suddenly ended and the transmission was cut off at the source.

Flicking onward, she found other signals. All of them were

in the same obscure dialect, and all of them were weak and barely audible. Each proved highly belligerent before they terminated their broadcast because of her interruption.

Exasperated at this failing, she followed the steps back onto deck and took down her binoculars before absently lacing the thong over her neck. Upon raising them she gave a tut, and then sighed. The performance of an action to stop them falling overboard now seemed a ludicrous precaution.

Candice gazed into the eyepieces. She focused and panned across the land, but she spied nothing even after completing a full circle. Candice sagged with an exasperated groan.

"Hello!" she bellowed. "Can anyone hear me?"

The words echoed across the plains and faded into silence. Candice let the binoculars hang between her breasts and cupped her hands about her mouth before hollering another greeting. There was still no response.

"Where the hell am I? Is there a good hotel around here? Where is the English embassy?" she shouted at the top of her lungs, mocking her solitude and trying to stay positive.

Candice returned below and slouched down into her slender bed. She hauled the thin blanket over her head, closed her eyes, and prayed that it would all go away when she woke up. Just in case someone turned up, she slid into her one-piece swimsuit and then jumped back under the covers.

Why had she listened to Joseph? He had been the one to suggest the merits of sailing to Japan, of the challenge and fun of such a trip. His words and the detailed route he had provided had been instrumental in making her decision to finally use her vacation time and undertake the trip she had been putting off for years. Now that it had ended in ruin, it was clearly his fault.

What was she to do? Was this real? Maybe it was some sort of hallucination brought on by something she had yet to fathom. Riven with a blizzard of questions, her thundering thoughts slowly dulled over the hours until through sheer mental exhaustion she slipped into a light sleep.

Her dreams were tainted and dark from her predicament. The nightmares fed upon her situation and bestowed added terror.

Several times, she awoke and thought that she was upon the waves again. The recall of her accident quickly banished all the pleasing notions that the strange event of being left landlocked was a product of mere fevered imagining.

CHAPTER TWO

Awakening with a start, Candice thought that her ship was being boarded. Her mind had left her with an impression that strange and eldritch beasts were scrabbling at her vessel, exploring this alien craft and seeking its owner.

She wiped the beads of sweat from her brow and slouched back into her pillow. When she closed her eyes, her heart began to steady and ease back from a racing pulse. A soft creak upon the deck had her eyes jerk open. It seemed that her dream had incorporated hints of reality. There really was someone on board, and now that she was listening properly, she could hear their soft measured tread as it crossed her boat.

Candice considered what choices she had. Perhaps she should offer a greeting? But what if they were hostile? She had no means of defence on board save improvised weapons.

Sliding cautiously from her mattress, she silently crept out and past the galley. Candice removed a sizeable carving knife from a drawer and kept her motions slow and steady so as to make as little sound as possible.

She could still hear sedate motions on deck, and it was this stealth and their use of the cover of night that made her malaise rise. If they were friendly, they would have called out to see if anyone were aboard and used lights to see what they were doing. Their very nature as silent trespassers in the shadows indicated that their purpose was nefarious.

Knowing the layout of *Cassiopeia* by heart, she closed upon the stairs that led to the aft deck. She pondered whether she should slam the hatch and lock it. If she barricaded herself within, she could seal the threat outside.

The clear sky showed a vault of stars and the large, silvery moon. Its familiar looking face was a welcome sight. For a moment, her panic ebbed, but then a wrenching tear filled the air as something was pried free from her boat. The item gave up its bolted hold with a final sharp snap.

The sound of violence made Candice flinch, and it settled her decision to lock herself away from the intruders. Her battlefield was the boardroom, courtroom, and the Internet. Her weapons were legal precedence, cash, verbal duelling, and inside information. She had no skills at brutish physical confrontation.

Stepping closer, she reached up to haul the overhead hatch along. With that in place, she could slam the small door shut and fix their latches with the padlock.

The pale skin of her extended arm seemed to glow in the moonlight, and it proved all the fiercer a contrast when a dark reptilian hand snatched her wrist. Small scales flowed onto a wiry forearm and there were three stubby fingers that were each tipped with a curved claw and a vestigial thumb. The nightmare entry of such an inhuman appendage made her shriek in alarm. Candice's arm flashed up and the blade etched a red gash in the tough flesh. The digits sprang open, and a hissing gasp issued from above.

Tottering away, Candice held the knife up in front of her. Her heart was stamping out a fearsome beat, her breath was icy and uneven, her eyes were wide, and they were full of fear. Candice continued to back up and now gripped the blade in both hands. The metal winked in the dim light as her trembling hands made the tip quiver unsteadily.

A humanoid form dropped down from the hatch. It landed at the foot of the stairs and folded into a tensed crouch.

Submerged in the shadows, she could not make out any features, and for a moment she prayed that the hand she had seen was merely a glove or piece of costume designed to frighten and intimidate.

The creature arose with a soft exhale. The silhouette of a thick tail wound out as its hunched form lifted into the moonlight. The soft beams revealed the head of a lizard. The elongated head was craned forward on a stout neck and dark unblinking eyes were fixed upon her. Its long snout was filled with tiny, pointed teeth that sparkled in the light.

A soft clatter drew her sight to its neck where she saw a necklace of crude bones. Candice spied a pierced humanoid ear amongst the collection and immediately turned on her heel so she could flee for her life. The grisly trophy confirmed that they were intent on homicide or mutilation.

Candice threw open her cabin door, jumped through, and slammed it shut. She leaned against it and threw the feeble latch before she started to retreat further into the shadows. Reptilian feet moved past a porthole. Then the sound of more scampering crossed the deck above her.

With a petrified whimper, she sank down, realising now just how many of these monsters were on board. Candice knew that by entering the forward cabin she had effectively cornered herself because no exits left the chamber.

Candice considered that perhaps the intruders were wearing costumes, because surely they could not be real. Nevertheless, even in the dim light, she could tell the difference between latex sculpture and real flesh, between papier-mâché and genuine scaled skin.

A punishing impact rocked the door, and it barely held. A second snapped the lock and the door flew open to jar violently against its hinges. The creature she had wounded stood and scanned the room. It picked her out of the darkness in an instant while two of its fellows stood behind it.

The beasts closed in, and their visage made them seem like demons from the darkest abyss. The sight filled Candice with a cold dread that gnawed at her bones. With a shriek, she sprang up. Waving the knife, she ran for the door and sought to drive them apart so she might make a run for freedom.

The lead monster skipped aside from her passage. The other two, being slightly slower to respond, failed to move as quickly. One of them sustained a graze to the shoulder from a whistling slash of Candice's knife, while the neighbour ducked down and kicked into her ankles with a brutal sweep.

Candice's feet were taken from beneath her. A pulse of white ran across her vision as she struck the carpet with a harsh thud. The impact forced her to spend all her breath in a pained croak, but she managed to maintain her grip on the knife.

Ignoring the injury, Candice fought to rise. The fear-induced adrenaline flow was keeping her pain in check, and instinct was now completely ruling her mind.

A clawed foot stamped onto her wrist and pinned it to the floor as gnarled digits tried to pull her weapon from her grasp. Candice yelled in mortal jeopardy and mashed her fist on the dense flesh of the foot. Trying to get it off, she bucked and jolted in order to slip free.

There was a whistle of air, and three lines of fire crossed her back. The scratches drew blood with the swipe, and they ploughed delicate furrows through her skin. As she released a scream of suffering, the knife was torn from her, and two hands clamped a tight hold about her neck. A tug hauled her straight into the air, and she hung from the creature's grasp with her toes barely touching the floor.

The blank gaze of the beast was almost lost beneath a knotted frown, and it snarled as she pawed vainly at the strangling grip. One hand let go and returned as a balled fist that sent knuckles dancing across her temple. The impact jerked her head aside and dazed her so severely that she could offer no resistance to its next vindictive action. With a whirling turn, the monster threw her into the wall. A brittle crunch sounded, and it was followed by a soft crumpling thump as Candice folded into a slack heap, her consciousness expelled by the collision.

CHAPTER THREE

Awareness returned with great reluctance. Her subconscious knew that if she awoke, it would open her mind to even greater stresses, ones that it had no desire to experience.

The dark shades of blackout shifted onto the realm of the night sky, and the throbbing pound of her bruises and cuts arose to afflict her stirring flesh. A straining pain filled her limbs, and as her mind deciphered the strange feelings, she opened her eyes to find herself spread-eagled in the air. Each limb was tied to a squat wooden post by a mesh of vines. The makeshift restraints were splaying her about one yard from the ground.

The vile creatures were all around her. The group was working together to ferry splinters of wood from her boat and arrange the shattered planks and poles beneath her. As realisation dawned, Candice screamed in abject panic. She screeched into the night as the prospect of being roasted alive was fully realised.

Straining against her bonds, she howled and hollered. Candice begged and pleaded as the impassive group continued to build their pyre.

Once the bonfire was sufficient for their needs, they gathered about her in a circle as another of them stepped forward from the scaly ranks. This one was clad in tattered skins. The hides were painted with strange flowing symbols and adorned with teeth, small skulls, and brightly coloured feathers. In its hands, it held a long and slender tooth. The dagger-sized incisor was of gargantuan proportions. With a vicious yank, he tore free her swimsuit and left her bared beneath the weapon as he chanted words in a strange hissing tongue.

The beast lifted the tooth over her in ceremonial fashion. Candice closed her eyes tightly and muttered prayers of her own. Her breathing quickened as the cold tip reached down and touched her chest. She gave a whimper as the shaman began to etch lines of eerie runes down her torso, sanctifying the forthcoming meal with light scratches that did not pierce her skin but which left angry rosy lines. The bite of the tooth was painful, but it promised to give way to far worse anguish and so Candice was quickly howling for help. The subtle distress of being written upon and the terror of being cooked sent her into a delirium of travail.

The slow meticulous scratch travelled around in winding paths, assailing her skin and counting down the time until the pyre was lit. Candice screamed and sobbed. She begged and struggled to try to do something, to do anything to avoid her fate.

The monster stopped its work when it arrived at her stomach. Her torso now ran with trickling rivulets of sweat that dropped onto the unlit kindling as tears rolled down her cheeks and frenzied drool slid from the corners of her mouth. Her head lolled back and she gasped for breath.

Stepping back, the creature pointed down to the dangling human and the others moved in. Some grabbed her hair, and with makeshift blades that were formed from large curved fangs, they began to cut tufts away. Others placed themselves between her thighs and worked on her pubic hair.

Candice continued to bellow for assistance as she watched them stripping away her locks. It was a distressing sight, and it was also highly unnerving as she felt them stripping her loins of their protective fur.

Sometimes they were impatient and yanked a few stubborn hairs out. When the beasts plucked her, she shrieked in pitches that made her throat burn as fiercely as her furious scalp and loins. Her skin clutched valiantly to the strands, refusing to let go, and every root that they assaulted became a riot of anguish.

Squealing as they finished stripping her of follicles in the most brutal of ways, she sagged and wept with self-pity at the loss of the last strands. Her savaged body now sparkled with a thick sheen of sweat from her energetic response to the shearing.

It felt as though every muscle and joint had been dislocated from her fight against her bonds, but she found fresh energy when they lit the wood. The sudden flare of warmth licked about her back and made her jolt with new desperate intent. Candice wailed into the night for someone to save her.

To her utmost horror, the fires did not escalate but remained at a hideous low intensity. Their intent for a slow cooking of their prize meal promised to extend this horrendous ordeal for an eternity. Crying out as her skin heated under the attentions of the fire, she bellowed and spat her hatred at them, to try to goad them into killing her swiftly. However, the lizard creatures had sat down to passively watch her. Their faces were bathed in the amber hues of the flames, their barren visages were fixed on her, and they all failed to respond to her pleas and insults. Exhaustion started to set in, and this reduced her cries to mere mewls and sobbing.

Occasionally they jabbed at her with their crude wooden spears. The flint tips painfully prodded her skin as they sought to revive her and stop her from passing out. The fires were starting to rise to the degree that she was beginning to feel serious pain welling in her underside. The heat lapped up between her legs and into her armpits, the more sensitive zones decrying the heat. She fought to bring her limbs in, to try to slip the vines but she could do nothing save buck and jolt.

Candice could not believe that this was happening to her. One minute she was a wealthy powerful elite executive enjoying an ocean trip, next she was an agony filled captive of inhuman monsters in a desolate land.

A chorus of whistles filled the air. They were followed by deep moist crunches as a flock of wooden arrows flew into the light and embedded themselves in the squatting diners. Some of them jerked back after having been slain by a missile. Others grunted and sprang for their crude spears or clubs as a fresh volley howled inward. Ignoring the wounds they received from the bolts, the monstrous creatures charged their attackers without pause or hesitation.

The sounds of hand-to-hand combat issued from the darkness. Candice could not see what was happening because her position in the source of the light was blinding her as to who her prospective saviours might be. Hissing death cries were accompanied by human shouts of distress. It was a sound that had Candice screaming for them to help her.

Silence fell after a few moments. Candice clenched her jaw and strove to subdue her cries as she strained to gain some insight about who were the victors. It was not easy to stay silent. The rolling waves of heat encompassing her body were still driving her insane with suffering.

A human male stepped into the weak light of the fire. His long brown hair was tattered and locked beneath a leather hat with a wide brim. His body was clad in loose clothes with a long leather overcoat laid over them. His rural attire was weather worn and bore numerous stitch marks from repair in addition to other scuffs and rips. The clothing was primitive — blend of tanned skins and roughly woven cloths.

In his hands, he held a blood-drenched sword and a wooden crossbow. Everything upon him pointed to truly backward origins, yet he wore a pair of army issue combat boots, plus there was a fighting knife buckled along the outside of his left leg, and dog tags hung about his neck. Upon scrutinising him further, she could see stripes of rank upon the arms of his coat, but the gold insignia was dusty and faded. Candice wondered if this man really could be from the military, because his face was haggard, stern, and forged into a perpetual sneer that melted the instant he saw Candice.

"Hey! You guys! Over here!" he roared with a distinct American accent.

Candice gave a sob of joy as he ran over and began kicking dirt over the weak fires. He dropped his sword and yanked free his smaller blade. The stranger then immediately began to saw at her bonds, but despite an obviously keen edge, the blade was having trouble with them. Despite the delay, the fading of the heat on her body was an intense relief for Candice.

"Damn Bonjitt vines. Tougher than goddamn steel cable," he cursed softly, and then started to apply more brawn to the task. After a few more saws at the vine, he paused and looked around, wondering where his forces were.

"Hey! Stop fucking about and get over here!" he roared over his shoulder as he returned to the task of freeing Candice.

"Thank you, oh thank you, thank you," said Candice with imploring gratitude and fresh streams of tears.

Other men ran from the night, and their manner of dress was akin to the first. The group were laden with small pouches and bags. Their clothes were old and decorated with personal trinkets. Each face was hardened by the elements to resemble tanned leather, and their wild manes of hair were held at bay by hat or headscarf. They looked a little like some mode of post-apocalyptic cowboy, and each of them bore a spear, while some had a crossbow or bow as a secondary armament. A couple of them were marked with rank, and all of them were adorned with US issue dog tags.

As they freed her, she could hear them talking. Their voices were tainted with the tone of various Stateside origins, but the accent was subdued and held at bay by the encroachment of numerous other influences. Candice's pondering as to their background vanished as their words chilled her, and in her enfeebled state, she could not respond to the statements that made her heart flutter.

"I don't believe it! Dude! A woman. A real, live woman!"

"Oh we've struck pay dirt here, guys. I told you it was worth nailing them lizards. I tell ya, my instincts never fail," announced the leader, who then cradled her arms as her legs were set free.

"And those idiot scaly freaks were going to just kill her? Don't they know what one's worth?" asked one of them. The younger man was staring down at her while he removed his hat to wipe his brow free of the sweat of combat.

"They know, all right. That's why they were going to eat her. Those dumb ass monsters think our chicks are sacred."

"To them, or us?" queried the youth.

"Us, retard. Christ, you're an idiot, Erin," interjected another as he started to scavenge amongst one of the creature's meagre belongings. Others had acquired several rough sacks from the foe, and they were currently sifting through the contents.

The slurred youth cast an insulting single finger in his direction and replied as though to dispute the questioning of his intellect.

"So, they were trying to dig at us by eating something sacred?"

"No, they think eating something gets them its power," said their leader with an irritated sigh.

"So by eating her, they gain what they think we worship?" asked Erin.

"Of course."

A mocking round of applause for his conclusion issued from the shadows. The enlightened man took a bow with a sneering grin of derision before frowning and turning back to the leader.

"Wait a minute. How the hell did you find this out, Cap?"

"I was talking with that lizard tracker we met in Berniesburg. Told me all sorts of stuff about his tribe after a few drinks. I thought it would be handy to get some actual info on them, seeing as we were entering the Wild Lands."

Another man strolled past the youth and slapped him on the shoulder in a mock chastising fashion before he looked over the nearby bodies for signs of anything of value.

"So while you were getting robbed blind by that card shark from the Southern Wastelands, the Cap here was taking care of business."

When Candice was freed of her bonds, they threw out a blanket and laid her down. They stared at her with awe and watched as she twitched from acute shock.

"She's pretty badly burned. You think she'll make it?" asked one.

"It's only superficial," announced their leader. "The soot's making it look way worse. She'll be fine. Ge-"

The words were interrupted as another of the warriors ran onto the site. He was panting and his voice was shaky from disbelief and excitement.

"Captain, there's a fucking yacht just over the ridge. A yacht! A new one! A real beauty."

A numbed silence fell as though they had found a treasure beyond description. The impact of the discovery was broken as their leader began to snap commands with a practised ease.

"Okay, you dogs, get the hell over there and strip that fucker for every scrap of the hard stuff that you can carry. We ain't got long before the Mitama'll be storming in here to get it. Come on, move it!"

The sound of frantic sprinting and joyous whoops and cheers started to fade as they charged for her vessel. The Captain knelt down beside her and spoke with severity. His voice was angry, but his eyes betrayed fear.

"When did you arrive? When?" he demanded, but Candice could barely move. Her throat was parched and her voice was lost from the grating effects of her screams.

"Tell me, you stupid bitch! We could all end up dead!" he hissed.

The man shook her so violently that her wounds returned to haunt her, making her croak and almost swoon. He calmed down, let go, and offered his question so it might be easier for her to answer.

"Yesterday?"

Frightened of what he might do if she did not reply, Candice managed to sedately shake her head.

"No? Today?"

Candice managed a nod. The man scowled and thought for a moment. He calculated in his mind before rising to broadcast his decision.

"Right, you maggots, she came through the Vortex today. We've got perhaps two days before the Mitama get here from the outpost, so I want us out of here by noon at the latest so we can cover our tracks."

"Are you sure, Captain? Surely we should just take the woman. If we get the metal, they'll follow us for sure," came a faint, yelled reply.

The sound of them scavenging on her boat was ringing out in the background. Candice felt that she should protest this looting of her possession, but she was too grateful to be alive to care. Besides, Cassiopeia wasn't going anywhere anymore.

"You want to be rich don't you, Corporal?"

"Of course, but what's the point of being a rich stiff?"

"Stop crying. They'll never get us if we hide our tracks. All we have to do is off-load the loot a bit at a time when we reach the town, and it's not a request, it's an order! So get moving!"

Candice meditated upon their words to distract herself from her residual pains and mental discord. She knew the word Mitama. It was *essence*, the emanation of a God or spirit. They held this *Mitama* with great fear, suggesting it was some sort of martial force that sought metal. But why metal? Why was such a worthless commodity so precious to these people? Dwelling on the group's visage, she had only seen metal in its essential forms—as tips for spears, swords, knives, and the barest parts for the crossbows. No other hint of it had been seen, no badges, buckles, zips, nothing. Their dog tags now resembled the gold jewellery of pirates, a reserve of wealth worn for emergencies, to at least ensure a decent burial if nothing else.

In addition, why were live women so precious? What did they intend to do with her? Why was she so valuable? What was this Vortex? If it was the electrical storm that had dumped her here, then was it artificial, or was it a natural occurrence? Maybe it was something like the Bermuda triangle, but that was stupid. The triangle had been explained away by rationale science. She was fishing into absurdity.

The turmoil of unanswered mysteries was ended as the Captain took her arms and pulled them behind her back. Too weak to resist, she felt a sheath of leather being slotted over the limbs. The triangular sleeve was pulled up so that her hands emerged from the point and the wide base was stretched between her upper arms. Laced straps were flung over her shoulders and crossed between her breasts before they were fastened back on the sleeve.

The Captain put a boot onto the sheath and tightened the laces until her arms were pulled toward each other and her shoulders coursed with mayhem. Candice gave a long moan of discomfort as she was restrained.

Tying off the laces, he lifted her ankles up to her snared wrists and caught them within leather restraints. The knots were placed out of her reach, and the bonds hog-tied her in a twisted pose, one where she could barely move. Any attempt to straighten her crooked legs now increased the pull at her shoulders.

"After all those times we've secured an outlaw with this stuff, I never thought I'd have the good fortune to be lacing a chick into this. Someone up there must have really taken a shine to me."

He finished his work with a couple of wide straps that encircled her shins and thighs to pull them even closer together. Another strap embraced her chest and rode beneath her breasts to drag her sheathed arms into her back.

With his prisoner secured and turned into a neat immobile package, the Captain sprinted off into the night to join his men in the salvage operation. Candice was left to her worries and concerns and the utter befuddlement that the conversation had infected her mind with.

Despite her oppressive bondage, Candice managed to find solace in sleep, and when she finally stirred, the sun was rising from the horizon. She closed her eyes and tried to banish the view. If she tried hard enough, perhaps she could banish the illusion of her trammels, the dead lizard creatures, the smouldering pyre, and the sounds of her yacht being dissected. When they refused to fade, she wept quietly to herself.

The sound of heavy hoof-like impacts made the ground tremble, and Candice looked up to the nearest ridge. She closed her eyes and muttered to herself as what she saw defied belief.

The Captain was riding a monstrous form. The Dinosaur was a quadruped with heavy trunk-like feet and a short tail that brushed the ground. It had a bony face with a horn on its beaked snout and deep-set eyes. It had a series of horns extending back from its skull to protect the neck and attached to these were a set of reins. The Captain sat in a large saddle that had many hefty sacks and bags attached all around the beast's flanks. Several poles lifted up from around the saddle to hold the shade from Candice's lounger. Other stitched curtains were stretched between the vertical poles to create a small den on the creature's back.

The beast plodded along and shook the earth beneath Candice with its immense tonnage. The Captain hauled the reins and brought it to a halt. Sliding from the saddle, he clambered down the huge torso and dropped to the dry soil.

"You must have been quite the wealthy broad back on the other side," he commented. "Kind of ironic that a rich chick from there, is going to make me just as rich, right here."

"Where . . . Where am I?" she managed to say. "And why have you tied me up?"

Candice pulled at her restraints. The leather creaked but contained her successfully. She wanted to protest more vehemently but was afraid of angering her saviours. This was a bargaining process like any other. She had to stay calm, win their confidence, and gain information so she could better deal with the situation.

"Can't have you running off, sweetie. There's all sorts of other nasties out there. Those lizards are only one of them. Vicious brutes. Evolved from Dinosaurs like we came from apes or something like that. But I dunno, I'm a grunt, not a scientist."

"D . . . Dinosaurs?"

"Yep, like ol' Betsy here. She's a Styracosaur. Better temper than a Triceratops, you know, the ones with the horns and the bony frill rather than these spikes, " he said and patted the side of his titanic steed. "Seems they didn't get extinct-ified out on this side. Weird, ain't it? Still, you'll get used to it."

"What is this place?" she asked.

"Heard it called Pangaea once, but who knows? Huh, actually, who even cares?" he said.

The Captain moved in to check her bonds. He stepped from side to side and scrutinised the laces and knots.

"I'm, Candice, Candice Me-"

"Not interested, babe," he interrupted. "Let's try to keep this on a business level, okay? Nothing personal."

"What do you mean? What are you going to do to me?"

"Absolutely nothing. That's the point. You're worth a hellofa lot to those who can afford it, and I ain't been out here with the Dino-herds and dust scrounging for the hard stuff all these years to miss an opportunity like this."

"You're going to sell me? Why?"

"Chicks is rare. Whatever the Vortex is, it's attracted to metal. Pulls planes, boats, subs, anything through when it's up to full strength. Caught our cruiser about, oh, ten years back. Fortunately, we got dumped out here in the wastelands like you. Most arrivals end up in the Kami Empire. So we try to get by, those of us who are left. Anyway, mostly military stuff comes through, plus the odd passenger ship or plane. That means we've a lot of men, not a lot of women, which makes you quite the commodity, and one we'll sell to the highest bidder when we get to Karlville."

"Please, please don't sell me, I . . . I can help you,"

"How? You can't shoot, you can't fight, you're fresh from the world and were obviously a city gal. What use are you?"

"Pleeease," she whimpered as tears welled in her eyes.

"Don't worry, babe. You'll have it easier than us. While we fight, kill, swindle, rob, and scrounge, you'll get a nice rich pad again. Course, you'll be harem material, but hey, beats slogging out a living in this dusty shit hole," he said, and patted her bound arms.

"You can't do this to me! It's not right!"

"Don't let the dregs of the uniform fool you, toots. Uncle

Sam ain't here no more, so we're out for ourselves. The hard stuff and other valuables off your boat plus your sale'll set us grunts up for life. No offence, but it's us or you."

"Then keep the ship, do with it whatever you want. If it'll make you wealthy, it's yours. Just let me go."

"Well, why be rich when we can be really, really, stupid rich? Metal's rare here. It just don't really exist. People mine and pan for it like they used to go for gold and diamonds back home. So, you can imagine what the contents of your yacht'll fetch. Chuck your value on top of it and well . . . easy street at last."

"Look, I . . . I can –"

"I've had all the talk with you that I care to, babe. I've told you more than you need to know, and better than you deserve, so it's time to shut it," he decreed.

From his coat, he drew a spongy ball that he proceeded to force into her mouth. Candice struggled to stop him, but he pressed his fingers into her cheeks to part her jaws and ruthlessly crammed it into her maw. With her mouth packed with the ball, he then tied a belt around her head. The leather slipped between her parted teeth and held the bloated intruder in place so she could not eject it. She snorted and tried to push the gag out, but it refused to move.

"Up we come. We've a long ride, and the Mitama'll be on our asses all the way," he said.

The Captain lifted her up with ease and held her along his shoulders as he climbed back up onto the steed. She was placed in the rear of the saddle, and a couple of dense straps were pulled over her body and wrenched tight to hold her in position. Each breath revealed just how fierce their grip was, and Candice wriggled and pulled at her bonds.

Flicking the reins, the Captain turned the beast around and had it trudge back towards the yacht. Candice could see that every scrap of metal had been removed. Every cleat, every pulley, every bolt, rivet, guardrail, even the propeller and engine had been dismantled and extracted.

A number of the domesticated Dinosaurs were currently being loaded up with the loot. Their huge size and massive strength easily bore the items that would have crushed a horse and even made a lorry struggle.

"Are we done yet, Corporal?" asked the Captain.

"Just fastening everything down for the trip," replied one of the former soldiers.

"Okay, mount up, we're heading out."

The men immediately clambered into the saddle and steered the beasts after the departing Captain.

Through the rest of the day, they trekked across the land. Gagged and bound, Candice could do nothing save rest in the arms of her straps and wonder what her future was going to bring. She had always created her own destiny, always known what to do and where she was going. Now nothing was certain. Her skills, her talents, her luxuries, everything she knew was useless here. This was a brutal frontier world where only the strong survived. Civilisation was tenuous at best, and she was only valuable as property.

This world was almost bereft of metal. The strange hole that existed between this world and Earth dragged it through—mostly to the place that the Captain had mentioned with such fear. When it appeared elsewhere, she assumed this "Mitama" were sent forth to reclaim it. Therefore, this world had some sort of established Empire. Military vessels were treasure troves of steel, attracting the vortex and creating a distinct gender imbalance. The Dinosaurs had not been rendered extinct, and some had evolved into primitive humanoids. That meant that the Humans here were all from Earth or descendants thereof. With the coast of Japan so close, the first arrivals had to have been from there. That might explain the radio signals. Was this Empire, and this Mitama, of oriental heritage?

Her deliberations were interrupted when the belt around her head was removed and the ball drawn out. She licked her lips and gasped with relief.

"Here. Drink," he said, and offered a canteen to her.

"Come on, please, I-""

"Well if you don't want any then," he interrupted and started to push the cork back in.

"No! Wait!" she exclaimed.

He opened the top and presented it to her lips. She gulped down as much as she could before he took it away and re-sealed it. The Captain took up the gag, and Candice writhed and threw her head from side to side to stop him restoring it.

The Captain grabbed her head and held her firmly. His other hand started to shove it back between her lips as she burbled and fought to stop him. Her words were cut off and the orb was packed back into place before the belt was added.

The group continued to march across the land. Several times, Candice saw a member of the unit near to the side of Betsy. He was a young soldier with a dark bandanna about his head. Even though he was wearing a set of welding goggles to protect from the sun's glare, she could see that he often spent prolonged periods scrutinising her body. She sometimes saw him covertly massaging his groin as he did so.

Candice considered that if she could talk to him, she might be able to convince him to take her for himself and flee. She could escape from one of these ex-soldiers much more easily than from all of them.

"Shall we make camp?" yelled one of the men.

"No. We go all night. Stay awake, and stay alert. Anyone sees what we're carrying and they could try and ambush us."

"But Captain, I'm nuked. We were up all night stripping the boat."

"Then hop down and grab some Z"s, private. We'll move

on without you. Oh, and say "hi" to the Mitama for me."

There were no more objections. The Captain draped a blanket over Candice's restrained body to offset the chill of the night and they continued onwards. When morning came, whole areas of Candice's body were numb from her confinement. Her jaws ached terribly, and she was desperate to move. The impositions were driving her mad with frustration. She had never before been bound, never before been utterly deprived of motion and speech.

"Okay, there's a pond over there. We'll rest up for an hour or two. Let the mounts graze and drink. We'll take ten-minute shifts on guard duty."

"I'll get a fire going for some hot food."

"You want to draw an arrow to our position as well, shit for brains? Jerky'll do for now."

"Oh Christ, come on, Captain."

"We'll eat like kings for life if we make it, so stop griping and think of what's at the end of this run."

The column walked into an area where there were a few trees, some strange ferns, and a brief carpet of grass. They halted at the edge of a large pond and dismounted. The beasts were allowed to graze and drink, and the soldiers either set down blankets to sleep or took up sentry positions with their crossbows.

Candice was drawn down from her position and set at the water's edge. The Captain tied a thick collar about her throat and tied rope to it. He then lifted up a strut of bamboo.

"No trouble, or else!" he warned harshly. "Understand?"

Candice nodded fearfully as she stared with dismay at the cane. The Captain gave a nod of approval and set the weapon aside so he could unfasten her bonds. Her legs dropped out and started to course with pins and needles. She whimpered onto her gag as the sleeve finally released her arms.

Candice's limbs languished on the grass and could not

move because of their long containment. Tears trickled down her face as she endured the awful process of recovery.

"Okay, here you go," he said.

Candice opened her eyes and saw a plate before her. There was dried fruit, some vegetables, and some salted meats. It was possibly the worst meal her Epicurean palate had ever witnessed. Nevertheless, she was ravenous.

Despite how deplorable the quality of the food was, as soon as the gag was removed, she managed to move forward and quickly devour it.

"Get some water in you, too," ordered the Captain as he took hold of the rope that held her collar.

Controlled by her most pressing needs, Candice crawled over to the water and started to guzzle scoops with alacrity. When she had taken all she could, she flopped onto her back and stretched out. A tug to the collar brought her back upright.

"Right. Into the pond and get all that soot off you. I want you looking presentable when we hit town," he said.

"Can you take this damn collar off now? I won't run, I promise," she said with as much conviction as she could.

Candice gave a startled cry and dropped back. She clutched the burning stripe of vicious feeling that now pounded along her thigh. The cane returned and assailed her exposed buttock. She gave a squeal, curled into a ball, and held her body as the ghastly effects continued to torment her.

"Any more requests?" he said firmly.

Candice shook her head from side to side while she grimaced and waited for the ferocity of the strokes to pass. As soon as she was able to move, she pulled herself into the water, if for no other reason than to deny him a target.

Kept on the end of a leash, Candice moved deeper into the chilly pond and started to wash away the grim, sweat, and soot. The swipes she had gained from the cane were already rising into short trenches and were tender to her every touch. The Captain lounged on the bank and watched her carefully with the cane in one hand and the rope held in the other.

"Now there's a sight I ain't seen in a while," chuckled one the troops.

"Keep your fucking eyes on the land. This ain't no peep show," growled the Captain, giving a yank to draw Candice towards the bank.

The sentry gave a huff and turned around. Keeping his crossbow cradled, he continued to watch the horizon.

"Can I at least have some clothes? That way I won't distract your men," she asked.

"No, you can't. I don't want your attire getting in the way of a good sale. Don't forget your ears, either," he added.

Candice lowered into the water and attended her lobes and the swirls of her ears. She stood up with cool streams of water running down her skin and dripping from her breasts.

"Clean enough for you?" she asked petulantly, and took a salacious stance to bare herself to him.

"It'll do," he stated and started to reel her in.

Candice was starting to seriously question whether the Captain was straight, or at least if he had any other emotions in him other than greed. When she was back on the grass, she settled down on all fours and then dropped onto her side.

"I'm going to take a quick nap. But I'm a real light sleeper. So any bullshit and . . ."

Candice jerked her legs out and gave a holler as the cane was brought down to cross both of her exposed buttocks. The flesh gave a ripple and then the lucid stripe erupted with pain. She grabbed her cheeks with both hands and dropped her head to the grass. Candice quivered and ground her teeth in endurance.

"Got it?" he asked.

Candice gave a vague nod, and then her head leapt back

up from the ground to release another long howl of dismay. The cane had caught the backs of her upper thighs and bestowed the most excruciating travail yet.

"I asked you something!"

"Yes! Yes! I understand!" she exclaimed.

"Right, then," announced the Captain.

The man removed his sword and knife and set them by his side. Leaning against a tree, he pulled his hat down over his eyes and relaxed. Candice lay quaking on the grass.

She held the fresh welt and gently caressed the tender flesh as the skin paled and rose before being surrounded by an angry hue. When she was sure that the Captain had drifted off, she moved into a slim patch of sunlight and cuddled up to her own body for comfort. She was collared, punished, shipped like an inanimate toy, and destined to be sold. She could not handle this situation. She was way out of her depth. She just did not have the faculties to cope.

With her eyes clenched shut, she tried to picture society functions, garden parties with senators, lords, and ministers, picnics in private gardens, anything to stop from dwelling on what was happening to her.

The sound of the great beasts tearing up great bushels of grass and chomping on them was accompanied by the sound of unearthly insects and the occasional subdued conversation between the sentries.

"Okay, fill up them canteens, we're out of here," bellowed the Captain.

Candice saw that the man had risen, straightened his hat, and was curling up the excess rope to her collar. His announcement had roused Candice a little, and then a stern yank to the rope made her flop over and brought her fully awake.

"Come on, up!" he ordered.

Candice pushed herself upright and placed a hand over her

pussy and a forearm across her breasts. Her nudity before the Captain had been unsettling, but now that she was no longer bound and she could see the group packing up and flicking licentious stares her way, her nervousness was growing. As she stood up, she felt a sudden pressure within her and tightened her thighs together. Candice looked around, trying to locate a private spot to relieve herself.

"What's your problem now?" he asked with an exasperated sigh.

"I . . . I . . ." she began, and found great difficulty with the words. How could she actually be made to ask to do this?

"Well? What?" he demanded.

Candice moved a little closer to him so she could whisper the words and not broadcast the fact to the whole group.

"I have to go."

"You're going all right. To town. Like I said. Moan again and I'll gag you!" he snarled.

"No, I mean, I . . . I have to *go*."

"So? Go on then," he stated bluntly.

Candice looked around the area with mortified alarm.

"What? Right here? I can't!"

"Suit yourself then," he replied with a dismissive tone and started to head towards the steed.

"Okay dammit! Okay. I'll . . . try," she hissed.

The Captain stopped and turned around. Holding the rope, he folded his arms across his chest and leant against a trunk. Candice could find little concealment so had to move behind a pathetically small shrub. She squatted down and tried to relax. Looking up, she found the Captain still staring at her with an amused smile on his lips.

"Do you have to watch?" she enquired venomously.

"And trust you not to try something? I'll count to ten. If you ain't going by then, tough."

Candice closed her eyes and her jaw flexed with animus at

this constant derogation.

"One . . . two . . . three . . . four . . ." he announced.

Candice fought to repel her anger, because it was making her tense and she needed to relax if she was to succeed. She tried to drop her barriers, but the exposure and the feel of the collar around her neck and the welts on her rear were not easing the task.

"Five . . . Six . . ."

She pictured flowing streams, waterfalls, running taps, anything to try to assist her. If she did not handle this now, she might not have another opportunity until nightfall.

"Seven . . . Eight . . .

Candice imagined dams bursting as she concentrated on relaxing her muscles. She prayed that her body just comply and stop being so stubborn. She had to go. Why was it being so damn obstinate?

"Ni . . . Ah, there we go."

The sound of running fluid sounded and Candice continued to keep focused on her task while hoping that she woudn't tense up again and fail to finish. The flow dwindled and finally stopped.

"All done?" he asked.

"Yes," she muttered.

"Sure?" he enquired.

"Yes!" scolded Candice, and took one of the leaves from the shrub to wipe herself.

"Every drop?" he added with a nefarious smirk

"Yes! I said *yes*, you bastard!"

Candice dropped the leaves and stood up. Again, she tried to conceal herself a little, but after the spectacle she had just provided, it hardly seemed worth it. She flexed her fingers and absently scratched them.

"Itchy?"

"A little. Why? What do you care?"

"Never mind then. Oh, by the way, that's Bitchweed you just used. It's a weed, and a bitch if you get it on you. Bad choice of T.P., babe."

"What? You . . . Why didn't you warn . . . What'll it –"

He drew on the rope with a stern haul, and Candice had to perform a sudden leap to clear the plant else she stumble right through it. She staggered forward and dropped to her knees. The Captain gave another haul and as she grabbed hold of the rope to stop the brutal haul at her neck, she was brought to his steed. He tied the rope to part of the saddle and then approached her with some strings of cord and the cane between his teeth.

"What . . . what are you . . ." she began as she started to back warily up.

The rope twanged taut and stopped her retreat. The wrench on her collar distracted her, and the cane was free and flashing round to impact against her hip in an instant. Candice collapsed to the ground and raised her arms protectively as he stepped forward and hurled the weapon high to rain more chastisement into her naked nubile form.

The attack never came. Suddenly, her hands were grabbed and steered behind her. Before she could resist, she was rolled onto her front and a knee settled into her back. She cried out in protest, but by then the cord was already being tied about her wrists. She struggled and tried to get free, but he simply applied more weight to his leg. Candice was pinned down, and she felt him let go of her wrists. She gave a groan of distress as he grabbed her elbows and dragged them together. The cord was woven around them, and Candice begged him to stop.

The Captain got up and grabbed her upper arms. His brawny grip yanked her back up onto her feet and she flung her torso from side to side as she tried to shuffle free of the accursed bonds. Her breasts were thrust provocatively forward, and she had no means to shield herself from the eyes of others.

"Pleeeease, not like this. I'll behave. Just give me something to cover myself!" she whimpered.

"Right!" he growled, and immediately retrieved the gag.

Candice pulled back against the rope and tried to get away as he marched towards her. The Captain grabbed the rope and gave it a fierce haul that countered her strength and made her stagger recklessly into him. He grabbed her tight and presented the ball.

"No! No! I'll not ta—mmmmph."

The petition was cut off as he forced it back into her mouth and applied the belt to stop her ejecting it. When he had finished, he took hold of her with new strength. With her torso held under his arm, he went down on one knee for extra support and laid her across his thigh. The Captain then started to apply the bamboo strut to her rear and thighs. Candice kicked her legs against the ground and fought to writhe free of his powerful grip as the mordant stem whistled down and struck her skin. She screamed against the gag as burning lines were painted across her hindquarters. Finally, the chastising assault stopped and he pushed her off his thigh. She dropped to the ground and lay shivering from the rigours of her punishment. Her rear was resonating with effulgent misery and her fingers held meekly to the worst regions. Why was she being treat so harshly? She did not deserve this—she was a refugee here just like they were.

"Move out, boys!" he announced.

The Captain prodded Candice's quivering body with the cane. She gave a weak whimper and barely responded.

"And unless you want to be dragged, you'd better get up as well. You could do with a little exercise after being bound for so long."

Candice tried to rally her strength, but the attack of the

cane seemed to have depleted her vitality. It took enormous effort to get her knees under her, and even more to force herself upright. As soon as she had regained her feet, the rope jerked her forward when Betsy began to wander off.

Weeping in despondent misery, Candice walked after the Captain. Her rear was still pounding from the effects of the cane, and her jaws and shoulders were again aching from the effects of restraint. Her nakedness was also a terrible bane, and the bonds prevented her doing anything other than stumbling after the beast with her body wantonly exposed to view. How could he do this to another human being?

She gave a whinny of complaint and skipped from foot to foot as her soles suddenly moved from the sparse greenery and onto the hot blasted surfaces of the plains. It took a few minutes before she had adjusted to their heat, and her anger flared as the others laughed at her predicament.

As she was made to saunter along, her face became red with humiliation as the other men openly moved closer to comment on her physique and leer and blow her prurient kisses. Candice was soon trembling with suppressed fury.

A distraction started to gradually rise in the form of an irritating itch in her fingers and between her legs. The annoying presence started to get worse and was not relenting, in fact, it was getting more intense.

Candice started to give the odd convulsion as the itching came in sudden waves to her pussy. She scuttled forward and rolled her hips with her thighs pressed tightly together. She gurgled onto her gag and gave pips of distress when the itch returned with ever increasing potency. The leaf had left some sort of sting, and the villainous Captain had said nothing.

The effects were driving her insane, because the itch could not be attended. She could scratch the affected fingers and ease the gnawing presence, but her pussy was unavailable to her. The itch started to become a brief stab that made her fold at her middle and cry out. A tug to her collar as the rope was drawn taut gave Candice the choice of falling over or charging forward to catch up. When she did so, the rapid movement of her legs only made the effects double in intensity.

"What's up, hot tits?" chuckled one of the men.

"Doing a little dance for the boys?" asked another.

Candice glared at them with rancour and then arched up and back down as another series of itching attacks chewed on her tender pudenda. The men laughed aloud at her travail.

"Bitchweed, right?" scoffed a voice.

Candice was no longer looking up to see who was talking. She needed to keep her entire attention on walking and maintaining her fortitude against the terrible irritant.

"Of course, could be worse. That "tard Swenson, for instance."

"Oh yeah. That skinny tool actually tried snacking on a few, didn't he?"

"Hey, remember when those puke jarheads we joined up with used it to wipe their redneck asses?"

"They were bouncing around like pogo sticks after that one."

"What about that one who tried to wash it off in that stream . . ." said one, his words trailing off as he succumbed to laughter.

"And didn't know it was full of Rippyfish!" announced another amidst riotous guffaws.

"Cured his ass ache, all right!"

"Took it off to the bone!"

The men laughed heartily for long minutes as Candice continued to suffer. One of them wiped the tears from his eyes and calmed his chuckles.

"It's okay, jugs. It wears off soon enough."

Candice fixed him with an indignant glower and continued to try to endure.

The stiffness in her legs and body faded due to the exercise, but as the day wore on fatigue began to set in. She was very fit, but marching naked and bound across this wasteland was more than she could handle. Her spasmodic reactions to the toxic plant had also sapped her energy reserves.

The itching was subsiding at an infuriatingly stolid rate, but her feet were starting to stumble and her senses were beginning to be affected. The hot sun beat down on her and her equilibrium started to fail her. She tripped several times but managed to regain her footing before she fell. The pain of stubbing her toe was maddening, because she could not stop to let the pain go away or even comfort the abused extremity. Even her most intense pulls to try to break free of the guide rope were not noticed by the huge monster drawing her onward to her slavery.

The column came across another watering hole. This one was far less giving than the last. The ground was dried and cracked, and only a meagre puddle remained at the heart of what was once a significant pool. The grass around it was thick and coarse and was dying from drought.

"We'll take five!" bellowed the Captain.

The steeds were allowed to settle and munch on the desiccated grasses while the riders stretched their legs for a moment. Candice lowered onto her knees and rasped for breath. Her leg muscles were hot, and they quivered from the long trek. Her thoughts were hazy and her skin was raw.

The sun was blocked, and this drew her attention. She opened her eyes to see the Captain towering over her. He presented a canteen and a warning.

"I'm going to ungag you now. If you make one sound, just one, you'll be gagged, and caned, and next Bitchweed we come across I'll rub it on your tits, all over your ass, and all over your pussy. Right?"

Candice nodded desperately as her face became a mask of

chagrin at this heinous possibility.

The Captain removed the belt and ball, and then offered the canteen. She drank her fill and arched her chest with a moan of delight as some of the flow slipped from her lips and ran down her naked chest. She dearly wanted to beg him to unfasten her raw arms, but his threat was too terrible to tempt.

He pushed the cork back in and slung the container over his shoulder. Candice jumped to attention and gave a hissed wail as he pinched a nipple and drew her back to her feet by the hold. She jiggled and battled to keep her words in check as he drew her to the beast and then bent her over at her middle. He nudged his shoulder into her stomach and then hoisted her up. With Candice over one shoulder, he climbed back up into the saddle and sat her in front of him.

Candice arched and gave a whimper as her welts protested at being used to support her. With her legs splayed across the cool leather, the Captain shuffled up close to her and grabbed the reins.

"Move 'em out!" he roared, almost deafening Candice in the process.

The journey commenced with the Captain leading the column. The wind whistled over Candice's exposed body and made her nipples rise as goosebumps rushed over her skin.

Candice stared out across the plains and felt almost secure for a moment. She locked on the feeling and tried to nurture it. She was in a new world. As absurd and impossible as it was, she had to face it with determination and bravery. To survive she had to adapt, and quickly. She had nothing to offer save her body, which was apparently precious and highly valuable. Her gender was her weapon, her defence, her single advantage. If she were to thrive here, she would have to exploit it. This squad of former soldiers had shown her that all previous allegiances were gone. Conscience was a fool's indulgence. Acting without regret for the sake of survival was the creed she had to live by, the mantra she had to recite every second of every day. Morality had to be given up.

Swallowing once for courage, she closed her eyes a little and let her fingers reach up and back. She brushed her captor's groin and with gentle motions started to caress him. The Captain did not object to her attentions and merely let her continue. His acceptance encouraged her, and she started to pick at the laces. It was not easy. The cords that held her arms had made her digits numb, and the Captain was not going to let them loose.

With a little work, she finally succeeded and reached in. Her hand took hold of his stiffening member and pulled it free. Candice filled her mind's eye with every arousing thought she could in order to assist her. With his cock in both hands, she started to shuffle her grip back and forth. The head of his manhood was resting on the small of her back, and the velvet skin traced delicate swirls upon her.

Candice moved slowly so as not to alarm him and brought her legs up so she might carefully shuffle around. Once reversed, she stretched her legs back down along the saddle and briefly considered orally serving him. However, the Captain was suspicious and would no doubt take offence, probably thinking it some ploy to horribly castrate him. With as sweet a smile as she could muster, she leaned back so that her arms were pressed into the saddle and her naked chest was arched up for him.

For a moment, she feared that he was going to ignore her, but then she felt his hands touch her hips. He held to them and drew her closer.

The detailed erotic conjurations that were racing through her psyche had managed to titillate her, and when his cock nestled between her lips, he found her damp with excitement. Clearly reassured by this response, he pulled her even closer.

41

Her pussy opened to him and devoured his full and extensive length.

Candice bit her lip and held back a wanton cry. The feeling of him charging into her bound and owned body was surprisingly intense. When he nudged to her deepest recesses she broke into a quivering fit and gasped for breath. Her legs curled up and locked around him. Her thighs tightened in fits as he began to shift his hindquarters and thus commence a dilatory ravishment.

Candice clenched her hands to the saddle as her eyes rolled and her mouth opened. His hands took hold of her breasts and began to fondle them. The brushes to her nipples were exquisite, and Candice gave long soft exhalations of rapture.

No word was exchanged between them. The Captain was taking advantage of prized and sublime female flesh, willingly offered. He was savouring every part of her, the texture of her skin, the curve of her hips, the softness of her breasts, the warm inviting channels of her pussy.

Candice was equally enamoured. She had begun her seduction as some sort of test experiment in her ability to adapt to this world. She had not even considered how pleasant it would be. Business and the acquisition of wealth and power had been her equivalent and alternative to sex. Such sources of pleasure were now gone forever. She was property here, a carnal plaything, an expensive bauble. Surrendering to that fate and in casting herself into the bliss of being owned was proving exceptionally rewarding.

After all her pain, her torment, her emotional battering, the feel of a hot throbbing cock slowly devouring her was awe-inspiring. Her whole body was alive with ecstasy the likes of which she had never known. She played her internal muscles and rolled them upon his shaft. The Captain gave a startled gasp and squeezed her breasts in his fists. The playful distress made her clench even more fervently to him and this escalated their dual pleasure still further.

Candice strained against her cords, but it was not to escape them, rather it was to revive their effects, to make her bound skin throb as she held her thighs to the Captain and gave herself to him with licentious frenzy.

He pulled on her assets and Candice complied with the goad. She hoisted her body up and he watched her as she straddled his manhood and rode herself against the twitching shaft. A broad grin of lewd indulgence crossed her features as she regarded his look of utter delight. It must have been so long since he had been with a woman. He had apparently pushed the possibility so far from his mind that he barely had a libido left. Now the sultry, elegant, and pampered body of Candice was attending his desires, and so his eyes were glittering with rapture. The revelation of just how much delight she was bestowing inspired a strange sense of benevolent generosity. After all that he had done to her, she only wanted to please him.

Candice licked her lips and moved one of her breasts towards his face. With such an offer, the Captain could not even pause. His cock gave a flick as it swelled with new arousal the moment her stiff teat brushed his lips. He licked the flesh of her breasts and tickled his tongue to her nipples before engulfing them. He moved from one to another, his mouth trying to do the work of two when he could not attend them fast enough to sate his need to taste her.

The Captain started to grow within her as orgasm loomed. Candice could also feel climax beckoning, and it was of a potency that she had never before encountered. Previous coitus had been fleeting, and was more conducted to access a new avenue of influence at work. Masturbation was a waste of her time, because why play with herself when she could be working on her portfolio? Now an orgasm was looming that threatened to destroy her. Already her pleasure was of such levels as to mock the zenith of every previous climax she had ever had.

Candice flicked to rigid attention and shook with strain as she distinctly felt the ripple of his ejaculation. The movement fired along his cock and poured into her pussy. His cock jolted with pulses of reflex as he clutched to her and crushed her in his arms. The stern clinch forced the breath from her lungs and stopped her drawing more. Candice wanted to screech to the heavens as she was submerged in a sea of excruciating bliss. The deprivation heightened the event, the feeling of such control, of such ownership of her delectable body. Her charms were a treasure that made the combined wealth of earth feeble by comparison. She felt like her ribs were about to collapse and her mind boil as he thrust into her and growled with endurance. His orgasm was long, and every second of it was fully explored before he let go and dropped back.

Candice copied his motion and flopped away so that his sheathed manhood was bent up to press against her sex. With a series of small shuffles she started to retreat. His hard flesh dragged against her clit and made her body quake until he finally came free. Even then, she could still feel him within her, and it was more than just his semen. There was also a residual sensation of what his cock had felt like when it was filling her body.

Her senses were reeling. The world seemed to lurch from side to side with the indifferent plod of the beast. Candice gave a sudden cracked giggle.

"What's so fucking funny," said the Captain with sudden paranoia and asperity.

"Nothing, my sweet Captain. A week ago, I was on my yacht, sailing for Japan, considering an argument with my lawyer about a possible IRS probe into my offshore accounts. Now I'm in a new world, on the back of a Dinosaur, fucking a man who's tied me up, beat me, humiliated me, and wants to sell me as a slave."

"Hey, it's –" he began, his temper having cooled.

"Nothing personal," she interrupted lethargically, and then hauled herself back upright. With her breasts still glistening with his saliva, she looked down her body and then along his. The Captain propped himself up on his elbows and met her eyes. She addressed him with cool and sultry tones.

"I know. So you said. But you saved me from a particularly ugly demise, and despite what you've done to me, I'm grateful, and I always pay my way."

Candice gave a wide smirk and with a wiggle of her shoulders, she lowered forward. The Captain gave a shiver as her mouth engulfed his cock and locked lips to him. He was of a size that had him pressing to the back of her throat before she had even fully taken him. She did not have her hands to help her with the task, so she decided to work even harder to coax another orgasm from the former officer.

With her lips firmly fixed to him, she pulled her head back and flitted her tongue about his summit before dropping back down as far as she could. She arched and gave a cough as she gagged a little but quickly beat back the response. Possessed by her newly roused passion, her mouth began to toil more swiftly. Piston plunges were accompanied with flashing tongue work. Her pace started to increase as she grew more confident and used to the motion. Her neck was aching, but she did not care. The feel of him again growing against her lips was more than enough to keep her fixated on her quest, and as his hips lifted up from the saddle, she felt liquid warmth flow into her maw. The taste was like nectar to her libidinous palate and Candice was suddenly mesmerised. Her eyes rolled as she swallowed the viscous treacle and her head fired back and forth while her tongue became a wild rambunctious serpent of oral gratification. The Captain's hands sank into the saddle, and his knuckles went white as his legs shook. His whimpering mewl was a glorious treat to her ears as she hauled every droplet she could from his body. Finally, when he was depleted, she did not end her fellatio. Rather, she left him in her mouth and let her tongue lethargically curl around him. Eventually she pulled free and placed kisses all around his organ.

"What is it?" he asked.

"What do you mean?" Candice answered with distracted attention.

"You were going to tell me your name."

"Candice," she replied.

There was no point applying her surname. Her family and everything pertinent to it were on another world. Even her first name was almost redundant here. She declined to ask him his and merely continued to adore his shaft and taste the lingering flavour of his seed and her own juices.

"I still can't let you go," he stated.

"I know that."

"Oh you'll fetch a mother of a price," he said with a jovial chuckle.

Candice looked up. Her serious expression caused his smile to falter for a moment.

"I intend to. I've never been a runner up. I don't tolerate failure or weakness in myself. I clawed my way to the top on Earth, and I assure you I'll do the same here."

"Well, I'll wish you good luck, Candice. I hope someone nice picks you up, 'coz there's some real sickos around these parts."

A sudden anxious desire suddenly flooded through her. It grabbed hold of her lust, warped it, and turned it into a craving that she could not control or reason the source of. There was one way to acquire it, and in a flash, she considered the possibilities. Could she stand it? She had to find out.

"So I've noticed," she commented.

"Hey, don't think that a quick fuck and a blowjob give you the right to give me lip!" he scolded.

"Then get me back in my sheath. Gag me. Strap me down nice and tight, right behind you. Where I belong!" she replied.

Candice lifted up onto her knees to regard him.

"You want that?" he asked, and his eyes were glittering with prurience.

"Does it matter? The real question is, do you?" she answered.

It was plain in his eyes and in his voice. Perhaps he had a predilection for such things, or perhaps he just wanted to have something so valuable, so precious, tied up and ultra-secure behind him. She could not even understand why *she* wanted to be bound, so how could she figure out someone else's motivations?

"You think you can handle it?" he enquired.

Concern at damaging his valued asset was taking precedence over debauched indulgence. Candice decided to push him on and increase her own containment. For some unknown reason, the need to be crushed into submission, strapped down, and transported was riding over all other considerations. She tried to remind herself of how appalling it had been, but all she could think of was how comforting it would feel, how safe and possessed, how abandoned to another she would be. It would be painful, downright distressing, but that was what made her want it even more. Candice did not tolerate half measures.

"You think you can tie me down securely this time? Not that feeble cuddle you applied that first time!"

"Right!" he said with an enthusiastic grin.

The Captain swiftly cut her cords with his blade and then sheathed the weapon. He grabbed the reins, folded himself back into his trousers, and brought his steed to a halt. One of the others drew up beside him.

"What's up, Captain?" he said and gave a dubious look from the Captain and to Candice. Suspicion was clearly dawning, so Candice decided to help her captor out. She launched forward and slapped him across the cheek before pounding her fists to his broad chest.

"She's getting to be a handful. I'm putting her back in the sleeve."

"Right. Need a hand?"

"I've got the situation under control, private!"

The soldier lifted his hands defensively to retract his accusation, took his reins, and turned around to head back. The Captain grabbed Candice and dragged her over his shoulder so that he might dismount with her. He threw the sleeve and the collection of straps off the beast and let them land on the ground. Candice wriggled and fought his grip with token effort so she could maintain the pretence of her rebellion.

"You fuckers! I'll get you *all* for this! You see! You'll all pay! I'm rich! You can't do this! Lousy fucking grunts! I hope you all get eaten by the lizards!"

As she continued her fake tirade, the Captain pinned her down and started to force the sleeve back onto her arms. He tightened the laces and then caught her feet. She continued to flail around in the dust and spit out imprecations in lurid detail. The men watched and smiled with amusement as the Captain began the task of tightening the sleeve in earnest. Candice hollered as the leather drew her arms closer together than ever before and the cross straps were hauled impossibly tight. When he added the straps for her legs and chest, she was squealing her abuses at them all. The Captain turned them into an exhaled croak as he hauled the belts with vituperative force. Her flesh bulged on either side of the straps, and she was rendered unable to even twitch.

"Motherfucking yankee scum fuck cu — mmmmmghff."

The ball was stuffed into her maw and the troops applauded at her sudden silence. Candice quivered with arousal as she was trussed and the belt reapplied. As he added it, she could feel a distinct bulge prod into her side from between the Captain's legs.

"Okay, the show's over, we've still got ground to cover," he announced, and then dragged her struggling form back up onto the saddle.

"So, you want it nice and tight, huh?" he said to himself, and then ruthlessly applied the holding straps. Candice gave a licentious whimper as she was crushed into position.

The sliced cord was threaded through the back of the belt responsible for holding the ball in her maw and it was then stretched back to the cuffs that were holding her legs. A brutal haul lifted her head up and craned it back until she gave a mew of dismay. The Captain tied off the cord and left her trapped in the demanding pose.

"Now for the really fun bit!" he stated while opening a canteen.

Candice shivered as cold sprinkles of water were dropped along the straps, the cord, and the sheath. Almost instantly, she gave a croaked cry as the bonds began to constrict. The pressure built up swiftly and she was hauled into the saddle with ever more potency as the cord withered and pulled her head even further back. Her cries were not of true pain because although there was indeed severe discomfort, for some reason, the tighter the bonds became the more aroused she was becoming. Her loins were burning with frustration. She wanted to be touched, to be ravished, played with, and the fact that she was not only inspired her depravity even more. She was caught on a bizarre decadent spiral that she had no means to escape.

"Are we happy?" he asked, and his hand ran along her trapped body.

Candice surged against his delightful caress, but no motion showed through her bondage. She wondered where these bizarre impulses had come from. She had never even noticed an inclination towards such perversity, but now it was loose and consuming her. Could it have been some sort of neurological hiccup from her passage through the Vortex? Had she always secretly borne this desire? It was possible, and after all, things a lot weirder than finding out she had a love of bondage had happened this week.

She felt like she was in a trance while she languished in her bondage. Her breathing was deep, steady, and rhythmic, her thoughts were flying high, and her body trembled with pleasure from the compression that kept her subdued and immobile. There were no decisions to make, no fight to undertake, no plotting, no thought, nothing to do but dwell in her tight containment and wait for her release. Candice was so obsessed with the potency of the feelings that were coursing through her that she could not dwell on what her sale and slavery might bring or what new hurdles she would have to face. What if her owner did not like tying her down in the manner she now so loved to be? Candice knew she would be able to rectify that. Rebellion, struggles, fighting back, all would have her utterly secure again in no time. The thought melted her heart as she imagined a life of ravishment and containment, with nothing to live for but her next orgasm as she wriggled against impossibly tight bonds.

The leather started to relinquish its severity as the heat dried it out. It allowed her to breathe easier and she managed to relax into the constraints a little more. The crushing hold was wondrous to endure, but she could not withstand it for long. Even now, areas of her body were going numb, and her joints and neck were significantly smarting. The havoc that was being created from prolonged exposure to containment was a heady aphrodisiac, and she gave delicate mews of pleasure against her gag. The moans grew more distinct when the Captain let his hands stroll over her and appraise her physique.

"Too bad I can't get to your pussy. I could make you come in this. You'd love that, wouldn't you? All turned on by being tied up and a nice juicy orgasm," he teased.

Candice groaned and gave futile jerks against her restraints. The notion of it was too intoxicating to dismiss and his words made her frustration a truly terrible companion.

"What was that? Still not tight enough? Well, water's a bit valuable, but we're on the home stretch for town, so I think I can waste a little more," he stated.

Candice's muted responses suddenly became a sharp exhale as the air was crushed from her. Water spattered the leather, and it instantly contracted. The Dinosaur hide groaned as its pressure built to new and terrible levels. Candice's eyes rolled and she panted for breath as she sank into masochistic rhapsody.

"Good girl," he commented, and fondly patted her craned back head.

Leading the convoy, the Captain leant back onto her body and removed his cock. One hand dropped onto Candice and the other snatched his rigid manhood before beginning a dithering masturbation.

The Captain would bring himself towards orgasm and then stop. He let his lust subside and then began again so he could draw out his onanism. Finally, he could hold off no longer and with shivers of ecstasy, he finally came.

The day passed slowly, and the effects of the bondage started to weigh more heavily on Candice's limits. The discomfort started to grow worse and made it harder to relish her predicament. When it continued to become acute, she was bitterly regretting her actions. What had she done to herself? Why had she done it? Why had she allowed such stupid, foolhardy, and reckless endangerment of her body and sanity? With all pleasure smothered by the mayhem of the restriction, all she could do was curse her words and the man who had done this to her. She was ashamed of what she had done, and wept quietly in her miserable lot.

She watched the day passing with rancour. The sun was moving terribly slowly. Every second was a purgatory that only made her anguish rise to new levels. Every part of her was aching and numb, all she could feel was pain in every part of her form and she had no way to communicate it.

The Captain took the reins and hauled at the beast. Candice sobbed with joy that she was finally going to be released, but these were the moments that were the worst as she was left waiting for him to finally notice her and set her loose. The possibility of being left in the pose all night could not even be considered because it was too nightmarish.

"Ready to come out?" he asked.

She could not nod because of the lead that hauled her head back, so she burbled her pleas as best she could against the gag.

"Is that a yes?" he teased.

Candice's fury made the incoherent words more distinct.

"Or would you like to stay like this all night? No problem, mind?"

Her protests were long and vehement as she wept and wriggled against the straps. Candice fought to communicate just how much travail she was in.

"You'll be good?" he enquired.

Candice broke down into a weeping fit. She could not withstand another instant of this duress and all he was doing was teasing her.

"Okay, okay. Eyes bigger than your belly, huh?" he stated and thankfully began to unfasten her bonds.

He carried her down to the ground and released the cord.

Her head dropped to the ground and she wailed against her gag as her whole neck seemed to explode with mayhem. She was gasping for breath and fearing further instances of removal when her legs were released and dropped back to the ground. Her knees and muscles churned with protest. They had grown accustomed to their agonising position, and now they were answering change with even worse havoc.

Candice convulsed and shook with stress as the lingering effects slowly started to subside and normality returned. The sheath was unbuckled and slipped free, and her inert arms flopped around like landed fish as ghastly pins and needles struck.

The Captain rolled her onto her back and watched her distraught expressions with an amused grin. When she started to recover, he presented food and water.

"I'm going to take off the gag. If you make one word, or try to escape, you'll spend the night back up there. And if there's a morning dew, well, I'm sure you get the picture," he said.

The gag was pulled free, and after she had exercised her aching jaws, she sat up and scarfed down the meal. Candice watched the Captain while she ate, and saw him take four wooden stakes from a saddlebag along with rope and a mallet.

He proceeded to ram the spikes into the hard ground and spread them in a wide square pattern before he tied the ropes to each of them. Candice could see what was coming. As she ate, she watched him work and pondered whether to risk flight. It was pointless. She would just have to endure until a better opportunity offered itself.

"Get over here," he ordered, and beckoned her with the hammer.

Candice arose onto her feet and with unsteady steps trekked over to him.

"Lay down and stretch out. You'll spend the night here so

I don't have to keep an eye on you," he stated.

Unable to defy him because of fear of being returned to the saddle, she did as she was told. Candice's ankles were bound and left in a wide split that made her inner thighs protest a little. The Captain then took her wrists and stretched them up and out to the stakes. With a stern haul, he stretched her body and made her moan at the racking effects before the ropes were tied off and she was left trapped and spread-eagled.

The men set out blankets and had cold meals before they settled down for the night. This left one sentry on duty.

Candice closed her eyes and tried to adjust to the demands of the position and relax. The night air made her skin chill, and she shivered as she stared up at the stars. Naked and staked out beneath the twinkling view, she wondered which one was the sun she knew. Was she even in the same galaxy, or the same dimension? Perhaps alternate universes did exist, and she had slipped through the cracks to end up here. On the other hand, was the Vortex some sort of wormhole? There was little point considering it. The trip was one way, and she now had to ensure her survival and success in this world. However, all that was for later. Right now she had to rest and regain her strength. It took some time, but eventually she managed to begin to drift into sleep, and her dreams were saturated with visions of restraint and ravishment.

CHAPTER FOUR

L ying upon the sun-baked soil, Candice was roused by the feel of hands upon her body. She stirred from slumber and opened her eyes to see a familiar silhouette beside her. The soldier that had been fascinated with her was clasping at her cleavage with a libidinous severity. The punishment of her breasts brought soft whimpers to her lips. For a moment, she thought he was only going to continue with his indulgence of fondling, but a furtive look about as he unfastened his trousers enlightened her that he was going to take his pleasure further this night.

He slipped his arms under her, grabbed her hair, and drew back. By twisting her head back, he caused her torso to rise until Candice was clamping her jaws together in an effort to weather the fierce pain in her scalp and spine.

With a series of exploratory jabs borne of inexperience, he sought access and then slowly forced himself into her. The soldier clearly relished the feel of her internal spasms as he introduced himself. The manhandling had been an outrageous act, but the ravishment was more than she could stand. She gave shocked pips of distress as he thrust into her and then she snatched a breath to spend on a cry so she could draw attention and perhaps acquire salvation.

A gloved palm dropped onto her face as he sought to stifle her, and the smothering palm made it near impossible to draw breath. Wriggling in her bonds, Candice strained against the tight ropes with increased vigour and desperately sought to break free. Her lungs were burning from starvation as his attempt to keep her quiet promised to suffocate her. She jerked beneath him, her lungs fighting to reach the air. Her fingers clawed at the ground, but they were unable to access any knot.

There was a deep resonant crunch, and her attacker flipped aside as a boot lanced into his side and threw him away. The soldier rolled into a crouch and cradled his throbbing side. A moment later, he yanked a blade from the sheath on his back and arose. His cock was still jutting from his trousers and a scowl of anger was spread across his face.

Candice turned her head and saw the Captain standing beside her. His face was bland and stern. He glanced down, and Candice gave an imploring look of gratitude. Again, he was proving to be her saviour, and her affection for him swelled again, as did her desire to feel him replace the villain's manhood with his own sterling phallus.

The Captain looked back to his opponent and drew his own blade. He stepped back and presented the wicked knife before him as he readied to meet any sudden charge. "I told everyone that she was to be left alone,"

The sudden noise roused the others from sleep, and they began to look up and bear witness to the argument. Their interest forced the transgressing soldier into continuing with his rebellion. These men all lived by a very harsh creed, and he was unable to back down in front of so many. It would make him look weak and the situation was one that the Captain had probably forced with his loud broadcast.

"So what? We ain't in the same army anymore. All that's gone! We don't have to listen to you!" he barked, trying to rally support for his cause.

"You want to give the orders, you little runt?" asked the Captain.

"Suppose I do? Who's going to stop me?"

"Well if you can take me out, then no one will. Question is, have you got the guts to take me on and the balls to finish me off? You've always been a snivelling coward. I can't think why we ever let a cry-baby like you join up with us. Maybe it was out of pity, I don't know, but this ain't no kindergarten, so tuck that tiny maggot away and let's see what you've got."

The incensing words struck their desired mark, and with a hiss of indignation, the soldier leapt over Candice's prone body and hacked out with a wide slash. The Captain skipped back and let the weapon sail past while keeping his own blade back in readiness. He kept poised while waiting for the decisive opening.

A truculent jab met nothing but air as the Captain sidestepped it. He immediately snatched the advantage that the rash and over-extended thrust had given him. One hand clamped to the presented joint and jerked his opponent onward. The soldier's balance was crippled and he was pulled over.

A swift sweep of Captain's foot stripped the 's soldier's legs from beneath the rebellious soldier and he was thrown face first into the ground. He landed with a jarring thud, and with a savage twist of the captive limb, the Captain created an arm lock. His knee dropped onto the man's spine to hold him, and the knife fell from the imprisoned hand.

With a roar of effort, the soldier tried to break free of the immobilising hold but had little chance of success. The Captain's weapon arm jerked high and then plunged. The blade gave a deep thud as the point punched through his opponent's ribs and sheathed itself to the hilt.

There was a croaking cry, and the man offered a wild spasm that devolved into a twitching fit. The Captain rotated the weapon and then yanked it free.

Cassandra's eyes were wide with horror at the sight of the slack form. The Captain loomed over the victim, and the blade was wet with red. He bent over and disdainfully wiped it clean upon his victim.

"I'm in charge here. Always have, always will. Understood?" The Captain revealed his victory to the entire band and ensured that they were aware that the murder had been committed because of the questioning of his authority. The responses were swift and genuine.

"Sure, Cap."

"You're the man, Captain."

"Never liked that little prick anyways."

"You okay? He didn't cut you, did he?"

"No, I'm fine," he answered and walked over to the slain man's bedroll. He took up the blankets and walked over to Candice. He laid them out on her and began to tuck them under.

"You alright?" he said softly.

"I am now. Thank you," she replied.

It seemed absurd to be thanking someone who had staked her out in such a way, but *their* coupling had been with her consent and active participation. The other man had not even considered her opinion and had almost killed her with his molestation.

"Anytime. Now try to get some sleep. No one else'll mess with you tonight," he said, and stroked her cheek once before returning to his bed.

Warmed by the blankets and the affection he had shown, Candice nestled into the soothing arms of her restraint and returned to sleep. It was only a few hours to dawn, but the rest she gained was very refreshing.

A breakfast of preserves was hand fed to her by the Captain and she sucked on his fingers and cast adoring eyes at him. He then released her from the ropes, and after packing everything away, she was carried back up into the saddle and sat before him again.

Candice lounged back into his arms and idly watched the

land passing by.

"You've not even asked what's been happening on Earth since you came here," she said.

"What's the point? There's no going back. We've all had to focus on life here and completely forget that world and everything we left there. Any news would only make us pine or fear for something we can't affect or ever have again."

Neither of them spoke after that. They just took the pleasure of each other's proximity while they could, because their time together was almost over.

The land started to become a little more fertile, and a huge mountain range started to manifest in the distance. At first, Candice thought it was a bank of clouds, but then she began to see the outline of the jagged peaks and the snow that covered them.

"Karlville," he announced.

Candice looked up at him and then followed his hand to where he was pointing. The land ahead had a few farmsteads with smaller breeds of Dinosaur in corrals or grazing peacefully. There were small fields of crops and some small orchards. A narrow river could be seen beyond these, and by it was a small frontier style town.

Candice moved closer to the Captain and embraced him as she watched the settlement grow closer.

The town was a strange parody of what she was used to. The buildings were comprised of wooden planks, and there were shops, saloons, hotels, everything one would expect to see in any western. Nevertheless, there were marked differences. Instead of horses tethered outside, there were Dinosaurs. Some were small, like horses. Some were covered in bony plates or had spikes, or were of the type the Captain and his men rode. All had saddle and harness, some had saddlebags, and others had cradles set upon them to create a lofty travelling perch.

The lights she could see were a mixture of simple varieties — oil lamps, lanterns, and lights taken from ships and planes. There was the odd neon sign, but mostly they were painted wooden affairs.

The town's population were largely drifters, by the look of them. They were dressed in rough attire, with obviously scavenged and adapted items. Almost everyone had a sword, and most had some sort of bow or crossbow. Some of the townsfolk had better attire, and everything relating to modern technology was gone or had been employed to a different purpose. Parts of boats and planes could be seen in the structure of the buildings, and the salvaged items still bore slogans, initials, and insignia.

The indigenous population could also be spied on occasion, but instead of tribal Indians, they were the strange lizardmen. Candice held tightly to the Captain as she saw them, recalling the horror of her previous encounter with the race.

The Captain tipped his hat to one side, and Candice looked to see the town sheriff standing before his office. The building had wooden shutters around every window, and the rear was made of dense bricks, revealing the existence of a jail and therefore some semblance of law. The outer wall had wanted posters plastered all over it, and the sheriff himself was a huge burly man in dark clothing. He had a bushy beard and a bald head. A massive two-handed axe lay behind him, and he had a pair of automatic pistols in shoulder holsters. He gave the Captain a brief nod and continued to watch the population with a vigilant and uncompromising glower.

The most opulent building by far was the Iron Mongers establishment. What would have been a low-class business on Earth was a highly prestigious one here, and it looked more like a huge bank. The building was made of brick, had guards visible within, and its tall chimney released a steady plume of dark smoke. The Captain turned to his troops and beckoned to the closest. The Corporal flicked the reins and had the massive steed catch up to them.

"Offload the loot. Try to get him down to twenty percent this time. Tell him we'll take our business elsewhere if he don't," said the Captain.

"What if he still don't accept it?"

"For melting all this down, twenty percent'll be a real windfall for him. If he doesn't want someone else to earn that cut, he'll take it."

"Right. Where'll you be when we're done?"

"I'm going to take care of her. Leave a couple of the boys to wait while he smelts it all down into bars, and we'll all meet at the Forlorn Hope."

"Nice."

"We can afford the best, so why delay?"

The Corporal gave a joyous salute and turned his steed around to convey the message to the others. The Captain continued onwards and finally pulled up by another fortified building with guards and a wooden stage set before it. Rising from the roof was a tall scaffold that was probably some sort of radio antenna. It was the first hint of communication tech Candice had seen so far.

"Come on, girl. This is it," he said.

"Goodbye, Captain," she replied, and kissed him on the lips. "And thank you."

He looked startled for a moment and then helped her down from the saddle. He tied the reins about a dense pole and escorted her to a heavy door. Taking out his fighting knife, he hammered the pommel on the surface. A hatch flashed open as he was still sheathing the knife.

"Waddya want?" came a sharp reply.

The Captain took hold of her upper arm and dragged Candice's nude body into view.

"Fucking hell!" came the astounded reply.

The sounds of many bolts being removed sifted through the door and the foot thick portal was hauled back. A thin and elderly man emerged. He was dressed in fine clothes and had an Uzi at his side along with two large men who bore machine guns.

"You better be selling," he said with a scowl.

"You're as smart as you are ugly. What cut are you looking for?"

"Fifty fifty, that's the rules, lad."

"Screw that!" exclaimed the Captain.

"Watch the mouth, son. Slaves needs feeding, they needs watching, they needs guarding, they needs tending. It ain't cheap. Overheads my boy, overheads."

"One—she'll sell within the week, so don't give me that bullshit. Two—this is a woman. Woooomaaaan. Right? This ain't no day labourer, skivvy, or some scaleback slob. Three—well, just look at her. She's young, gorgeous, smooth, and fragrant. You'll take ten off the final sale and that's it, pal."

"Twenty five."

"I ain't bartering here, you withered old fossil. I said ten. That's it. You want to have a woman to sell. You take my price, or the only time you'll see this luscious ass is in your dreams." he said, then twirled her around and grabbed the back of her neck. He forced her down and nudged her legs apart with a few taps of his boot to her calves.

Candice slid her legs apart and presented herself for view. She quivered with sedate lust as she was shown off like an object.

"Ta . . . ta . . . twenty," he barked after a few stammers.

"I said ten," purred the Captain and slid his hand between Candice's thighs. He let his knuckles graze the soft skin and then his fingers rode against her pussy. Candice shivered and released a long ululating groan of rapture as he stroked her. Her thighs clenched in fits, rippling her muscles as her hips started to sway with his steady precise manoeuvres. His grasp on her neck tightened to keep her bent over, and Candice's eyes drifted shut. She surrendered to the fierce pleasure of being fondled and so brazenly shown off.

"Fifteen. I have to make a living too, lad," growled the old man.

"Deal."

The two men slapped hands together.

"Heh. Bring her inside, boys. I'll get on the radio and announce the sale," he said.

The two guards shouldered their weapons and grabbed her wrists. The old man started to scuttle back inside, cackling to himself.

"Heh, a woman. Can you believe it? A real woman! Oh I'll make a pretty penny on this one. Fifteen bars of pure steel. No, twenty. Thirty! Heh heh."

Candice was brought inside, and she looked over her shoulder to see the Captain walking away. The door was closed and refortified, leaving her in near darkness. The guards drew her in and past rows of cells. The thick wooden doors were all barred from the outside, and small blackboards to one side listed the name, ethnicity, age, height, and weight of the occupant.

The old man opened another door and presented the interior with a bow and a wave.

"Your chamber, madam," he crooned.

The guards moved her in, and her arms were drawn over her head and thrust into a pair of iron manacles that hung on chains from the ceiling. A matching pair of fetters drew her legs apart and kept them shackled to the floor.

"Leave us," ordered the old man.

The guards departed and closed the door behind them. The old man just stared at her licentiously as their heavy footfalls departed.

"Well, my dear. Do you have a name?"

"Candice," she said softly.

"A cute name, for a very cute young lady."

He moved forward and circled around her, assessing her nude body with practised skill.

"Well, I'd best make sure my estimates are accurate," he said with a grin.

The slaver closed in behind her, and his hands started to explore her body. Candice pulled at her bonds and quivered as she felt a gentle touch circle her breasts, pass over her hips, and then move up and down the inner and outer surface of her legs. He cupped her rear, squeezed her muscles, and all the while his panting breath brushed against her skin.

"Oh, you are superb, my dear. Superb. In all my years as Slavemaster of Karlville, I've only ever sold four women. All were off that Oceanographic ship and were frumpy and lumpy. You, however. Oh yes. You are the one I've been waiting for."

"What will they want me for?" she asked.

"Maybe prestige. Nothing says *look how stinking rich I am* like having a woman on one's arm. Maybe for breeding, to give some noble or wealthy merchant some heirs to his cartel. Maybe just for sex, and plenty of it," he said with a snigger.

The Slavemaster moved closer and lifted himself up onto tiptoe so he could see her lips. "Please show me your teeth, my dear," he asked.

Candice yawned wide. She had always taken care of herself and eaten right. Consequently, there was not one filling.

"Oh it just gets better!" he said. "So, we've seen all of you, except for . . . ah yes. A little unorthodox, but I'll indulge myself."

Candice watched him lower carefully onto his knees and take hold of her hips.

"What . . . what are you . . . oooooooh! Oh!" she said as she answered the lap of his tongue along her pussy.

His spry tongue trailed through her and took several more savouring licks before he started to attend her clit. Candice jiggled and gasped for breath. He was exceedingly skilful, and his tongue was long and deft. She clawed at the chains that held her and her head draped back. Her chest rose and fell with heady gasps, and she moaned and whimpered. Candice gave a delighted cry as he suckled on her clit and then thrust the full measure of the warm, wet organ into her as far as he could. After tasting her depths, he returned to lapping at her clitoris. His hands were soft, and his delicate attention began to tickle her inner thighs and caress her rear.

Candice could feel orgasm looming. She started to tense, and her gasps grew more rapid. Her arms flexed and started to bring her up onto tiptoe. She grabbed the chains and held tight as she braced for her climax.

The man flicked his tongue tip to her clit and then hauled at it with a sudden potent suck. Candice dragged herself into the air until the chains to her feet stopped her. She screamed into the air of her cell as his tongue swirled and danced, cavorting within her.

"Stop! Stop! Pleeease! I . . . I can't take anymore!" she cried.

The old man devoured her clit again and gave it several sensuous nips with his teeth. Candice's words became a howl of utter ecstasy that reverberated through the room.

The Slavemaster drew back, and Candice dropped back down to hang limp from her shackles.

He looked up at her slack face and grinned. "You taste delicious, my sweet. A darling pussy. Ripe and succulent," he said happily, then awkwardly managed to rise before he shuffled out of the room.

Candice watched him depart with bemusement, wondering why he had been so generous to the property he was going to auction off. Did anything in this whole bizarre world make sense? The door was shut and barred, and she heard the scratch of a chalk noting her details without.

An unknown duration gradually passed. As she grew used to the silence, she started to make out the sounds from other cells. Sobbing, prayers, struggling, and the rattling of chains. The other slaves were not happy with their lot. They were less valuable than she, and their fate was far more precarious because of it.

The door opened, and the Slavemaster entered with two young men in fine but practical attire. Each youth had a cattle prod tucked in their belt, and Candice immediately decided to comply with whatever they wanted.

Candice was released from the cuffs, and she stood and rubbed her sore wrists. The men drew their prods and fell in behind her as the Slavemaster beckoned her out. Candice was shown up into the higher levels of the building and brought to a room where the barred windows allowed sunlight to pour in. There was a single bed with cotton blankets and soft pillows. A simple dressing table had a large mirror, numerous brushes, and other cosmetic items arranged atop it. There were a couple of chests of drawers, a porcelain toilet, and a wooden bathtub. The tub was full of hot soapy water that had been heated by the bucketful from a nearby stove and it let curling wafts of scented steam drift into the air.

The door was closed, and the two guards cradled their prods and took up positions on either side of it. The Slavemaster moved to the bath and perched his wiry frame on the edge. He reached in and stirred the contents, causing more mounds of bubbles to form. "Come on, my dear. You want to get cleaned up, don't you?" he offered.

Candice looked to the two sentries and then wandered over to the Slavemaster. She climbed into the bath and immediately sank down into the hot waters. Candice gave a long moan of bliss as the wet heat enveloped her physique. It was a stark difference to her last bath in the pond.

Candice sank beneath the waters and shook her head to soak her scruffy hair. When she arose, she sat up with clusters of bubbles running down her slick skin.

From beneath the bath, the Slavemaster took up a natural sponge and presented it to her. Candice took it and started to work it over her skin to strip off the sweat. The process made her skin tingle, and when Candice glanced to her side, she saw the eyes of the guards upon her. Their fingers were clenching to the prods, and there was a distinct tightness to the front of their trousers.

With a nefarious grin, she leaned back and let the sponge run over her exposed breasts. She circled the flesh and focused upon her nipples. The nuggets stiffened and she gave a satisfied purr as she attended them. Her arousal grew stronger, and with eyes half shut, she let the sponge drift down between her legs. She started to stroke herself beneath the hot waters and shuddered as pleasure rushed through her. It did not matter that the Slavemaster and his cohorts were right by her — in fact, she wanted to exploit her gender and make them livid with desire. They could punish her at any moment, but she could also torture them.

The Slavemaster did not intervene and merely let her continue to masturbate brazenly before them. Perhaps he wanted to test the resolve and commitment of his employees.

Candice dismissed such thoughts and focused on what she wanted to. She conjured fantasies of being tightly bound, of being crushed into a package and held captive to another's desire. The fantasies swirled through her head and made her dizzy with arousal.

She released the sponge and let her fingers continue where it had left off. Her digits danced on her clit, and her breath started to speed up and deepen as she grew nearer to climax. She gasped, her other hand grabbing the edge of the tub and holding onto it as her chest arched up out of the waters and her legs jiggled beneath the surface. With a cry, she answered her relief, and with bared teeth, she hissed and fought to endure the delight as she continued until she could take no more. Candice sank back down into the inviting waters and closed her eyes.

"Quite a show," commented the Slavemaster. "Whatever price you fetch, you'll definitely prove worth it."

Candice gave a small chuckle and sat up. The Slavemaster produced a towel from one of the drawers and opened it for her.

She arose and wiped the suds from her body with her hands, ensuring that she folded at her middle to wipe her legs and thereby give the guards a wanton view of her hindquarters. Afterwards, she stepped from the tub and draped the folds of the towel over her shoulders. The Slavemaster enveloped her within it and then headed over to the door.

"It will take a few days for the relevant parties to get here, so you have freedom within this room to do as you wish. Please attend to your hair and look after yourself. Food will be brought to you."

The trio left the room, locked it behind them, and she was left to her thoughts about the future.

Candice spent the next four days relaxing as best her confines permitted. There were no clothes, but she was getting used to being naked. In this eerie realm, it seemed to be her standard mode of being displayed, and she was becoming strangely at ease with it.

She used the set of scissors she found in the drawer to even out her hair. She turned it into a spiky carpet on top with shorter hair at the sides. She plucked her eyebrows, shaved her body, and ate heartily of the strange dishes they provided. The meat had to have been reptilian in nature and came in a variety of odd textures and tastes that had no earthly comparison. She exercised, but this was done more to ensure she could sleep rather than to keep fit, and she spent much time staring out of the window and watching this odd new world go by. If she squinted, it looked like frontier times, save that the horses were about ten times too big.

Often she indulged herself and teased her body. She could not stop from fixating on her new predilection, and thoughts of being bound, on a leash, and invaded by the cock of the Captain could not be dismissed. She knew she was inadvertently conditioning herself to such things, but she could not stop the process. Every orgasm was charged with images of constraint and made her more intrigued and desperate to enact such things. Sometimes she tried to focus on more normal and vanilla scenarios, but they just were not up to arousing her anymore. She needed vice to titillate her, and only when the standard fantasy suddenly developed ropes, chains, leather, a crop, a cane, and a ravishing, only then could she attain orgasm.

Her whole life had been turned upside down by taking the route Lei had suggested. After everything that had happened to her, she could barely recall him. It was as though he belonged to another's memories. Candice remembered that for someone who had only been around for a couple of months, Lei had slotted himself flawlessly into their close-knit social circle. Normally they were highly exclusive about their choice of companions, and their elite little clique denied access to virtually everyone. However, Lei had a charm in his words that caused them to open to him. The enigmatic man had stepped into the heart of their group and seized the reins that guided them when they had some moments to squander on leisure. His nature was so reassuring and inoffensive that she had even allowed him to call her *Candy* for short, something she steadfastly refused allowing anyone else to even contemplate.

Notions that he was attempting seduction were

unfounded, and to this, Candice remembered applying a shade of regret, because she had more than a fleeting attraction for him. Again, this was a rare thing for the former version of herself, and the intensity of the budding affection had been surprisingly strong.

When he had suggested the voyage and given her an exact route, she had thought that he was seeking an invitation to join her on a lethargic cruise, just the two of them. Instead, it transpired that he had pressing appointments during the time of her vacation, so he had delivered his suggestion in the mode of a friend, one who sought to generously pass on a favoured pastime for the enjoyment of others. Candice had considered that next time, she would ask him to accompany her.

It was strange how fate worked when it had the inclination. Lei had been new to their country club, and while she and the other executives chatted, he had asked a simple passing question on his way to tee off. Even now, Candice could not recall exactly who it was that had invited him to sit with them, and that in itself was strange, because such an invite was unprecedented. They were elite, and so they universally dismissed every such attempt to enter their company. However, within the space of a couple of hours of talking, it seemed that they had known him for years.

Joseph Lei had been hunting for possible acquisitions for a Japanese conglomerate. They had no reason to fear that he was sizing them up, because all of their personal holdings and companies were powerful, stable, and immune to takeover. Candice herself had been worth millions and was senior vice president to three separate magnates. She could have easily taken the highest positions from these companies should she have wished, because her advice and skills were invaluable and without equal. Nevertheless, she had not wanted to be a figurehead. If something went seriously wrong, it was always the face and name at the head of the company that took the full blame. As an apparent second in command, she could enjoy the rewards of her position without having to take responsibility.

Whenever she had merged with a new firm, she'd made sure to spend time covering her position by allocating any possible blame elsewhere. The higher she rose, the more she chose to employ the odd private investigator or to bribe certain people into gaining her some blackmail material, just in case she needed emergency leverage one day. There was no point rising through the ranks if there was any danger that it could be taken away by some ambitious upstart or a superior caught with trousers down or hands in the till. It was better to sacrifice a little time, money, and effort to ensure complete safety.

Perhaps the change in her life was not so stark after all. She was still worth a fortune, and had to be crafty and ready to do anything to succeed, but now, physical delight and sensual fulfilment was her reward. It made the dull material acquisitions of her old life seem feeble, and Candice felt glad to have been exposed to chance at rebirth.

One night she was awoken by the sounds of a ruckus outside. She slid from her bed and wandered to the window, rubbing the sleep from her eyes as she went. She looked down and saw a group of men staggering down the street, holding bottles, singing loudly and badly. As she managed to focus, she saw that it was the unit of soldiers. They had new and fine clothing, were clearly inebriated, and were revelling in their good fortune. She sank down to her knees and held to the windowsill as she tried to see if the Captain was amongst them. The group stopped and held to each other for support. One of them hoisted his bottle to the building.

"Cheers, Candy! Woohoo! Here's to ya!" he bellowed and then took another long swig before falling over.

The Captain was spotted as he laughed and gestured for

one of the others to pick up the unconscious form. He looked up at the building and panned across the windows. Her room was unlit, so she could not draw his attention. Candice merely stared down at him wistfully and smiled as he gave a salute and then continued on his way. Candice returned to bed and cuddled up into a ball to dream of the time she had spent with him.

On occasion, she saw small groups arrive. Servants and bodyguards accompanied the wealthy men, and they arrived on the back of a beast or in large coaches. The Slavemaster always emerged to talk with them, and then they would head off to one of the hotels. It was clear to Candice that her time of being without an owner was rapidly thinning.

Candice was just finishing her breakfast of one huge boiled egg, some toast, and a glass of bright green juice when the door to her room was opened and the Slavemaster appeared.

"Is it time?" she asked.

What was the point of fighting her fate? Throwing things around, acts of rebellion or escape attempts were pointless. It was far better to just behave and try to affect her destiny for the better.

"I'll give you a moment to prepare," he said softly.

Candice finished her meal, wiped the crumbs away, and quickly ran a brush through her short hair. She stood up and took a deep breath.

"Okay, Candice. Let's go," she muttered to herself.

The guards fell in beside her as soon as she left the room. She was shown back down to the ground floor and then to a short passageway. There was a set of double doors up ahead, and around them she could see seams of light. The sound of people conversing and the passing of the monstrous reptilian traffic could also be discerned.

Candice's hands were lifted up, and rope was used to bind them to a wooden track. The overhead rail ran forward along the ceiling, through the righthand door, and then it returned through the other. It connected back to the beginning and created a full circuit of enforced passage.

The guards stepped back, and there was a sudden clatter of motion. The pulley system in the track grabbed her bonds and started to tow her forward at a slow rate. Candice gave some energetic tugs at the coils but could not stop the mechanism. Resigned to her unveiling, she continued towards the portals.

The doors opened just before she reached them, and she had to cast her head around as the sudden deluge of light pained her eyes. Warm rays caressed her naked form. As her sight cleared, she found herself on the stage.

The overhead rail followed the edge of the stage and showed her off in full to all those who were present. Three rows of deck chairs had been arranged around the perimeter, and they were filled with a variety of men. They were of varied age, race, and appearance, but all of them had fixed their focus on her.

Beyond the chairs was a dense throng of the local population who were clearly anxious to catch a peek at a nubile female form. Candice scanned the crowd and hoped to catch a glimpse of the Captain, but he was nowhere to be seen. Every face was consumed with lust as they glared at her, and Candice found it strangely arousing to know that almost every person here would have her in their fantasies by nightfall. Dozens upon dozens of hands would be clenching to throbbing pussy-starved cocks and pounding them with fervour as images of her tottering bound physique ruled their thoughts. The notion made Candice suddenly quake with iniquitous glee.

The Slavemaster stood in the centre of the stage with two burly warriors on either side of them. Their machine guns were held ready to dissuade any illegality or interruption of the proceedings.

"Fresh from the other side. Untouched and unspoiled. As smooth to the touch as she is easy on the eye. Gentlemen of the eternal wastelands, I give you Candy."

The words broke the trance that her sex hungry body had brought on. There was some spontaneous applause and much muttering as people discussed her physique and charms. The track stopped and left her standing at the forefront. She briefly considered being annoyed at being called *Candy*, but the woman she had once been was gone, so perhaps she should adopt her former reviled abbreviation to suit the new identity she was crafting for herself. Only Lei had called her this, and Lei had been the key to opening the rift and throwing her into this new reality. Candice was from Earth, a ruthless businesswoman who relished her pampered wealthy lifestyle and had no time for sex. Candy was a slave in Pangaea, a woman who delighted in restraint and being owned and used for the prurient and depraved appetites of others.

"The bidding will begin at fifty bars of stainless steel!"

A large rotund man who was swathed in furs instantly met the amount. Another quickly added a bar, and then another man added two. The bidding was fast and furious, and the Slavemaster was having trouble keeping up. Candice watched them all vie for her. The amount quickly reached one hundred bars, and then a tall European man in dark attire raised the bid to one hundred and fifty. The crowd gasped, and a number of the bidders turned and scowled at him for dashing their hopes of owning her.

"I have one hundred and fifty from Mauris da Rimini. Do I hear one sixty?"

"Two hundred!" snapped a fierce looking man in velvet. The sounds of astonishment from the crowd grew more distinct. The Slavemaster coughed and had to clear his throat before announcing the bid.

"Two twenty," calmly decreed Mauris.

Candy looked at him and studied his body. It looked as though she was going to be his. The other man was sweating and nervous. His expression betrayed that he did not have the funds to match his opponent.

Candy chose to regard Mauris with new eyes. He was definitely attractive, and she could easily picture herself being his carnal plaything.

There was a sudden thundering of heavy footfalls and eight beasts charged into view. The monsters were about nine metres high and looked like little Tyrannosaurs. Their arms were more developed and had two spindly fingers and three large clawed ones. The beasts had sections of dark barding all over their body and fanged head, and these plates of armour were formed to protect them and still allow easy movement. Each piece had many strange ideograms and symbols etched into them.

On the back of each beast and riding in an ornate saddle was a toughened figure. They were lean and muscular with suits of black lacquered armour that looked like a bizarre cross between the battledress of Samurai and the panoply of a Medieval Knight. They had snarling bestial masks and curved swords on their backs. At their sides were automatic pistols, and in a saddle sheath was an assault rifle. The rear of their saddles bore a tall pole from which fluttered a red banner that had a strange golden symbol embroidered on it. Candy could vaguely process the ideogram. It was a little distorted, but could well mean *A-Katsu*, which translated as *I Conquer*.

The warriors reined in their beasts and trotted to a halt. As one, they drew their assault weapons and cocked them with a threatening attitude. The guards on the stage lowered their own firearms and started to back away, leaving the Slavemaster alone and unprotected.

"Lord Hachiman. Fire Warlord of the Mitama demands this slave. She is to be Kami-tsu-ko."

"But we have a-" began the Slavemaster.

The warriors hoisted their weapons and drew aim on him. The Slavemaster raised his hands and started to retreat with a series of supplicating bows. One of the soldiers climbed down out of the saddle. The crowds parted instantly at his approach and dragged chairs aside to permit him access to the stage. He climbed up and stepped before Candy. She could see the glint of his eyes behind the mask, and she felt terribly afraid.

"You are the one called Candice?"

For a moment, she was too stunned to answer. The sheer outlandish nature of their appearance, the mixture of modern, primitive, and extinct had been startling, but to hear that they were aware of her identity was even more confounding.

"I asked a question, slave. Answer me!" he snarled.

Candy nodded, and there was a flash of movement as he drew his sword. Candy gave a panicked squeal and then noticed that he had cut her bonds and sheathed the blade before she even really saw it. The warrior grabbed her and pulled her down onto her front, whereupon he quickly applied handcuffs. The restraints had a set of similar fetters attached to them, and her ankles were locked into the adjustable fixtures to hog-tie her. He produced a ball gag and started to force it into her mouth. She wiggled and tried to stop him, but the soldier was tolerating no denial of his will. The orb was stuffed in and the buckle tied tightly about her head.

Candy gave a mewl of protest as he hoisted her up onto his shoulder and carried her back to his steed. The terrible riding creature was frightening to behold. The eldritch armour, the ranks of flesh-rending teeth and terrible claws all made it a monster to terrify.

Candy was laid across his lap, and the man yelled an order

in a strange dialect of Japanese that she could not understand. The small force brought their beasts about and then galloped off. Candy watched the crowd dwindle and vanish into the trail dust of the beasts. She had lost another owner, and now her fate was again a mystery.

The soldiers left the town and charged into the plains. Candy tried to stay still and relax, but the bounding gait bounced her upon the soldier's armour and the hard saddle. She had resigned herself to being auctioned; she was ready to accept that. This strange force had ruined that plan and left her with a new and uncertain fate. How could they possibly have known who she was? Had the Captain told them? Was he in serious trouble for having looted the yacht and stolen her before the Mitama reclaimed what they believed was theirs?

Candy could soon see a herd of various Dinosaurs up ahead. Several of the Triceratops breed were drawing a large wooden wagon upon which resided the remnants of her yacht. A number of other such beasts marched around it, and they were all heavily laden with baggage. Several dozen of the bipedal carnivores were marching along in a formation around the prize, each with one of the warriors on their back.

At the head of the column was a massive conveyance that looked like a small fortified house on wheels. The armour-plated shell had splendid decorations and an abundance of metal that signified the occupant as someone of great importance. The coach was drawn by a team of six armoured herd animals, and at the side arose two titanic forms. The sixteen-metre-high Tyrannosaurs were bedecked in sections of ornate steel armour and were ridden by warriors in equally flamboyant protection. On the beasts and on the coach were banners bearing the same martial symbol as that upon her abductors.

One of the group responsible for escorting her galloped up

ahead and addressed the drivers of the coach. A horn played a swift series of notes, and the column ground to a halt.

Candy was brought to the side of the massive coach, where slender windows had silken drapes swaying on the inside. The soldier released her ankles and helped her down onto the ground as the other riders dismounted and went down on one knee before the coach.

Several deep metallic notes issued from within the portable abode, and a section started to lower from two stout chains, much like a drawbridge. Candy could see that the inside was lined with carpeted steps, and the armoured panel exposed an intricately carved wooden door with a gold frame.

Soldiers rushed over and formed a line three abreast at the foot of the steps. The door swung inward, and a form emerged from the shadowy interior. The warriors instantly went to one knee and bowed their heads. Candy was too entranced by what was happening to act. It was a failing that caused the soldier who had stolen her away to grab her shoulder and yank her down onto her knees before he joined her.

The woman that emerged was a lithe and tall beauty. Her hair was jet black and tied into a long ponytail that fell to her waist. Her face was hidden behind a black veil, and her elegant physique was clad in a vinyl kimono with curling red embroidery. The tight black fabric opened across her chest to expose her cleavage and split at her hips to allow two flaps to reach almost to the ground. Her exposed areas of leg were covered in fishnet before vanishing beneath stiletto-heeled thighboots. A pair of vinyl opera gloves matched the attire, and around her throat was a tall leather collar with ornate swirls upon it. Its height almost made it akin to a posture collar.

The woman had a bullwhip coiled in one of her hands, its dark leather fading by degrees to its red tip.

Behind her came two naked women with muscular bodies.

One was dark skinned with long dreadlocks, and the other was a tall red-headed amazon with braided hair and fierce green eyes. Both were extensively tattooed with swirling patterns, dragons, and other esoteric imagery.

The woman reached the bottom of the steps and walked around Candy, glaring down at her.

"So, Commander. This is the female?" the woman with the bullwhip asked. Her voice was as calm and alluring as her body.

"Yes, Lady Uzume. She was in the process of being auctioned when we arrived," the commander answered without even raising his head.

"Prepare her for her journey to the Empire," she said flatly, then turned to saunter back up the steps and into her coach.

The women followed and the door closed. The drawbridge was hauled back up into position, and as soon as it locked into position, the guards sprang into action. Candy's hands were freed and one soldier each grabbed an arm as others rushed to acquire implements for her processing.

A strip of one-inch-wide steel was brought to her, and Candy struggled against her captors as she saw the large steel dildo at one end and the collar at the other. The collar was hinged at the back and bore a lock at the front with a ring hanging just below it. At the sides were two small ports with a screwed thread inside, and on the rear of the plate that bore it was a heavy semi-circular hoop. Riveted to the upper portion of the strip were two leather straps with locking buckles, and down the outside surface of its back were a number of small rings that had been welded into place.

A hand reached into the crease of her buttocks, and she shuddered as petroleum jelly was worked into the opening. The fingers dashed in and out and left a lingering lubricant.

The dildo charged into her anus without delay. Candy gave a cry from the sudden shocking entry, but the men just tightened their holds and kept her subdued until she had grown used to its sphincter stretching presence.

The steel strut was placed to her back, and the length ran along her spine and moulded it into a proud stance. This was enforced as the thick posture collar was snapped into place and the lock sealed.

Those holding her arms took stronger hold of her shoulders. Hands grabbed her thighs and hoisted them up, dragging her torso into the air. With her breasts hanging beneath her, another pair of men moved in and tightened the belts into place. The thick leather jaws squeezed above and below her breasts and when they had finished, the flesh was welling with a light strangled discomfort.

The processing for her voyage continued swiftly, and they were obviously experienced at it. Candy wondered how many other women these soldiers had manhandled and restrained for this Lady Uzume.

They set her back on her knees and sat her up. Her arms were brought outward, and two metal poles were screwed into the sides of her collar. The leather manacles at the end encircled her wrists, and her arms were thus left slightly crooked and utterly immobile.

A bowed pole of steel was presented to her back. A small plate had been welded to the metal at a ninety-degree angle and it had a hole through it. At each end of the beam was a matching leather cuff, and the pole was placed to her lower back. A bolt was slipped through one of the exterior rings, then through the hole in the plate. A large nut was then applied and tightened thoroughly.

Candy gave a whimper as her legs were delivered to the fetters. The pole spread her legs exceedingly wide and held her feet just a little bit below the level of her rear.

Stretched open and utterly vulnerable, Candy wriggled against her bonds. She could not sway from side to side because of the spinal plate. Her knees and elbows could wiggle a little but there was no way for her to bring them in or escape the distant cuffs. Her head was fixed forward by the demands of the collar, and this left her with a singular view. The pulse in her breasts was becoming more distinct because of the slight crimp that made them swell and stand out and to attention.

The guards hoisted her up by the poles and became her pallbearers. Candy watched the ground pass beneath her while she was carried face down and over to one of the giant herd Dinosaurs.

Candy was wondering how they were going to get her up onto the beast when a heavy clip grabbed the hoop at the summit of the back plate. The hands released her, and she swung down from the support, her whole bodyweight being supported by the posture collar and the bottom of the curved backplate. The dildo was ground deeper into her and her lower jaw was pressed firmly shut. Her body swung back and forth like a pendulum, and this allowed her to see the area and catch hints of her fate.

As she swung, she managed to get a look upward at what was holding her. A small gallows had swung outward to release rope from its tip and grab the rear of her bondage apparatus. There was a large pale canopy fixed over it, and a plain saddle awaited her at the top. One of the guards was poised by the gallows and began to operate the winch at its base. As she started to rise, she found that she was bouncing slightly, and that a dense spring must have been set between the back of the collar and the rope.

The mechanism continued to crank her up past the dense torso of the beast, and as she bounced, she tried to figure out what the spring was for. Was it just to ease her suspension, or was there a darker intention?

When Candy rose over the saddle, she saw what was

waiting for her and what her bouncing was intended to assist. She could not stop an astonished gasp when she saw a significant dildo jutting up from the saddle. The toy was glistening with a thick coating of gel and was distinctly ridged.

When the top of the spring bumped the wooden beam, the gallows were drawn around and locked back into a forward-facing position. Candy's breath quickened as the winch then began to lower her inexorably towards the toy. She peered down with her eyes but could see no further back than the head of the steed because of the controlling collar.

The toy touched her pussy, and she gave a snort as the lubricated head opened her body and entered her. The winch lowered a little more and the ridges bounced her flesh upon their troughs and peaks. Candy's belly quivered and her hips shook as she was lowered still further and was more deeply speared by the succulent carnal weapon.

The winch then retreated until the head of the toy was just within her and then it was locked into position. From either side of the saddle came fresh lengths of rope, each with a spring attached to the end. The clip atop these coils was stretched out and snagged her fetters, leaving her anchored by a trio of spring loaded points.

The guard clambered down from the saddle and left Candy hanging upon her own personal conveyance.

The same trumpet issued another order and the column started to move off. The beast started to stomp forward, its back swayed slightly, and each step affected the saddle and the spring. Candy gave a long moan as she started to gently bounce up and down. The dildo thrust deeper and then the overhead spring hauled her back up. Every step of the beast was translated into another penetration or wiggle of the dildo.

Candy quaked in her bonds and hauled at them as the apparatus slowly ravished her. The teasing started to curdle her with pleasure, and scarcely an hour had passed before she was being forced through a most vexing orgasm. The dildo was slow, and the play was hesitant. When she loitered on the verge of release, she was bucking and trying to speed the next plunge of it into her. However, she was forced to be patient, because any wriggle only upset the natural rhythm and stalled the process. With tears running from her eyes and beads of sweat decorating her brow, she had to wait for the next thrust. When it came, it ferried her closer and left her gasping for breath while her senses burned from the deprivation. Another thrust and she was almost there. A quick second thrust would achieve climax, but she had to wait. Cursing her restraint, Candy stood poised for the next step of the Dinosaur. When it came, the ridged dildo slid into her and then the spring hauled it back out. The springs on her fetters stopped its complete removal, which was something she actually craved, because she was livid with anxiety as she was caught in release but could not hurry it. Every dithering stab of the glorious toy brought another chapter of a very slow and drawn-out climax. It almost drove her mad. On and on she was made to endure the excruciating bliss and when it finally started to ebb, she was still being bounced upon the shaft.

Exhausted, she had to continually ride the toy until her body had once again started to climb towards inevitable orgasm. Candy whimpered and begged softly to herself, trying to find some way to stop her body responding to the steady piston plunge of the device. She managed to hold her reactions at bay for a while, but the apparatus was relentless and soon she could not help but start to give in to her pleasure. The orgasm was just as savage to endure as the first, and with her channels raw and aching, she was left to continue her dancing passage.

Every orgasm that she was made to withstand left her pudenda increasingly chafed and sore. This made the ride slightly painful until her arousal could be cultivated to provide additional lubricant. The vexed membranes of her much-plundered pussy were not of a disposition to easily provide such passion. It took concentrated fantasy and dedicated thought to gain arousal, and the pain wracked orgasm only served to make her even tenderer.

The pleasure became harder to acquire, and when it was, it was corrupted with discomfort from her sore belly and her aching bound body. Candy was almost delirious from the ordeal when the convoy finally stopped for the night.

Candy was left hanging on the tip of the dildo, her pussy burning from overuse. She regulated her breathing and tried to remain calm as she listened to the sounds of the column making camp. Finally, she felt someone climbing up the flank of the beast. The slight movement was brought to her loins as a wiggle that made her winch and choke.

The winch hauled her up, and she gave a sigh of wanton relief as she was finally freed from the machinations of the toy. Candy was then lowered back to the ground. Her body settled onto her rear and her mouth was finally permitted ease, because now that she could relax, she did not have to constantly bite to the ball gag.

The belt at the back of her head was opened and the ball drawn from her parched lips. A waterskin was brought to her, and she suckled on the nozzle. The cool waters were a definite treat. She was dehydrated from her ordeal, and she gulped down a significant quantity before they took it away. A bowl of rice and vegetables was slowly fed to her with chopsticks, and after a little more water, the gag was again restored to her.

Candy was expecting to spend the night as she was, but then her aching wrists and ankles were set free of the cuffs. The enervated limbs dropped and hung from her torso. Her back was still kept rigid and straight, but the pleasure in being able to close her lewdly parted thighs was a delightful one.

While life trickled back into her extremities, the poles that bore the cuffs were unfastened and she was hoisted back onto her feet. The regal woman she now knew as Lady Uzume moved into her sight. On her shoulders were two fluted plates of steel armour, and from them draped a long satin cloak. She had replaced her bullwhip with a long riding crop that had a carved bone handle. The two naked women were at her side, and each had a curved sword in their hands.

A leash was clipped to the lowest ring on Candy's back, and the crop flashed around and into her buttocks. Candy gave a cry and staggered forward until she reached the limits of the lead. A single yank made her stop and caused the back-plate to shift and the steel shaft in her anus to tug at her sphincter.

The two nude guards moved ahead and stood just before Candy to help guide her passage as the Lady gave her another flick of the crop to force her to walk forward. Soldiers followed the noblewoman, and together the group began a tour that both apprised the noblewoman of the camp and also served to exercise Candy's weary form.

The soldiers bowed deeply as she passed and did not rise until the Lady had passed them by. It was obvious now that the woman was of no small standing, which meant that Candy's new master had to be even higher. Was she going to be sent to some majestic palace of depravity? The obvious fetishistic inclinations of Lady Uzume and the meticulous bondage they had applied suggested that perhaps her lot was going to be a very interesting one. They had a serious predilection for domination, and Candy was starting to become a little concerned about the punishments they would apply to her. After all, she was still a relative novice. Their expert attentions might be too much.

They passed areas of the perimeter on several occasions where Candy saw warriors standing like dark sentinels, watching the land with night vision goggles and assault rifles. Candy could see lights on the horizon in the direction they were heading. The twinkling line was too pale to be from fires, and suggested that their destination was using electricity. Again, the bizarre merging of technology and primitive devices was bewildering.

A circuit of the camp was completed, and she was shown back to a large tent at the very heart. The entrance had two sets of guards standing rigidly on either side and they bowed as the four women marched in.

The interior of the tent was warm and scented by the clusters of incense burners that left a purple mist hanging in the air. Thick drapes created several distinct areas, and the floor was bedecked in rugs and piles of embroidered sumptuous pillows. There were some low tables and decorative fixtures upon some of the tent supports, and several sets of manacles hung from the roof beams, but what astonished Candy was the human element that was brazenly present.

On each of the four main tent poles was fastened a naked woman. Their arms and legs were held to the wood by individual straps of leather, and this left their elegant torso and large breasts free and open. The belts were riveted to the surface and were clearly permanent incorporations. Leather hoods that bore only a small hole for their mouths smothered their features, and the hoods had tall and stern posture collars that kept their heads upright and to attention. The collars also had a curling metal strut that sprouted from the front and from the sides, and resting upon each of these ornate supports was a dense white candle.

Facing blindly inward, the four human chandeliers served to illuminate the tent with a soft glow. The flickering light also drew attention to the shining silver rings on their nipples and the other piercing that could be seen running through their clitoris.

They were not alone in their inert servitude to the Lady. Opposite the entrance to the tent, there was a small wooden platform that was about a foot high. The platform bore a rich purple seat, and kneeling behind it was a woman whose body was clad in a catsuit of the same soft fabric. A pole arose from the platform and rode up between her thighs and along her back. This strut embraced her with a collection of leather straps that flashed around her featureless hooded head, around her chest and her hips and over her thighs. Her arms reached out and forward and were inserted into the rears of the living armrests. The two women who served in this capacity were kneeling with their hindquarters thrust up into the air to be filled with the backrest's hands. Their shins were strapped down to the wooden platform and their high posture collars were connected to the floor by a short pole. This kept their leather entombed faces glaring blankly down and their noses just short of polished surface. The arms of these pieces of feminine furniture were held together beneath them by sleeves of leather that culminated in a single tight mitten that was in turn fastened to the wrist cuff of the backrest. It looked as though any pull with their constrained arms would pull the fist deeper into them, so all they could do was stay still with their anus full of another slave girl's hand. She could see their buttocks clenching on occasion as they squeezed the extremity, which Candy could assume was gently toying with their internal tracts.

To one side of this organic throne were several large oval pillows. Curled upon them were three more women who each had a leather sheath containing their shins and forearms. These socks and gloves reached out and transformed both hand and foot into the semblance of a paw. The moulded apparel was highly effective and at the joint, there was a dense metal ring. A slim length of chain stretched from these limb-swallowing cuffs and reached to destinations that made

Candy's head swarm with lustful notions.

The ankle chains connected to the base of their butt plugs and attention was drawn to the large affairs nestled deeply between their buttocks by the small pliant tail that sprouted up to perky attention.

The wrist chains connected to a metal band that rested over the leather of the hoods that encased their entire heads. The hoods had slim eye slits, a crafted snout, and pricked up ears to give an implied canine visage that was convincing enough. Each woman had rings in their nipples and clit, and each had a small silver bell hanging from the hoop. The pups all looked up as they entered, and a jiggle of their rears made their tails wiggle and their bells issue soft chimes.

Standing to one side and just behind the throne was a brawny male. He had hints of an oriental heritage in his features that were themselves strong and imposing. His head was shaven, and tattoos of serpentine dragons coiled along the sides, down his muscular neck, and then travelled around his shoulder blades and pectorals. His nipples were also pierced with dark purple hoops, and a thick leather corset belt encompassed his waist. The leather bore an even pattern of dome-like studs and had the military emblem set on the front. A flowing robe of black with flames embroidered all along the bottom extended down to the floor and hid his feet.

The man held a leash that connected to a crouching female form. She was young and slender, with subtle breasts and a charming face. Not one hair existed anywhere on her body or head, and save for a steel collar, she was completely nude.

Candy was paralysed by a sudden wave of tumult. The images before her were of the most arousing nature, but also that titillation was coupled with utter dread and fear. She had been fantasising about dalliances with sadomasochism and submission, but it seemed that her owners were dedicated to it with every fibre of their being. Could she handle such a comprehensive and unwavering reality? Could she handle the severity and intensity of what they were going to do to her? What she had done with the Captain was pleasant and easy on her. She could have acquired the same from the person who bought her while still trying to affect her lot and work to better herself. This Empire was going to swallow her whole and would not relent in its use of her. She was one slave amongst countless. The worth she'd had in the wilderness was going to be useless here. Whatever they wanted of her, it would be done, heedless of her words or actions. If they wanted to mould her into furniture, or make a pet, or a chandelier, she could do nothing to stop them. The Captain and her previous prospective owners would always temper what they did to her with care and consideration for the well-being of such a priceless item. It seemed that this Empire had an abundance of woman, and she was far more disposable to them.

Candy suddenly wanted to flee, to run away and escape their clutches, to return to the safety of being auctioned so someone could protect her and cherish her as she explored her sexuality in relative safety.

Lady Uzume walked passed Candy, and the two bodyguards removed her cloak and armour. The sublime female form turned and relaxed into her throne. The backrest gave a soft moan as she was used to support the reclining noblewoman. Holding the crop like a regal sceptre, she placed her hands on the living rests and tapped her heel to the wood. The Lady and the male were both beautiful of form, and the man was exceedingly handsome. This beauty was offset by Candy's fear of what they might do to her and the lingering resentment of having been abducted from the auction.

The male leant over and released the girl from her leash. The nude form scuttled over and began to diligently lap at the patent thighboots. The noblewoman barely even registered the act of devotion.

"I require entertainment, my Nakatomi," said the woman.

The leash was removed from Candy's back, and the two women grabbed her wrists and drew them upwards. They were entered into a set of shackles whose height served to keep her on tiptoe. The collar was opened and the backplate drawn down and away. Candy gave a whinny of response as the dildo finally slid free from her rear. She pulled at the cuffs, but the chain that reached up to the ceiling was not going to let go.

Candy glanced to the noblewoman, whose face was still a mystery behind the veil. The image vanished as she screwed her eyes shut the moment a hearty smack caught her buttocks.

The dark-skinned woman began a swift spanking of Candy's rear. Her strong hand swept from side to side and laid hot flashes to the skin. Candy gave startled mews as the flesh started to heat and grow more sensitive. Each slap made the effects grow, and soon the almost pleasant nature of the chastisement was becoming harder to patiently endure. She started to jiggle on her toes and paw at the thick cuffs.

The spanking stopped and the other woman appeared before her. Without word, the red head reached up and suddenly squeezed Candy's nipples. The fierce pinches increased in effect, making her whimper. Candy shook from the severe havoc being applied to her teats, and the woman started to turn her holds and pull at them. Candy sobbed and danced on the spot as she was tormented for the amusement of her captor.

Candy gave a cry when a leather strap hurled inward and slammed across both of her cheeks. She lurched against her bonds and tried to turn around and evade another swipe, but the hold to her nipples was not going anywhere, so neither was she. Each movement she tried to make only increased the mayhem being ruthlessly applied to her assets.

The strap stung her again and then attacked the upper reaches of her thighs. This area proved far more tender, and Candy was swiftly hollering against her gag and begging for the woman to stop. The strap filled the room with the tune of rapid impacts and Candy cried out each and every time.

The Lady lifted her hand, and the assault stopped. Candy's nipples were released, and her tormentors moved to stand to attention on either side of her. Candy hung slack in her restraints, her head hanging low as she gasped for breath. Her rear and thighs were throbbing, and her nipples were aching terribly. The feeling of reprieve from the discipline had her suddenly sway with dark relish and clamp her thighs together as she quaked with lewd response.

"What do you think, Mikado?" said Lady Uzume.

The woman was speaking in the affected dialect that Candy could vaguely comprehend. The words and phrases that she could not, she could at least guess with fair accuracy.

"Attractive enough, but inexperienced. Her attachment to her previous life will make her difficult, but I think she has the makings of a fine concubine. Perhaps not Kamube material, but still a worthwhile addition to House Hachiman," he replied.

"Then we had best start to toughen her up," said the woman with a callous and yet amused tone.

"Nakatomi Jemma—hold her legs. Nakatomi Ammalia—the cane. I want to see how much she will take," announced the Mikado.

It took a moment for Candy to process and translate the words, then more time to fill in the gaps as best she could. The moment she did, it was already too late. The red head dropped down and hugged Candy's legs as her partner grabbed a length of bamboo from within a pile of cushions and skipped back behind Candy.

The words sank in, and with a gasp she tried to implore for

clemency. Candy was a novice, she had inclinations but no experience, and so she could not be subjected to such treatment, not yet. Before she even managed the first syllable, the cane hummed against the air and Jemma tightened her grip.

A searing line of hideous heat crossed her rear. Candy cast her head back and screamed at the horrible sensation. She tried to kick her legs free, but Jemma was incredibly strong and easily contained her berserk struggles. Ammalia repeated her stroke with venom. Candy's buttocks flashed to attention and she wailed again as she was afflicted. She clawed frantically at her bonds and tried to find a way in which to escape.

The cane sank into her cheeks and added another scorching dose of misery. The strokes were coming too quickly to grant her any chance to speak. The sheer level of travail being imparted demanded a long and hearty cry, and just as she snatched a breath, another swift stroke was applied to steal any complaints.

The woman continued her assault with steady rhythm and truculent might. Candy hollered and bucked, fighting to escape as she was mercilessly punished for no other reason than to see her distress. The cane caught the back of her thighs to coax forth the most mournful wail, and then it stopped as the Lady lifted her hand and ended the ordeal.

Jemma still held Candy's legs, and her strong back was flexed with droplets of saliva, sweat, and of the tears that were now coursing down Candy's face. Candy sobbed uncontrollably as her rear continued to pound with misery. The cane had engineered a swell of pain that lingered in the brutalised skin and was refusing to fade. Shuddering and trying to recapture her breath, she watched through bleary eyes as lines of moisture connected and ran down her quivering nude body.

"Mmmm, that was most enjoyable," commented Lady Uzume.

Candy wanted to spit curses at the woman, to vilify her for this brutality, but she was too exhausted from the punishment. She managed to look up a little and saw the pups all staring avidly at her, their thighs pressed together as they squirmed subtly from watching her display.

"Jemma," stated Lady Uzume.

The woman looked up and turned to regard her owner. Lady Uzume lifted her hand and held it forth, she then pointed down between her legs and shifted her thighs apart. The grovelling hairless slave girl moved aside and followed Uzume's right boot while continuing to lavishly draw her tongue up and down the material.

"Ammalia," said the Mikado, and placed his hands on his hips.

The two women rushed over and settled into place. Ammalia slipped under the Mikado's robe and rose up within. A slurp issued from beneath the material, and the back of her head started to ride out against the curtain of fabric. The Mikado stood still and to attention as the girl continued to swallow his cock. Her shoulder's rolled and shifted, revealing her dextrous hand play as her lips and tongue audibly toiled.

Jemma settled between the thighs of the Lady and reverently lifted the flap of plastic aside. The fishnet had an opening at the front that allowed her to remain on all fours and to humbly press her face into the pussy of the noblewoman. The Lady arched and gave a long murmur of approval as a deft tongue started to lap and adore her.

"Mae. Now that your tongue is nice and limber, see to our latest Kami-tsu-ko," she purred licentiously.

Candy's weary eyes opened wider as the nude girl left the boots of her owner and scampered over. Candy had rarely been with men, let alone with another woman, and she was suddenly startled by what was going to happen.

The girl reached up and drew Candy's slightly resistant

thighs apart. Candy stared down at her with alarm, wondering if she could go through with this. The worry vanished as a warm wet tongue rolled through her lips and started to lap at her clit. Candy's neck became limp and her head rolled back as she chewed on her gag and mewled with abject delight. The girl was an oral fiend that melted her with rhapsody. Her tongue poured deep and danced into her. It flashed around before she kissed and nibbled gently on Candy's clit. The broad width of her tongue poured against her roused morsel and made her quake with rapture and groan libidinously. The acute tip fluttered, and her full lips suckled to ravage Candy with ecstasy.

The loitering distress in her much-punished rear added to her enjoyment by catching her masochism and fanning her libido with the steady angry pulse of the contusions. The girl started to delicately caress Candy's thighs and legs, letting her soft hands drift up and down, tickling the skin as her tongue continued to thrash against pussy.

The Mikado gave a deep animal growl and he stiffened slightly. His ranks of muscles flexed and shifted as Ammalia slowed her motions and consumed his liquid heat with gusto. Lady Uzume sank her fingers into the bodies of her armrests and gave a long contented rasp as Jemma also brought her to orgasm.

Finally, after a few more minutes, Candy jolted and whimpered as the agile tongue of the fellow slave girl whipped her clit with its point. Her lips locked to Candy and she sucked with ferocity. The girl continued her work and made Candy jerk and holler as she strove to stay still and not kick the girl away.

The Lady suddenly recalled her slave with a slap to the backside of one of her armrests. Mae scuttled back and returned to lapping at the boots of her owner. Candy remained tensed for a moment and then slowly managed to regulate her breath. As the pleasure faded, so too did her vitality, and as energy drained from her body, she slowly slumped down to hang limp from the shackles.

"Mikado, I am tired from the day. Walk the pups and you may retire."

"Thank you, Lady Uzume. May the Moon God smile favourably upon your dreams."

"And yours, most beloved Mikado," she replied.

The man moved back, and his robes were drawn from the form of Ammalia. The woman was still kneeling and was shivering with pleasure as she licked her lips. The Mikado proceeded to the pets and took leashes from beneath their cushions. After attaching them to their collars, he drew the energetic hounds out into the darkness. They skipped and rushed around him, straining on their leashes as they eagerly anticipated some much-needed exercise after their long day of inert travel.

The Nakatomi arose together and after Jemma straightened the Lady's attire, they came over to Candy and let her down. Holding a wrist each, they ferried her over to the edge of the tent where a most unusual form of bed awaited her.

The slender rectangle had a padded leather surface, and it had easily been missed when she had entered. At each short end was a black lacquered pillory with smooth soft leather cushions riveted around the holes. Too weak to resist them, she was lain down and offered into the jaws. Candy gave a subtle whimper as she sat on her painful welts, but the women took firmer hold of her and rapidly locked her in. Her head was resting on the soft surface of the bed with her neck caught in a giving grip. Her wrists were kept on either side of her face, and she could just about graze her features if she stretched her fingers toward her as much as she could. Her feet were pulled slightly apart and her ankles trapped. Locks were added to the bed to ensure that no one could interfere with her containment, and the two women added a silken blindfold before they departed. Candy stared into the enforced blackness and listened as the Lady was undressed and escorted into bed with the two women. The sounds of licentious coupling arose and plagued Candy as she imagined what carnal deeds were being performed that she could not see. She wanted to ask them to let her watch, but these people were stern and uncompromising. If she did not try to remain an utterly obedient plaything, they were sure to punish her most severely. Already she had tasted what they did to their slaves for fun. What they did to correct them was bound to be far worse.

Cursed with frustration and fright, she listened to them lazily pleasure one another, and then the sounds slowly faded away. She heard the rattle of chains outside and some soft yips. The pups were being left outside the tent, no doubt tethered into place like guard dogs. Candy wondered what it must be like to be a pet, to have speech and civilisation taken away and replaced by the unwavering command of a leather uniform. Could she handle such a role? Her musings about what she had seen and what might lurk in the future for her slowly ebbed as the demands of the day took its toll and sent her into sleep.

CHAPTER FIVE

The clatter and bustle of activity as the camp was dismantled roused Candy a little and the removal of the ball gag
brought her fully awake. Still blindfolded, she felt her bed being lifted up at one end, and she was fed another plain meal
and offered water. Before she could speak, the gag was rein-
stalled. She was a body to these people, nothing more. Her
mind and her opinions were superfluous items that needed to
be quelled.

The blindfold was removed, and she gave a jerk of shock
as she saw the nightmarish faces of three soldiers before her.
The contorted masks had taken her by surprise and as she
calmed her racing heart, the pillory was opened. The guards
stepped forward and grabbed her before she could move and
then hurriedly dragged her out. Candy gave some minor
mewls of resistance as she saw her steed and the gallows waiting for her once more. A soldier had brought her spinal plate,
and the other sections were waiting by the beast so they could
re-join her. The guards yanked her forward and served her up
to the evil device.

Candy did not resist anymore. She did not need to earn
herself some sort of awful accompaniment to her distress just
for defying their intentions. The steel dildo was again smothered with fresh jelly to make the start of her day easier, and
she was attached and hoisted up until the other toy entered
her body.

Once again, the column started to trek for the distant hint
of structures on the horizon and Candy was being bounced

on the ribbed phallus. A command was bellowed out and the column broke into a trot. Candy's eyes widened with horror as she saw the lead animals charging off and those behind swiftly following.

The countdown to her own advance proceeded quickly and as the monster before broke into a dash, she screwed her eyes shut and braced for the inevitable.

Candy hollered and fought her bonds as she was swiftly bounced upon the dildo. It thrust deep and retreated promptly before she was dropped back onto it again. Bobbing along with the swift gait of the beast, Candy squealed as her pleasure was massively intensified.

She was danced into orgasm and then into another. All the while, the city was getting closer and closer. Candy prayed that they hurry up and get there, because she could not take much more of this infernal process. Calling for the column to reach the gates with her every breath, she was made to withstand three more potent climaxes before the steeds started to slow back to a steady march.

With the easing of their rate, her senses managed to process something other than excruciating ecstasy. Candy could now see that the Kami Empire had been built to be defended. A line of huge pagodas stretched out as far as the eye could see. They were both elegant and heavily fortified, designed to be both pleasing to the eye, intimidating, and functional as defences. From beneath their overhanging layers of roofs peeked the barrels for artillery and machine guns as well as cannon, catapults, bolt throwers, and other medieval devices. Stretched between the towering forts was a high stone wall. The battlements had guards marching behind them with bows, crossbows, and firearms at the ready. These troops looked a little different to the normal warriors she had seen. Their armour was heavier, and more inhuman.

Before she could gain a better look, the force was moving

into the shade of a huge and heavily armed gatehouse. The huge gates were made of riveted iron, and they ground back aside into the walls as the portcullis behind them was hoisted into the air.

The huge vaulted passageway led them through the shield wall and onto a halcyon scene of tranquil beauty that took Candy's breath away. Riding the dildo with the more usual steady rate, she took in the scent of greenery and moisture-laden air.

The realm beyond the wall was a marked contrast to the barren cracked plains. The soil was fertile and well irrigated. Plants and trees of every description thrived. She could see farms and ranches, fields of crops, and corrals of small Dinosaur herds. A wide road of smooth stone bricks stretched from the gatehouse, and it had been methodically constructed to a degree where the surface was as smooth as marble and the seams were barely visible. The road wove out into the land and branched off in numerous directions as stone bridges of exceptional beauty lifted it over streams and narrow rivers. It seemed that the foreboding shield wall of the Empire encompassed a huge country of verdant growth and prosperity.

In the distance, she could see huge palaces that were spaced miles apart from each other. Each one was ornate and spectacular and arose amidst forests and seas of colourful flowers and sprawling gardens.

Her steed stopped and someone appeared to lower her back to the ground. When she arrived, she gave a cry and struggled instinctively against her bonds when she saw who it was that had been responsible for attending her.

Lady Uzume stood with her small entourage and watched Candy as four of the lizardmen creatures handled her. The strange armour she had seen on the wall had been real flesh. The inhuman physique and features of the beasts was adorned with the same dense plates, and they all wore swords and blades on their person. Hundreds of others could be seen around the gatehouse. Some were drilling under the eye of human warriors, and others were helping to unpack the convoy.

Their clawed hands worked across her bonds, and she was quickly released. Candy closed her eyes and trembled with chagrin. The ghastly recollection of her near-death experience possessed her, and even though she knew these individuals meant her no such harm, the sight and proximity of them was mortifying. The dildo was hauled free, and she dropped to the floor and instantly jolted away from them. They turned and moved to reclaim her. Candy backed up with tears in her eyes and her fright now controlling her. Suddenly the two Nakatomi moved forward and grabbed her by shoulder and wrist. She was brought to her knees and held firmly in place. The feel of the women holding her down was a reassurance and her terror faded a little.

"You are dismissed," announced the Mikado.

The monsters bowed deeply and marched off to help elsewhere. Candy gave a sigh of relief as she watched them leave. For all the things that they had done to her, the Nakatomi were at least human, and their holds were less fearsome.

"Why such an extreme reaction to our Wani?" wondered the Mikado.

"Recall our arrival at the site of her crossing. Those salvagers killed a number of wild Wani. No doubt they were going to do her harm and she still fears them."

The powerful physique of the Mikado stepped before her. Candy kept her focus on the ground to hide the tears of her anxiety. His strong fingers took her chin and lifted it up. Her gaze moved up over his robe, over the belt, and along the crafted anatomical perfection of his torso before meeting his eyes. His expression was kind and reassuring and Candy melted against the holds of the burly women.

"Do not fret, slave," he said in pure unaccented English. "These Wani have been raised from the finest clutches of eggs. They are a warrior caste loyal to the death to the Kami Empire. You need never fear them. They defend our realm and leave us open for more . . . amusing pursuits. Do you understand?"

Candy gave a small nod. He smiled and stroked her cheek for a moment, soothing her angst. He then looked up to the women.

"Bind her," he commanded.

The pair dragged her back onto her feet, and Jemma caught her in a stern arm lock. Candy gave a whimper as the fierce grapple sank into place and squeezed.

Candy could feel the breasts of the woman pressing into her back. Jemma's nipples were distinct and hard, and this showed just how much she delighted in subjugating another slave.

Ammalia dashed off back to the coach. While she was gone, the Mikado continued to assuage Candy's fright with physical attention. His hands reached up and began to stroke and caress her breasts and body. Candy could not stop herself from relishing his interest, because his hands were educated and dextrous and his every touch was a joy.

"I think you are fond of our new slave, Mikado," lightly enquired Lady Uzume.

"She has a certain quality I find appealing, My Lady," he answered, and his touch became more passionate. He moved closer to her, and she wilted against Jemma as his lips brushed her neck and his hands cupped and began to knead her breasts.

Ammalia returned, and the Mikado moved back. Candy's legs were weak beneath her from the exchange. She was confused, distraught, furious, aroused, terrified—it was a mixture of feelings that made her head swim, and she yearned to be restrained because being bound would help her remain calm. By taking away her will and ability to move unfettered, they would reassure her that she was safe, and owned, so Candy did not defy them as a leather arm sheath was drawn up onto her limbs.

The tight sleeve pressed her arms together and caught her hands in a tight mitten. Cross- straps reached around her torso, and where they crossed in her cleavage, there was a large D ring. Fetters were closed about her ankles and a short hobble chain was stretched between them to limit her every step.

The Mikado opened his hand, and Ammalia placed a leash in it. He closed his fist, surveyed Candy's body with a lecherous glare, and then snapped the lead to the ring.

"Come, slave," he said softly, and with gentle pulls he guided her.

Bound to his desire and unable to resist, Candy felt a lot better. When she looked at the Wani, she felt trepidation, but the numbing dread was gone. She was a possession again. She was contained and protected.

From one of the gatehouses came a small unit of human warriors that made directly for their location. The soldiers followed a tall man in extravagant armour. He wore a billowing cloak, and his mask was that of a snarling demonic beast with twin sets of tall curling horns. Everyone save Lady Uzume bowed deeply to the new arrival.

"Welcome back, Lady Uzume," he said with a deep, resonant voice.

"How goes the day, Warlord Ashua?" she replied.

"Not bad. There was a robbery of a Toyo-tama shipment this morning, but my men assure me that there will be a swift resolution to the case. How are the heathen lands?"

"Backward and petty, but the will of Izanagi and Izanami chose to deposit our treasure out there, and retrieving it was not difficult."

"A mere toy boat seems a minor prize to warrant such commitment from House Hachiman."

"This was the real prize. A new female."

"Superb. Is she for breeding stock, or will she be a concubine?"

"We shall see how her training goes before we make that distinction."

"If she proves inadequate, I would consider it a favour to have the chance to buy some of her progeny."

"Of course, Warlord."

"Which brings me to another matter regarding your House. When you see Warlord Hachiman, could you try to get him to remind Take-mika-dzuchi that I cannot regulate the lands of the Empire if he keeps siphoning all Wani units to his battery regiments? He has taken the last three broods."

"Have you taken this matter to Warlord Toyotama-hiko?"

"He informed me that the Warlord had the proper authorisation to commandeer the new broods. Your master may have reasons for this diverting of troops, but I would ask to take precedence in the next brood releases."

"I will see what I can do, Warlord. Is my transport here yet?"

The Warlord turned and gestured down one of the roads.

Candy followed his masked glare and saw a strange procession coming their way. As they drew closer, she began to make out trotting human forms.

The women were from many different ethnic backgrounds, but all were exceedingly muscular and all of about the same height. Their arms had each been buckled up behind them into a tight sleeve of leather with a featureless glove at the end. A strap at the end of this glove connected to the back of the thick padded posture collar that extended out onto their shoulders. Their heads were lost within the confines of plain leather hoods that had no apertures save a small tube at their mouths.

Their collared necks were each fitted into a corner of a splendid wooden litter, and each corner was formed like padded stocks that had opened, swallowed their throat, and had been locked to leave them bearing the burden on their shoulders.

There were four of these large platforms, and each was stylishly decorated with many gems and precious metals woven amongst the numerous ornate carvings. The chair atop each litter was large and the cushions highly embroidered. A canopy supported by thin poles provided shade, and there was a strange lever to one side of each throne. The purpose of this lever took a moment for Candy to figure out and when she did, she gave a slight gasp of astonishment.

When the women drew closer, Candy saw that a pole reached down behind each them, and it thrust a large dildo between their buttocks. Manipulation of the lever operated gears within the litter, and caused a corresponding churning motion of their dildoes. This was the means with which they were stopped, started, and steered when they were being ridden.

Because they were currently without a rider, a beautiful woman guided each of the vehicles. Each wore a strict corset that ran from neck to hips, and they travelled on foot at the head of each platform.

The procession was stopped and each of the leading females darted around and knelt stiffly by the side of their palanquin. The backs of their corsets could now be seen, and upon them was a flat panel that would provide a step for the assigned rider.

The Nakatomi gathered the pups and had their long leashes reach up to the rear of the litters and lock them to it. Once the pups were secure, the women climbed up and took their separate seats.

Lady Uzume ascended and settled into place. The Mikado attached Candy's lead to the left side of his conveyance, and like them all, he then used the back of the slave girl to make his ascent.

The riders gave a pull to the lever and Candy watched the girl in front of her arch as the pole shoved the dildo deeper. The slaves gave a unified whimper and started to march forward.

The women bore their charges with steady smooth grace and did not seem to tire. Every hour or so, they would moan as the shafts were thrust deeper to bring them to a brisk trot for about twenty minutes. The team of scuttling pets easily kept up, as did Candy, but then again, she was not on all fours or bearing a palanquin.

Candy wondered how long they had been kept like this and could not stop staring at the lean powerful body of the woman in front of her. As she watched the pole rotate and churn the shafts within them to tell them which direction to follow, she wondered how she would fare in such bizarre captivity. The notion started to make her very uneasy, and she tried to stop pursuing such dark avenues by distracting herself with the landscape.

The land was rich in perversity and beauty. The Empire seemed to have an over-abundance of what the rest of the strange world lacked. Female forms could be seen serving in hundreds of mundane forms. She saw a team of women tethered and hauling at a plough as a nonplussed farmer ensured straight furrows. There were women bound in the middle of fields to serve as scarecrows. They passed other feminine powered traffic as well. Coaches, wagons, and gigs, all pulled by an endless variety of bound pony girls. Some had only token applications of tack, while others were lost within a dense weave of straps and buckles. They drew crops, produce, shipments of goods, and riders. All of them bowed deeply as the Lady and her entourage passed by.

They had been travelling west for a short time before changing their route to a northerly direction. Candy could now see the ocean in the extreme distance. Sometimes hills or a brief mountain range hid the view, but it was a steady sight.

She saw small towns and villages, and occasionally one of the huge palaces of the ruling elite. As the sun was starting to set, she found out which one she was heading for.

A perimeter wall of stone surrounded the palace. There were squat guard towers, each with a weapon emplacement atop them. She could see human guards patrolling the walls, and then their palanquins were steered around and toward a sizeable gatehouse.

The gates were comprised of a woven lattice of delicate iron. A squad of guards parted them to permit entry and then sank to one knee.

They entered, and Candy saw that the grounds were gorgeous. The flowers, shrubs, and trees were all meticulously tended and watered by slaves who showed customary respect to the Lady as she passed. There were glittering streams, pools, and waterfalls, each populated by a variety of brilliant coloured fish. In some of the larger ones, Candy spotted larger figures that swam around, and when they broke the surface she saw fellow women, adorned in tight, brightly coloured sheaths that devolved them into an aquatic state.

As they drew near to the huge palace itself, she started to see small groves in which there was situated some manner of bondage apparatus. The engines of restraint were engineered for practicality as well as to be visually pleasing. They were decorated with flowing designs and patterns that incorporated many jewels. Upon each of them was a contorted and distressed female form. Each was sternly gagged, and they shuddered as they strove to endure their ongoing containment. Sometimes she spotted a man or woman in salacious clothing tormenting them with toys, strange implements, or merely chastising them with a crop, cane, paddle, or just their bare palm.

They emerged through a wall of trees and onto a great courtyard. Large units of soldiers marched in formation while others trained against each other in areas of fierce hand-to-hand combat. Others were lifting weights and exercising vigorously to improve their bodies. All of them were dressed solely in a wide belt and a skirt of embroidered material. The average soldier had tattoos winding about their arms, while those giving orders or supervising had many more, and it was clear that that the extent of the designs corresponded to rank.

To the left of the courtyard were several massive barracks. The four storey buildings had arrow slits for windows and reinforced doors, while to the right was a set of stables. The long buildings had numerous female ponies and a number of men and women attending them. There were paddocks for training and exercise, and pens to hold those awaiting attention.

When the procession trotted into the complex, the living steps assumed their position while nude equerries appeared to free the bearers of the litter and take them away.

The Mikado removed Candy's leash, and she was shown into the palace itself. It was an amazing vision of opulence that was lit with ornate light fittings that were either run from electricity or fuelled with oil or candles. The halls had many treasures arrayed throughout. There were astonishing works of art, detailed statues, items of heraldry, tapestries, and numerous other exquisite items. They depicted acts of conquest, of war, views into distant times, often featuring divine entities. Others showed such deified beings at play and performing carnal acts so outrageous that they made Candy blush just to see them presented.

There were also objects of a more depraved nature. Items of restraint were stationed in alcoves or on pedestals to present lewd images. The living woman who was hopelessly tangled within the decorative fixture could not move or speak, merely linger in her ordained fate and pray for the day another slave was exchanged for her.

The halls and corridors were far from devoid of less restricted life, and the vast majority were women. Some were hideously bound in rubber or leather so that they ambled along as best they could against the demands of their punishing uniform. Others had token restraint, and some wore brazen fetish attire and strolled with a weapon of corporal punishment in hand.

The males she saw were often in military attire, while others had chosen to dress more provocatively. All who passed by offered a bow and a welcome to the Mikado.

During Candy's route, only one thing managed to truly rattle her. It was a set of descending spiral stairs. The stone was black, and it glittered as though laced with sweat. Burning brands provided a sinister light, and all around the archway that accessed the stairs were contorted carvings. The images of screaming faces and demonic visages were horrendous in their detail and highly disturbing. As they passed it, Candy gave a shudder as warm, sticky air wafted up from below and she heard the distant almost inaudible sound of hundreds of wailing and despairing voices.

Choosing to focus on the more pleasant images in the halls, she was taken to a door, and the Mikado placed the hoop of her leash into a sprung clip on the wall. Without saying another word he turned and wandered off, leaving Candy to stare lustfully at him as he strolled out of her sight.

When he was gone, she turned and looked at the clip. It was such a simple thing, yet with her arms bound it might as well have been a stout padlock for all her chance of getting free of it.

A few minutes of questioning and boredom passed before the door suddenly opened. Candy gave a gasp as a ghostly woman appeared. Her entire body was encased in a smooth gleaming suit of white latex. The cocoon had stiletto-heeled footwear incorporated into it, and the only breaches were for her eyes and her nostrils. Her jaws were stretched within the close hood, and a bulge from between her lips indicated a sizeable gag.

Candy's leash was taken, and she was brought within. The antechamber had several gurneys placed against the walls, and one was waiting for her in the middle of the room along with another of the albino rubber women.

The women worked quickly and removed all of her restraints. Then with stern holds, they dragged her onto the cold steel surface of the wheeled pallet. Her previous items were replaced with leather shackles that embraced her ankles and kept her wrists at her sides. Another encompassed her neck and another her brow to keep her head down and secure. The final straps formed a cross section over her chest that hauled her into the metal. Candy did not act to stop them. In fact, the outlandish image of the gleaming snow-white women made it seem like she was ensconced in some sort of dream.

When she was secured, they took a side each and pushed her towards the opposite door. Candy was brought through into some sort of medical chamber. There were large surgical lights on heavy articulated arms, steel cabinets full of instruments, in fact, everything looked like it had been looted straight from a normal medical bay.

The click of the women's heels replaced the soft squeak of the wheels, and they brought lights over and shone them down on her. Candy started to grow worried as to what was about to happen to her.

She heard another door open and the sound of footsteps. A

man leant over Candy's head and scrutinised her for a moment. His head was shaven, and he was in his late thirties, with a calm, emotionless expression. From what she could see of him, she noticed that he too was clad in one of the form-fitting catsuits, but his rose to a high collar and was zipped down the back.

He lifted his hands absently out to his sides and the two women obediently pulled a set of surgical gloves onto the extremities.

"Hafuri Ishin. Take her details. Negi Nokato. Attend her," he said.

"Yes, Imbe," replied two distinct male voices.

Another younger man in identical attire appeared with a clipboard that had a quill and bottle of ink fixed into it. She heard movement in an area that she could not see, and then there was a strange humming noise. A smooth shivering orb about the size of a fist laid itself to her pussy and poured sustained vibrations through her. Candy gave a squeak of surprise, lurched against the straps, and then sank back down. Her thighs trembled as the glorious sensations ravished her, and her eyes rolled as the mysterious Negi Nokato started to rock the vibrating head against her.

"What is your name, slave?" asked the Imbe.

"C . . . Caaandeeee," she purred.

Ishin dipped the quill into the pot and carefully entered the information.

"How old are you, slave Candy?"

"Twenty . . . six," she added.

The device came away and Candy gave a holler as her swollen clit was punished with a vicious pinch.

"Truthfully, slave!" sternly decreed the Imbe.

"Thirty-one," she corrected.

The vibrating instrument immediately returned and made her quiver with glee. The consequences of lying had been revealed and she was now committed to truth. Already she could feel herself rising towards a monstrous climax.

"Any medical problems, any allergies, history of recurrent illness or disability in your heritage?"

"No . . . nothing," she stammered.

Ishin noted all that she had said and then began to add her approximate height, weight, and physical descriptions as the Imbe expertly assessed each. He was clearly so practised in this field of slave processing that he could tell everything by sight alone, and all the while the toy continued to pleasure her.

With the end of her details, he stepped back and nodded. The toy came away and stripped her of its reassuring presence. The two women stepped in, removed the straps on her head, and then forced an O ring gag into her mouth. The stern hoop was covered in thick rubber and had a metallic ring on the upper surface. As she bit onto the device, it was buckled around her head. Candy's eyes then widened with dismay as the women started to hand strange tubes to the Imbe. The slightly pliant pipes were glittering with a layer of moisture and were coming towards her gagged maw.

Candy tried to throw her head around and prevent what she was expecting. One of the women moved in and grabbed the sides of her head to hold her still. With rubber gloved hands holding her firm she watched and burbled her pleas for them not to do this to her.

The pipe entered her maw, and she fought to stave it off with her tongue. She tried to shove it away, but the slick lubricant defeated her. She arched and gave a whimpering gurgle of dismay as it slid down her throat and was expertly threaded in so that it could access her stomach. Candy could see a distinct ring coming towards her as she retched and struggled maniacally, and the eerie sensation of being invaded ended when the ring met the front of her gag and with a turn, they were screwed together. Snorting through her nostrils, she looked up with terrified eyes at the perverse physicians.

Candy screwed her eyes shut and gave a sorrow-drenched gurgle as another pipe invaded her anus. This assault ended when a slight ridge travelled through her sphincter, and then there came a swift pumping noise.

The ridge swelled within her body and grew rapidly as she clenched her anus and tried to expel it. Her buttocks flexed and she lurched against the straps. Her canals were starting to ignite with a pulse of distress as they were stretched upon the welling balloon, but she was totally helpless.

The inflation stopped and she was left with a bloated trespasser whose width defied her attempts to get it out. She gave one squeeze to try, but as the most minor portion of the bulb stretched her sphincter far more than she could take, she gulped it back in again.

Penetrated fully, Candy heard a switch being thrown, and then came a strange chugging noise. The pipes gave slight twitches as something was pumped through them and directly into her body.

The toy returned and eased her with its pleasurable effects, but she was still startled by what was being done to her. She began to feel a little lightheaded and a warm prurient mood started to envelop her. Candy's resistance ebbed, and she started to squirm licentiously on the steel table. Her nerves seemed to become charged with delicious sensation, and the feel of the tubes within her became less abhorrent as the bliss of the toy grew in potency. It was a bizarre change, because she felt the possibility of orgasm vanishing. Her pleasure was intensifying, but whatever they were infusing her with was serving to keep her at an intense level of delight, but one that could ascend no higher.

The Imbe gestured again, and the two women moved in.

Each attended one of Candy's breasts, and their rubber-smothered fingers traced soft sensuous routes around the flesh, leading Candy to mewl with bliss. They worked their rounded impermeable fingers up to the summit and tickled her teats, which immediately stiffened. The women continued and left Candy livid with arousal as her sensitised nipples raged with delight. Candy closed her eyes and wallowed in the experience.

The fingers seemed to change places with something else, and there was a sudden stern click. Candy gave a little moan as a brief moment of discomfort affected her teats. It felt as though they had just been prodded with fork. The same sensation repeated on her clitoris, only this time it was a little stronger. The moment of shallow pain vanished as small sponges that were drenched in moisture took up the task of stroking her. She could now feel some sort of additional presence in the areas, a light internal tickle that was most delectable and made her even more amiable to their caresses.

The pressure in her rear began to grow more acute as she was slowly filled to capacity. The strange weight of being swollen from within by a field of influence that extended through the twists and turns of her colon was oddly pleasurable. A switch was flicked, and the two tubes ceased filling her. Another control was operated, and the anal shaft began to siphon away what it had given her. The sucking slurping tune of it devouring the fluids was distinct even through the muffling walls of her body. When all had been removed, the orb was deflated and the pipe removed. Candy quivered and unleashed a lecherous cry as the tubing fled her tracts. The feel of it sliding upon her sphincter was a most astonishing and alien one.

The oral tube was unscrewed, and she burbled and coughed as it came free and was then taken away.

"Osha Nachatiki, Imbe of House Ohonamochi, decrees this

slave fit for servitude and ready to be educated," announced the physician, and after his assistant had written the words, the younger man offered the clipboard to his master so that he might sign the document.

The two women appeared and started to wheel her away to the steady clack of their heels upon stone. Another door allowed her through, and she started to be ferried down passages that were comprised of the more classical oriental architecture of panels supported by wooden frames.

One of these panels was drawn aside, and she was brought into a large tranquil chamber. Her bonds were removed, and the women helped her up. She was still a little intoxicated from what they had introduced into her, so when she saw what else had been done to her body, she could only giggle.

A smooth silver ring now transfixed each of her nipples, and another was visible between her legs. She had barely even registered the process of piercing and she had to admit that the decorations looked very nice. She wiggled her chest to make her breasts sway and she watched the light sparkle on the metal.

The women summarily drew her to a bizarre pillory. The item was made of varnished smooth wood, and her neck and hands were slotted into the padded leather apertures. The slat was brought down and locked, leaving her trapped. Her body was now resting along a padded beam that opened into a wide V when it reached her hips. This left her hindquarters hanging in the air. The smooth wooden struts kept her legs stretched apart with straps that were fastened to her ankles, below her knees, and to her upper thighs. The women drew them tight so that they dug into her skin and made her unleash a purr of approval.

Another belt was drawn over her waist and another over her upper torso. Both hugged her into the horizontal beam and her breasts rested down the sides.

Wiggling her toes in the air and stroking the wood, Candy watched the two sultry women saunter away with the gurney and leave her to examine the chamber alone.

Lush potted plants occupied the corners and the floor had woven mats placed across it. There was a small rack set to one side upon which was stationed an array of items. There were several canes of different thickness, a strap, a paddle, a crop, and several large leather floggers. Immediately before her was a low table upon which resided several large leather-bound tomes and a small wooden chest.

The soft sound of the panel door being slid open reached her ears and then came the tune of footsteps.

A man in white robes with a leather sash pinning it to his waist suddenly marched passed. His long brown hair hung loose about his serene features, and two women followed him. They both had dark bobs of black hair and were exceptionally attractive. They had slim builds and wore only a tight leather skirt, stockings, and high-heeled court shoes. Their nipples bore silver rings, and short leather gloves covered their hands. Each also wore a plain steel collar.

The man moved to the table and sat cross-legged behind it. He opened the chest and removed a black ball. The orb had two silver chains emerging from one end that in turn bore two small clips. He lifted the ball, and one of the women accepted it. The pair then approached Candy and removed her *O* gag before one of them grabbed her jaws and held her mouth open while the other pushed the large ball in. When the sphere was in and paining her maw with its dimensions, they held her jaws to it and attached each clip to a nipple ring. Candy gave a squeak of dismay as she realised that should she spit out the heavy gag, it would be hanging from her freshly pierced teats.

The women marched back and stood like sentinels on either side of the male. Their arms were folded before their naked breasts, and their legs were rigid and slightly apart to create a most dominating stance.

"My name is Sato. I am Imbe to House Temmangu, the Great House of education and learning. These are my Kamube, and they will be assisting me in preparing your mind and improving your skills for life in the Kami Empire."

The man looked to the two scantily clad females, and they immediately strolled to the rack of weapons.

Sucking on the ball gag, Candy watched them each collect one of the heavy floggers and run their leather-clad fingers through the long bushel. With salacious ease, they flowed upon their heels, and with wicked gleams in their eyes they moved behind her.

"Your first lesson will be in focusing on other matters regardless of the distractions you may experiencing," he announced.

Candy gave a snort when one of the floggers hummed as its wide leather tendrils arced up through the air and then struck across her back. The varied lengths created an effect akin to a spank, but it was one that covered a vast area of skin. The smooth leather left a warm feeling, and the tentacles tickled her as they slid sensuously back. The leather trailed down between her buttocks to bestow a moment of sly pleasure before they fled and the other flogger assailed her.

The floggers then began to fall with lethargic rate. They were a minor discomfort, and her jolt of response to their arrival was more from the very loud clap they made when they landed rather than from actual pain.

"The first Kami, or divine spirits, that came to this world established the Empire which now dominates it. Each of the Great Houses is dedicated to that Kami, the ideals they personify, and all their descendants who are hereditarily elevated to divine status. You are now the property of House Hachiman. Warlord Hachiman is a Kami of fire. Fire Kami are the Warlords of our armies and police force who see to the security of the lands of the realm. There are Kami of water whose Great Houses patrol and farm the ocean and the rivers. The Kami of air see to communication, and the Kami of the earth farm, herd, see to heat, light, irrigation, fishing, building, hunting, and generally provide all the basic needs of the Empire," said Sato.

The women continued their precise application of the scourges, and Candy started to find it harder to ignore them. The skin of her rear and back was becoming prickly with angry sensation. The flesh was getting hot and chafed, and each stroke they applied only made it more intense. Candy gathered her strength and strove to stay focused on what the Imbe was saying. This was the information that would help her survive here, and she had to process it all and recall it accurately.

"Yatakagami is our Sun-Goddess and supreme ruler of the Empire. She has absolute power over all Houses, and only Tsuki-yomi, the Moon God, rivals her in influence. The Moon God plots the will of the creators, Izanagi and Izanami, who bestow us with treasures from the other world."

She had heard those last names before. Could these deities be personifications of two factors that plotted the trajectory of the vortex? This meant that they knew when something was coming through, but clearly not where it would materialise.

"The great rift brings us items for our use. The males from the other side work deep within our foundries and mines. Females are generally used to revitalise our breeding stock. We have a potion that we administer to them that makes them highly productive of female progeny that we then raise in our Houses as Kami-tsu-ko or use to breed even more property. When a male child is desired, they are bred from the priesthood or the Lords of the House and only from the best genetic stock. You have been brought here to be trained as Kami-tsu-ko, a pleasure slave dedicated to House Hachiman."

Candy gave a sob as a particularly energetic series of blows fell across her back. She strained a little against her straps and bit to the gag for strength.

"Your life is a cord with three strands. Emotion, thought, and conduct. To attain standing, your emotions should be full of gratitude and be without fear. Thought yields conceptions and beliefs, and you should be dedicated in thought and in emotion to the purity of your conduct. Your conduct should consist of you doing that which is pleasing to the superior powers and in refraining from acts that may be offensive to them. It includes worship of your superiors, and purity of deed and morality."

One of the women showed her sadistic streak with an up-handed flick that laid the leather tongues between her legs. The slap against her inner thighs was startling, and the lick of the tentacles into her exposed pussy was appalling. Candy's head jerked up and accidentally banged her crown against the thick wood of the pillory. Her jaws stretched wide with her holler and as she dropped her head back down, the gag almost fell free. It rolled out of her jaws and with a frantic suck she managed to lock her lips to the weighty device and haul it back in before it fell free. The women returned to flogging her raw back, and the Imbe continued with his oratory.

"The priesthood of every House is led by its Mikado. Below them are the Nakatomi, who are the mediators between Kami and slave. Imbe, like myself, are the preparers. The Hafuri are inferior grade priests that handle daily responsibilities. The Negi handle all mundane functions. Kamube such as those whipping you are former Kami-tso-ku who have pleased their masters and been elevated over those such as you."

A pair of simultaneous swipes lapped at her inner thighs. The stripes flashed around the wooden strut and assailed a large area of her legs. Candy gave a yelp and crushed her jaws to the ball lest she let it slip again.

"If you habitually cause offence or disrupt the pleasure of the House, you will be sent to Yomi. This is the land of darkness that resides beneath our feet. There, the damned suffer terribly and are subject to the most vicious treatment for the rest of their lives. Now we will begin with teaching you the sacred language of the Empire . . ."

The whipping stopped and Candy let her head drop. She rasped over the ball and stared blankly at the chain that reached under to grab her nipple rings. The sound of heels roused her a little, and she saw the women stroll passed her and return to the rack. She assumed that they were putting their weapons away and leaving her to her lessons, but then they returned to retake their positions behind her. Candy looked up with a start and swiftly scanned the rack. The cane and the paddle were missing from their previous locations.

Candy gave a whimper of despair as she realised that her education was going to be handled in a very strict manner.

The Imbe arose and again reached into the box to arm himself with a neatly woven length of leather cord. He walked over to her and pulled the gag from her mouth. He then knelt down and detached the nipple clips ,and Candy breathed a sigh of relief that the threat of them being used to hold the orb was gone.

One of the women appeared before her. Candy looked up over her alluring frame and met her eyes. The woman gave a brief wink and then turned on her heels. Candy stared with puzzlement at the rounded cheeks of the woman's rear. The leather was stretched tight across the mounds, and then suddenly it was pressing to her face. The woman thrust her hips back and upward, crushing Candy's face between her cheeks and pinning her head back. Candy's hands strained to reach in and move her away as her breath was stifled. The woman gave a slight wiggle and shifted so that Candy's nostrils could find freedom.

Candy snorted against the leather, and the scent of it poured through her senses. Her eyes stared along the smooth naked back of the woman and she increased her struggles as she felt one end of the cord being tied tightly around her left big toe.

The Negi then threaded it up through her left nipple ring, passed it through the right, and then reached back to her other toe. She wiggled them to try to delay his actions, but he merely grabbed her foot and bent it upward as far as it would go. Candy gave a croak as he drew on the cord. She wanted to implore him to stop, but they had managed to smother her words in the rear of another slave.

Candy gave a cry against the layer of leather skirt when he pulled on the cord. An internal anguish afflicted her nipples as the rings were drawn upon and forced her to start lifting her left foot. With his undeniable encouragement, she was made to strain her foot up as far as she could, whereupon he captured her other toe.

Any attempt to lower her feet would now drag on her rings and rack her poor helpless breasts. The woman shifted forward to release Candy, and with her cane in hand, she stepped back behind her.

The Imbe took his seat and let her get used to her predicament for a moment.

Candy declined to speak, because if she did, he might punish her further.

"I understand you speak Japanese?" he asked in that language. Candy affirmed in a similar tongue.

"Excellent. This will make your education very swift indeed. As you are no doubt aware, the sacred language of the Kami Empire has many similarities, but there are several distinct variations that have developed here over the centuries."

The Imbe then began to educate her in the new dialect. She had managed to figure out a few of the changes since her time here, so it was easier to process the tuition. However, during this they chose to prove to her that she needed to be able to focus and learn even against discomfort. Her soles started to cramp, and she shuddered as she was coerced into simply enduring it. Sometimes she tried to raise one foot a little and lower the other, but the pull to her rings made the nubbins flash with pulses of internal stress that forced her to give up. Such times almost always earned her additional strife.

When Imbe Sato tested her on a lesson by asking a challenging question that she would need to answer using the latest information, it was always done with consequences to ensure she tried harder. If the information was significantly wrong, she would scream as the cane hissed inward and laid itself to her rear or even the back of her thighs. Such chastisement was rare, but when it came, she was left sobbing and straining against her bonds. They would let her recover and then continue with her lessons.

If the failing was relatively minor, the paddle would slam to her cheeks, and when she had just earned a stripe from the cane, the burning trench would thunder with renewed fury when the paddle struck it. Even so, the ordinarily minor affliction of the paddle was accentuated because of the work of the floggers. Her rear was hot and sensitive to any abuses, and the paddle was a lot harder to endure than normal.

If she managed to excel, to make an intuitive leap and thus speed her enlightenment, she gained a most welcome reward. One of the women would settle on her knees and Candy would pant and moan as a dedicated tongue tip reached into her pussy and tickled her clitoris with swift swirls and rapid laps. The ring would dance around and shift, elevating her bliss, and once she had been given a minute or so of ecstasy, the tuition then continued.

Candy was elated to have at least gained a knowledge of Japanese and a rudimentary awareness of the nuances of this new dialect. Without it the resulting days, weeks, or even months in such stringent bondage would have been dreadful. It made her shiver with trepidation, and a sly licentious enjoyment to think of all those women with nothing save a basic western language to assist them. Learning the sacred tongue would have been hellish for them, and she was sure that the weapon arm and not the spry tongue of a Kamube would be the one that was most exhausted by the end of their lessons.

Finally, after a few hours of tuition, she was deemed to have successfully mastered the language. He entered some details on the clipboard and gestured to the two Kamube.

The women took their weapons back to the rack and unfastened the cord. One of them handed it back to the Imbe, and together they started to extract her from the pillory. They had to help Candy off the padded back, because her long confinement and the rigours of her lessons had left her weak. Hoisting her up between them, they locked one of Candy's arms along their shoulders and presented her to the Imbe.

After packing away the items, he took up the clipboard and strode toward another section of panels. He drew it aside and exposed a corridor into which Candy was taken. Her feet slipped beneath her and managed to provide only occasional support, but the smooth polished floorboards offered her bare soles no harm.

Another door was opened, and she was appalled to see a hall with several dozen heavy rectangular wooden crates spaced equally throughout it. Each was made of thick varnished panels that had flame designs curling over it, and each had a small vertical slot on the outside. Most of these slots were empty, but a few bore the clipboard and papers pertaining to another slave who was undergoing her initiation. There was also a bolted hatch at the foot of one of the shorter faces, and the lid itself was hinged to allow full access.

"Tomorrow we will begin your lessons in carnal action,"

announced Sato as he lifted the lid of a vacant case.

The women brought Candy over began to force her into it. The floor was covered in leather padding and there were some covert breathing holes in the walls. There were also several buckled straps that had been riveted into place.

Candy gave some token struggles that were inspired by nervousness, but they were nothing that even delayed the women in their goal.

Her words were quelled as she was brought onto her belly with her shins rising up along the interior. Her face was then pushed down towards the hatch where she saw that the inside of the small door bore a squat phallic toy that sprouted out above a moulded pad. It was formed from moulded latex, and her face was drawn toward it until she was made to engulf it. Her jaws were spread wide and her torso forced down into a more compacted format. Her chin was left resting in the contours of the pad, and this let her relax her neck even though her mouth was yawning wide around the stubby dildo.

Her arms were drawn out to the sides of the crate, and a restraint at wrist and elbow ensured they stayed pressed to the smooth wooden interior. Her feet were then pulled back down to press to her rear and three thick straps were pulled up and over her. They were tightened with wrenching hauls and two of them pressed her shins into her thighs and her ankles into her striped cheeks. The third belt lay across her upper body and made her nipples ache as her breasts were pressed forcefully into the padded floor. This belt also ensured that she was hugged into an enforced position and was unable to find any way in which to get the fake cock from her mouth.

Candy gave a whimper and struggled slightly as she tried to adjust to her position. Then she was then plunged into darkness as the lid was shut.

The locks were set, and she heard her clipboard scrape into position before the muted sounds of her tutors" departure reached her.

Breathing quickly, she pulled at her restraints and tried to back off of the dildo. Candy gnawed on it, groaned, and continued her fruitless attempt at escape. The interior of the box started to grow hot with her struggles and her racing breath. Candy continued her fight and then offered a flurry of berserk straining and hollering against the gag as she lost all patience with her containment.

The fight quickly exhausted her, and she sagged as she resigned herself to this terrible lot.

As she cooled her temper, she started to feel her old desires coming back to haunt her. Her time as a bound object with the Captain had created a penchant for this method of control, and Candy gradually managed to sink into a tranquil haze of contentment. The ferocity of the Kami Empire was intimidating, even frightening, and her abandonment to a lot as one slave amongst thousands would make her fight to elevate herself even harder and was infinitely more pressing. Nevertheless, she had advantages. Her freshly unearthed masochistic nature, her interest and adoration of submission, her looks, her ability at language — those all might be commodities to again make her valuable.

CHAPTER SIX

Candy managed to gain some decent hours of sleep even though her body was starting to go numb in places and her jaws were aching from being so acutely parted.

The sound of a bolt being drawn back had her shift a little, and she opened her eyes against the darkness. The hatch rose, and a blast of dazzling light attacked her sight. Candy gave a squeal and a jerk of response that the straps expertly subdued.

The dildo slid from her maw as the hatch was raised completely and a male hand entered to remove several clips that allowed the chin pad to be pulled out. Before Candy could lay her head down on the exposed wood, a bowl was pushed in.

The plain meal of rice, strange alien vegetables, nuts, and odd slivers of meat had an intoxicating aroma, and Candy quickly began to devour it. It was reassuring to know that they were feeding their property well and ensuring that they kept strong and healthy.

As Candy ate, she started to hear the other hatches being opened and the occupants fed as well.

She licked the bowl clean, and then it was pulled out. The chin cup again lifted her face, and the hatch began to come down. The dildo nudged her lips, and the operator gave some threatening pushes. Candy felt the tip breach her lips and touch her teeth. Closing her eyes to commit herself to obeying them, she stretched her jaws wide. The dildo pushed in, opening her out even more as she gave a protesting gurgle and whimper. The bolt was thrown and she wiggled and gasped while trying to accept the return of the huge instrument.

After being given some time to digest, she began to hear people coming into the hall and start removing occupants. Every time she heard people wander passed her crate, she hoped that it was Sato coming to release her and continue her education, but it was not to be.

The thought of being taught carnal acts was a very alluring one. She knew that the lessons would be conducted under some mode of bondage, with punishment set to correct her failings. However, what would the reward for exceptional performance be?

The top of her crate rose up and let light fall onto her body. Feminine hands once more operated her restraints, and Candy was hauled out of the box and onto all fours. She quivered and shook as pins and needles and the onset of myalgia coursed through her long restricted body. It was easier to stay still, because she was starting to become familiar with such effects. She knew all too well what to expect and thus what to ready herself to endure.

Imbe Sato and his slaves were again before her. The women still wore their leather attire, and now they held a three-pronged tawse in their gloved hands. The Imbe himself held a collection of slender red rope.

"Follow me on your hands and knees, slave," he announced.

The robed man turned and wandered out through one of the panel doors. The two women walked at her side, their weapons ready to pounce and lash her body for the slightest error. Candy kept her focus on the hem of Sato's robe, hoping to keep a supplicant face and prevent the retribution of the women.

Candy started to wonder what they had endured here, and how they had managed to acquire higher status. It was a pleasing image to think of them crying in the dark, locked in a crate, or being caned as they were harshly taught the native language, just as she had been. Nevertheless, they had since earned control over other slaves, and Candy had confidence that she could eventually acquire the same.

The passage had numerous doors along each side, and the sound of slurping and feminine whimpers seemed to issue from some of them. As she was shown down, she could see that the rooms had flickering candlelight, and sometimes she saw the image of a woman cast as a rough silhouette against the paper walls. They had their backs to her and were kneeling. They seemed to be bound and were attending something with their mouths, but there was no one standing in front of them. Intrigued, she continued to scamper along until the Imbe opened one of the doors and showed her in.

The box room had a lantern hanging in each corner. The decorative lamps filled the chamber with a flickering glow that cast their shadows against the door. To one side was a set of elaborately carved wooden drawers upon which resided several unlit candles.

In the centre of the chamber was a wooden post that reached to waist height, and the smooth pole had a replica phallus jutting horizontally from the summit. Candy could see that the slightly pliant rubber creation was flesh coloured and of decent dimensions.

The women closed the door and stood on either side of it with tawses at the ready.

"Kneel upright, slave. Hands on your head," ordered Sato.

Candy complied and watched as he started to unravel the rope and then brought it to her. Candy was intending to stay absolutely still, but the motions she was compelled to make came from the delicate sliver and tight clinch of the rope rather than from answering any real discomfort.

The rope loosely encircled her neck and slid down her front before it moved between her legs. She hissed with delight as it was brought up between her buttocks. The ridges of the coil slipped between the lips of her sex and rode the ring in her clit. She swayed slightly, then arched her chest with a gasp as he pulled it tighter and fastened it about her waist to create a stern and succulent weave about her hindquarters. The rope took hold of her ankles and returned to her crotch rope before heading up to encompass her upper body. A *figure of eight* weave hugged the base of her breasts and made her nipples tingle with added sensation as the slight cinch made them swell outward. Each arm was brought down from her head and the hand then set at the base of her shoulder blades. The rope took her wrists and upper arms and tightened to haul them against her back. Once both arms were captive, he secured the whole harness with some knots and some weaving that ate up all that remained of the length.

"Show me what you can do, slave," he stated, and marched to the side of the pole.

Candy's libido was charged and anxious within the ropes. Every movement brought the most delightful and covert shuffle of the crotch rope. Every shift that moved her clit ring and tickled her pussy was making her even more lustful and the welcome clinch of the harness across her form was an added enticement.

Candy trekked over and instantly began eating the phallus. She locked her lips to it and her body swayed with licentious motions as she sucked and moaned with heady glee. She imaged the Captain, imagined Sato, or the Mikado of Lady Uzume standing before her, watching her rope-constrained form performing wanton fellatio on their cock.

She sank back and flapped her tongue to its tip before spearing her maw amidst a long groan of hungry desire and satisfaction. Candy rocked back and forth, the suction making her cheeks hollow to the shaft as she worked.

The Imbe paced stolidly around her, assessing her actions. The scrutiny and the possibility of impressing the teacher made Candy even more wanton in her actions and she started to rub her breasts against the pole as her hips writhed and her head bobbed against the phallus.

"Not bad. Not bad at all," commented the Imbe.

Sato left Candy to continue working the toy and went to the drawers. When he returned, he pulled her off the device and unscrewed it from its base. In its place was set a replica of a pudendum. Sculpted from the same pliant material, it was completely translucent to allow the Imbe to see what her tongue was doing in full clarity.

"Begin," he ordered.

Candy was now a little worried. She knew how to handle a man's organ, but she was a little out of her depth with regard to a woman. However, she knew what she liked, and had felt a variety of techniques used on her by some of the slaves here. Her inexperience made her question whether she could perform to the required standard.

Candy poured her tongue into the replica and started to try to do all the things that had felt so pleasurable to her. She suckled, she thrust deep, she lapped, and she flicked her tip to the toy's imitation clit. The Imbe moved in and pulled her off once he had seen enough.

"Hmmm, adequate. With a little training you will do better," he said, and Candy gave an inner sigh of relief that she had at least not failed.

"Kamube!" he snapped.

The women rushed over, and one of them knelt down beside Candy as the other took up a position behind her with tawse in hand.

"Watch and learn," said Sato.

He stepped back with his arms at his side. Candy shuffled aside to watch as the woman took her place. It was a strange sight, to see a transparent disembodied sex and the long slender tongue that was ploughing into it. The woman performed with obvious skill, and Candy felt a little giddy as she watched the practised organ at work.

"Your turn," interrupted the Imbe.

The woman ceded her place to Candy, remained on her knees, and stared at the toy. Candy tried to copy what she had seen to the best of her ability, but her tongue was not as adept. She lacked the stamina and flexibility of the veteran slave, and she paid the price.

The Imbe instructed her what she was doing wrong or how she could do better, offering guidance on what she should do. These words were punctuated by the swipe of the tawse.

The slender tongues slammed against her rear and thighs, imparting vicious blasts of mayhem that made her sink her face into the replica and mute her cries with the material. The tawse regularly struck, and she was shivering with strain as her aching tongue sought to keep up with the lessons.

Sometimes she was given a moment's reprieve to rest as the other slave was brought in to give another visual demonstration.

Tears trickled down her cheeks from stress as sweat began pouring down her labouring frame. Her tongue felt ready to drop off from its exertions. It was becoming almost impossible to conduct the most basic manoeuvres because of it.

Candy gurgled and sobbed as she was continually chastised for her weakness, and the need to try to flee often arose as the tawse skimmed her rear and left her quaking with despair.

The ropes held her body in check, and if she did try to escape, she knew she would only earn an even more vicious punishment. Only once the Imbe was satisfied that she could take no more did he permit an end to the lesson.

"I believe you have the correct idea. But you must learn to adapt to the wants of your partner. Watch their reactions carefully and act accordingly. Now, let us move onto the next stage of your training."

Sato closed in and Candy let her eyes drift shut as she felt the brush of his hands upon her body. Knots unfastened and the coils slowly lifted away until she was free again.

"You may rise and follow me, slave."

The woman with the tawse opened the door, and as Candy followed the Imbe out, they again fell in behind her. She was escorted down the passage and to the end. The wall there was made of stone, and a large wooden door was set in it. The Imbe pushed it open, and the sound of a multitude of bodies in motion poured out along with cries and gasps from dozens of tormented female throats.

The large stone hall had a vaulted ceiling with hundreds of depraved sexual frescoes. Men and women were depicted as an endless tangled sea of limbs, all interlocked and performing an encyclopaedia of carnal acts. Two large chandeliers hung from stout chains, and each was a starburst of metal that embraced a spread-eagled woman. They were each strapped into the frame and their bodies had many lines of dry wax running down their bare skin and hanging from their undersides as frozen opaque icicles. Their heads were hidden within a leather hood, and the twenty large candles arrayed about them continued to fill the room with radiance.

The walls were hidden behind red drapes, and the flagstone floor offered a large wooden stage. Three steps led up to it from every side, and set across the surface were precise ranks placed five across and five deep. The positions were marked by a circular cushion of padded leather that gave comfort to a female slave. The edges of the padding were fastened into place by a close ring of dense eyelets that pierced the cushion and entered the stage. At the middle of the cushion arose two distinct dildoes that were solid and had metal panels arranged all over them.

The women were held to the toys by restraints. A steel

collar, cuffs, fetters, and a waistband all had semi-circular hoops of steel welded along them. Chains had been fixed permanently to these anchors, and they reached down to lock to the rings at the perimeter of the cushions. The chain that reached from the front of each woman's collar kept them slightly hunched over, and their arms were drawn out to the side. Their waists had a chain at front, back, and sides to keep them permanently impaled, and their ankles were held wide to keep them in lingering kneeling splits.

The women were wriggling and riding the dildoes as the toys oozed liberal lubricant. Sometimes they tensed and gave a cry against the leather plate that had been buckled across their entire lower face.

Candy was shown to a vacant spot where the chains reached to open steel bonds. She looked across the struggling forms and wondered what was going to happen to her and more importantly, how she would do.

In place of the sensual rope, the women started to add the cool steel restraints. Her wrists were stretched out, the collar embraced her neck and bent her over, and her legs were stretched wide. Gloved hands took her hindquarters and manoeuvred her into place. As soon as her pussy and rear touched the head of the devices, they started to produce a cool lubricant that eased their entry. Candy gave a moan as they pushed her down onto the shafts and the waistband clapped shut about her waist. Situated just over her hips, the barrier meant that there was no way for her to rise up enough to get away from the toys.

The Imbe took up the empty gag and pushed the large ball that was supported on the interior into Candy's maw. He tightened the buckle around her head, and the leather pressed to her face to create a near airtight seal.

"The probes that are inserted into you are controlled by a very sophisticated computer program. They are also very sensitive to even the minutest motion. They will demand that you satisfy an alternating list of various responses and movements. If you succeed, you will be rewarded. If you fail, they will punish you until you get it right. We will return at the end of the day to see how you are doing."

Candy yanked at her bonds and yelled against the gag. She could not handle a whole day of such barbarous tuition. Sato had to understand that.

The women gave her a gloating look of amusement as they no doubt recalled their own time in such distress and then turned to follow the Imbe back out. The door closed and Candy continued to try to find a way to get off the toys or to slip her bonds. She stared up at the ceiling and wished that these people would be a little more mundane in their sexuality. Why couldn't they just tie her down and make her learn with a real manhood instead of torturous toys? She guessed that when she was used by one of them, they wanted it done right, and they had no time for her to learn at the expense of their own satisfaction. Obviously, she would not know the physical affections of the Kami until she was good enough to warrant it.

Her hopes that the Kami would be just as adept and the skill of their attentions would justify all this abuse vanished when the probes suddenly released a charge. It tricked her nerves and made her channels clench to them with all their might.

Candy cast her head back and yelped from the pain. She thrust herself up, but the chains held, and the waistband dug at her hips. She jiggled and tried again while hauling at the wrist cuffs. The probes attacked her again, and for longer this time. Candy gasped for breath through her nose, tried to ignore the presence of all the other women, and started to ride the toys.

A lesser shock came, and then another. Candy cursed the

devices and struggled again. She yearned to know what they wanted from her, and it was a dreadful process of trial and error to figure it out.

The pleasure she took in being able to ride the devices was constantly interrupted when they shocked her and demanded her compliance. It was infuriating and frustrating that no matter what she did, she could not stop them or even figure out what it was they wanted. She was out of her depth. She could not cope with this session.

Candy fought on, squealing and crying as she was tutored. Slowly, as time continued to pass, she started to gain some insight into the will of the toys. They were shocking her in areas that were not reaching the desired standard. As her pussy and anus grew more sensitive from the abuse and the stimulation, she started to discern what was happening. They wanted her to use every muscle, every part of her to pleasure them. They were demanding a level of coital skill that was unparalleled. It was almost impossible to do, because she just did not have the experience necessary to operate individual muscles. Nevertheless, the machine did not care. If she failed, it made her suffer, and if she still did not satisfy it, it continued and escalated its effects until through sheer manic desperation she eventually made it.

The day was impossibly long and trying. The toys would require a certain attention, a certain pace, a certain manipulation from her body. When after endless frustrating trial and error she reached it, Candy then kept that rate and started to work herself towards climax. Each and every time, the evil program stopped just before she could acquire orgasm and applied nightmarish flickering waves of shock, making her screech against the gag and suffer until her pleasure had been totally destroyed. Then a new program was activated, and she was made to try to figure out what it wanted all over again.

Candy thought she was going mad from the abuse. She

stared through water filled eyes at the other slaves as their nude bodies pounded and writhed while they tried to satisfy the machines. It was a surreal image, one that made her addled senses process it as a dream or hallucination. She just could not be in a porn-painted hall, being taught how to fuck by brutal machines with a dozen or so other nubile, enslaved women.

The whole army of probes suddenly fell still, and at some unspoken command, they stopped issuing lubricant and started to retract into the floor. Everyone dropped to the cushions and relaxed as best as their bonds permitted.

The door opened and six men entered. They had exquisite tattoos along their arms and wore only leather trousers and heavy boots. They were of various nationalities, and each had a whip curled at their sides and a large bowl of food rested in their hands.

They proceeded to each of the women, and after a warning that if they spoke they would have their probes increased in effect, they had their gags removed. The women were spoon-fed a portion of the ample contents, and after their meal their gags were restored. Two of the women begged and cried out for help and mercy. The men forced their gags back in and made a note of the disobedient slave's location in the grid of captives.

Candy bit her words and accepted the sustenance when she was freed of the gag. She almost let something slip when the gag was offered back to her, but she managed to stay quiet and let it in. She was exceptionally glad that she had. The men departed and the probes rose up. Some of the women tried to avoid them, because they were coursing with a charge that brought a terrible flash of misery to any skin it touched. Many of the women immediately plunged themselves onto the toys. Candy gave a squeal as her inner thigh touched one and then she decided to copy the clearly more educated slaves and dropped recklessly onto them. The shock instantly stopped, and when the toys were fully extended to stop her getting off, the programs began again.

The women who had broken the imposed vow of silence were much more energetic in their responses to the probes. The priests had indeed upped the power of the devices and failure on their part now earned severe ramifications.

Candy winced to see them sobbing and in torment, but they had been warned. The Kami Empire did not tolerate disobedience, and there were harsh penalties for any who did not live up to its commands. It was a lesson that all of them were learning very quickly and very thoroughly.

She often stared up and examined portions of the ceiling, seeking to fan her arousal and make the task of appeasing the inanimate lovers a little easier. She also started to run over what she had learned, refreshing it, and keeping it vibrant so that it would stick.

Did all the palaces maintain these areas for members of the medical and educational Houses? If so, then in every one of the huge sprawling domains she had seen there had to dozens, perhaps hundreds of women, being taught how to survive under the rule of a single deified individual, and survival meant pleasuring them and their depraved whims. They had become deities of sexual excess and had designed an entire priest class to ensure that they got precisely what they wanted.

A pair of robed forms marched into the chamber. One held a two-inch-thick rod of bamboo, and the other had coils of purple rope. They moved through the ranks and unfastened one of the women as all those around her offered sorrowful and imploring looks to the men.

The lithe and tanned physique of the girl was dripping with sweat, and she hung limp as they hoisted her onto her feet. Her head was held low, and her blonde hair hung in sodden locks.

The bamboo pole was placed horizontally to her back and the other priest began to use the rope to secure it. Her arms were drawn over and then back under the strut. The tight waistband of rope that was formed grabbed her wrists on either side of her navel and left her arms folded acutely upon the pole. A crotch rope reached up between her buttocks and was attached to the strut, and then the rest of the rope was speedily looped and knotted around her upper arms, elbows, and chest. When the restraint had been applied, the priests each cupped an end of the pole in their hands and helped her out.

They provided very little actual assistance. Rather they stood ready in case she fell and left her to trudge stolidly out of the hall that had robbed her of so much energy.

The same event happened again a short time later, and Candy realised that those women who were maintaining a flawless rate for a prolonged duration were being excused further education. The sight of a third woman being taken out in rope and bamboo convinced Candy to try even harder. She concentrated with all her might to fulfil the demands of the machine.

Three new females were drawn into the chamber to replace those who had successfully mastered the lessons. The introduction of fresh pupils meant that Candy had no idea how long the others had been here, and thus no clue as to how long it had taken the victorious women to master their lesson.

The rods again retreated, and a team of priests entered to feed and provide water to the enervated ranks of women. Those who had violated the silence before made very sure not to repeat their error again. Whether this would earn them a decrease in their shocks was not known.

The gags were replaced, and the men simply departed. However, the rods did not rise.

Candy looked around to try to find out what was about to happen and saw a number of the more veteran pupils curling down onto the cushions to try and sleep. Candy copied their motions, adopting the same comfortable position that they had no doubt spent time working out prior to her arrival or observed on the slaves who had been veterans when it was they who had arrived as novices.

No one spoke, and Candy surmised that again, harsh consequences were awarded to those who broke the quiet. The sheer level of physical exertion that had been demanded through the day left her little strength to even try anyway, and so she was asleep in moments.

CHAPTER SEVEN

For four days, Candy dwelt on the infernal rods. Each day she fought and struggled to succeed but could not maintain her rate without error for long enough to warrant release. Each time she saw men entering, her heart leapt, but even though she was not earning punishment, they were always there to collect someone else. She started to despair that she would never make it out of this room alive, or sane.

The sexual frustration was as much a horror to endure as anything else. The constant stimulation throughout the day and the complete denial of relief was a grievous strain on her. The chains that held her waistband and cuffs allowed her fingers to come within mere millimetres of her pussy but denied her the chance to alleviate her yearning desire during the night.

Her anguish finally ended as she was riding the probes as usual, seeking to predict or meet the requirements of the foul program that tormented them all when another team of men entered the room. Candy looked away and refused to plague herself with another denial, instead focusing more devotedly on meeting the rather trying and chaotic program she was being forced to match.

The probes deactivated and withdrew from her body. The hands of the priests started to open her shackles, and Candy started to weep with elation that her ordeal was finally over. Was this it? Was her education at an end, would she actually be allowed to serve her masters now?

The bamboo was pushed to her back and her body turned

so that the rope could encircle it within a tight network. She shivered as they worked, because the input of something other than her schooling was delightful. Every touch of the rope was exquisite, and she wore an inane grin all the way through the process.

With the priests on either side of her, she was escorted out of the room and through a side panel that accessed another series of stone corridors. The route passed by as a blur. Candy's senses were too scrambled to truly process where she was going.

Naked slaves drew a heavy portal aside, and she was shown into another large chamber. The walls of the room were lost in darkness. There was no light save for a pale spotlight that shone down from above and created a pillar of radiance. She could vaguely detect large solid columns forming a circle around the room and the occasional hint of movement in the darkest depths.

Standing behind the light were three men. They each wore loose trousers beneath a wide studded belt. The dark silken garment was tucked inside tall, polished boots, and their arms and entire upper torso were covered in tattoos so that their muscular anatomy seemed almost totally coated in rolling colourful patterns and numerous strange symbols. Their heads were shaven, and their expressions were stern. One of them held a clipboard, and another bore a slender riding crop.

Candy was brought into the brilliant column of light and pushed down onto her knees. She bowed her head and waited as the two priests retreated.

Without a word, the unarmed priest stepped forward and knelt before her. He laid her back, and she closed her eyes against the radiance pouring down on her.

Candy shifted her folded shins around, straightened her legs, and lay supine before him. She felt his hands touch her breasts and she gave a sultry gasp and a wriggle of bliss. After so much deprivation, it was a distinct elation to be touched by human hands.

The rest of the world seemed to vanish as the dazzling light made it impossible to see what else was happening in the gloom. It did not matter, because right now, she needed a ravishing more than trying to figure out who else might be watching.

Possessed by her libido, her thighs curled up around his body and her torso started to rise. Hands grabbed the ends of the pole and forced her back down. The pressure on her folded extremities brought a flicker of havoc that added to her passion. Candy surged beneath him, and with mewling gasps, she squeezed her legs about the silken folds of his attire.

Lips brushed her neck and started to work their way up. Candy felt them clear her jaw, and his tongue circled on her lips. She opened her mouth and curled her tongue within the cavern of her maw to try to entice him in. The tip of his tongue brushed hers, and she hesitantly emerged. Their kiss was long and vivacious. Every small shove he made onto the pole to see if she would break from their coupling only made her more devoted to it. She hoisted her chest up as best she could and stroked the roused stiff points of her breasts on his bare torso.

His hands left the pole, and she felt him reaching into his trousers. The head of his cock trailed through her pussy and continued to rub her vulva. Candy clenched her teeth and gave purring mewls of delight. When he slowly stole entry into her channel, she arched suddenly and gave a holler of bliss. He rested his elbows by her side, and her head leapt up to adorn his neck with lavish kisses and a trailing tongue. He thrust slowly into her, and Candy applied everything she had learned on the toys to his manhood. Every trick her muscles could do to excite and stimulate him was employed, and she actually found herself being grateful for the harsh tuition she had received. To feel this obvious veteran of enslaved female attention responding to her efforts was very confidence in-spiring.

Candy felt him move against her with arousal and start to return her kiss. His cock started to swell within her as she drew him towards climax. When she felt him come within her, Candy was turned into a vibrating wreck of response that stalled her efforts. The feel of him ejaculating instantly trig-gered her own orgasm, as though only through pleasuring another could she now acquire her own release. The long overdue orgasm was mind bending in its savagery, and she squealed beneath him as his drives continued to plunder her spasmodic pussy. His arms squeezed to her for support, and he brayed with ecstasy as he added another few lingering drives.

The male withdrew and brought a sudden jerk of response as his flight dragged his shaft against her ultra-sensitive chan-nels and restored a blast of sensation. The man caught his breath and then stood up before leaving the column of light. Candy tried to rise and failed. She applied more effort, and with stiff and awkward motions, she managed to get back onto her knees before them.

"Nakatomi Hachille. Your decision?" asked the man with the clipboard.

"She is worthy," he panted.

Candy realised that she was being tested. This was her final exam. She would either graduate from this room as a full Kami-tsu-ko, or would no doubt start from the beginning all over again. The thought of having to endure the entire process anew was too terrible to even contemplate. Some of it had been fun, even highly pleasurable, but she wanted to get out, to earn respite from discipline and to explore what else this palace had to offer its concubines.

The next of the Nakatomi stepped into the light. He wandered behind her and flexed the crop between his fists. Candy swallowed for strength as she anticipated a session of punishment to verify that she could endure.

The Nakatomi with the clipboard stepped forward, and his free hand drew forth a flaccid member. It became obvious that they were going to test two of her skills at once.

Candy reached up with her mouth and enveloped him within her maw. She curled her tongue around the organ and then gave a snort as the crop slashed in and crossed her rear. The impetus of the stroke was heinous, and the havoc made her pause as she tried to survive its effects.

The Nakatomi gave a tut and marked something on the clipboard. Candy was mortified, and instantly her mouth became a devoted oral demon. She attended him with everything she could think of as the crop continued to whistle against the air and slam into her rear. Her body jerked with each swipe that left a terrible burning line, but her mouth steadfastly refused to be delayed or thwarted by such pains. Her head rocked back and forth while he started to grow against her tongue and slowly stretch forth to give her more to work with. He was soon fully erect, and Candy was swallowing him as far as she could. Her mind was curdling from the input, the utter abandonment to the desire and pleasure of one priest as she struggled against her tight ropes and stayed devotedly on her knees. All the while, another of them was hacking into her buttocks to impart raw trenches and a level of background distress that was starting to make her dizzy because of its might.

Desperate to succeed, she continued her efforts and fought the urge to just throw herself aside and grovel for their mercy. Nevertheless, she knew that they would show none. These men had earned their places in the priesthood and would not dare risk losing what they had achieved because of something as insignificant as the whines of a trainee slave girl.

Locking to her goal, Candy was elated to feel him swelling against her wild tongue. She swallowed him even deeper and increased her suction as the crop became more vicious in its applications. She gave a shriek of dismay as it started to catch her upper thighs, and as she suffered terribly, she felt a sudden shot of warmth into her maw. Every fibre of her being wanted her to flee. Her animal instincts were bellowing for her to preserve her body from the crop, yet she continued her work, devoured his seed, and gave him every piece of bliss that he could handle.

"I deem her worthy," he impassively stated before jotting an entry on the clipboard.

"Nakatomi Nushi?"

"I concur," said the man, his breath now coming in pants because of his long workout in punishing Candy's helpless buttocks.

Candy sank back and let his cock pour from her mouth. She settled onto her rear, gave a yelp, and straightened back up when the welts seemed to erupt with new and shocking fury.

Kneeling before them, she rolled her tongue around her mouth and savoured his taste as the man returned his cock into his trousers and added the other passing grade.

"The Nakatomi of House Temmangu assigned to House Hachiman have concluded this slave worthy of Kami-tsu-ko status. Send this to the archives and despatch a Hayachi to inform Warlord Hachiman that his new slave is ready."

The man clapped his hands together and guards appeared from the shadows. They took hold of each end of the pole, hoisted her up, and drew her from the room. As she was leaving, she saw another young girl being brought towards the testing chamber, and Candy recognized her as one of those who had been in the training hall, one who had been there even before her own arrival. Such a sight gave Candy a small glow of satisfaction from knowing that she was still doing better than others.

Several sets of spiral stairs led her ever higher into the domineering palace of the Warlord. There were numerous long passages and large halls, and all were decorated with bound women and spectacular art. The men of the higher floors were almost all officers and had the same equal mixture of oriental and western heritage. It appeared that the ranks bestowed to the Hachiman priesthood also corresponded with their military ranks. They wore a standard mode of attire while marching around the corridors, and it was comprised of close-fitting trousers of dark hide, heavy boots, and a wide belt. Their exposed torsos bore tattoos of an extent befitting their rank, and they generally bore a crop, a whip, or the leash to a slave girl.

A lengthy passage presented itself, and doors were spaced equally along both sides. Candy was shown to one of these and her ropes were swiftly untied. The pole dropped from her back and she was ushered in.

Candy found herself in a sizeable chamber that was decorated in a sumptuous and pleasing style. A set of large windows were wreathed by thick curtains and allowed glorious sunshine to fall in. Several thick rugs covered the floor, each intricately woven with strange and colourful patterns. There was a long wardrobe with several mirrored doors, and an extended dressing table with plush velvet stools that presented an array of bone handled brushes along with elegant glass bottles of perfume and cosmetics.

Several ornate shelves bore books and other mementoes, as did the top of a couple of chests of drawers. There was a large double bed with pale satin sheets, and two sets of leather manacles were fixed at both head and foot. Upon seeing these items of restraint, Candy then noticed the subtle rings that had been set in the ceiling and along the walls to provide similar moorings should they be required.

There was one other door in the room, and it opened to reveal her roommate and the shower and toilet that lay behind her. The girl was in her early twenties and had long auburn hair. She was shorter than Candy and much more slender. Her face was round, with full lips and sparkling pale green eyes. She wore fine denier stockings with high-heeled court shoes. Her arms were clad in opera gloves of the most delicate leather, and the same fabric created a scanty thong and delicate choker. Her breasts were on open display, as were the silver rings transfixing her nipples.

"Hello. You must be Candy," she said warmly.

"How did –"

"One of the Hafuri told me that you were coming. I'm Yakami."

"Pleased to meet you," said Candy.

"You're really from the other side?" she enquired enthusiastically, and settled down on the bed. She patted the covers to invite Candy to join her.

"You're not?"

"Heavens, no. I was born and raised in the palace. I've never even met someone from the other side."

"Really?"

"Of course. Surely they told you about all that during your preparation?"

"The men work, the women are often used as breeding stock."

"Indeed. It's very rare for them to let a woman from the other side become Kami-tsu-ko. You must be very special," she said timidly.

Yakami's hand reached out towards Candy's shoulder. It was not threatening, but the unexpected approach of a total and nearly nude stranger caused Candy to instinctively shy away.

"I'm sorry, did I offend?" she asked.

"No, I'm the one who should apologise. All of . . . this . . . it's all still so alien," said Candy, indicating the room as she spoke.

"Here, let me pleasure you. You could do with some relaxation after your education, and I can see quite plainly by your rear that they were harsh with you. It must be because they want to make sure you're properly trained."

"We're allowed to . . . I mean . . . we can just . . ."

"Oh yes. This is our room, and we can do as we wish here."

For a moment, she hesitated, but then she embraced her lessons and her new life. Candy smiled and flopped back onto the covers. She ignored the ache in her welt-coated bottom and shuffled back until she could sink her head into the soft pillows. Closing her eyes, she relaxed her punished and weary limbs, then readied to accept the girl's advances.

Gentle hands parted her thighs, and the fingertips trailed up and down the inside. Candy gave a moan of elation that deepened into a resonant purr as she felt Yakami's lips brush the skin and tickle it with small swirls.

Yakami's lips parted to let her tongue drift upon the same areas and then her attention rose higher. She skipped from thigh to thigh, giving Candy a few more moments to ready herself before she started to kiss her pussy.

The elegant pecks became more focused, and Candy's fingers sank into the sheets as a deft tongue stole entry into her body.

The girl started to delve into Candy, exploring her as she quivered and panted for breath. Yakami suckled on her clit, and when it was sufficiently roused, she started to attack it with a most passionate tongue tip.

Such skill brought Candy to orgasm in moments. She clutched to the sheets to endure the ecstasy, and the girl's hands rode up and down her splayed legs. Candy pressed her rear into the covers and made her welts churn with new life. The words to ask for restraint rose in her throat, the inherent need to have the girl bind her, punish her, force to endure the pleasure.

"Enough! Stop, please!" she barked.

Yakami moved back and continued to kiss and lick at her legs. Candy recomposed herself. She had been taken aback by having something she had asked for actually being obeyed. She was so used to having her pleas and words falling on deaf ears and her prayers going unanswered that Yakami's cessation was most unexpected.

"Have a shower and come to bed. You could do with a nap before dinner," said the woman.

Candy slid from the covers and went into the bathroom. It was then that she realised that she had not agreed with Yakami or even considered the words. She was obeying more because of her indoctrination in submission. When someone told her to do something, she complied immediately and now it appeared that the effect worked even with regard to fellow slaves.

The bathroom was equally as plush as the bedroom. Her owners kept their pets pampered and in a luxury that rivalled what she had become used to on Earth. The fixtures sparkled and were of a most decorative nature. Each faucet and basin was like artwork. Even the glass panes that formed the shower cubicle had been engraved with depictions of clouds, with birds and dragons weaving amongst them.

After cleansing her body with the luxurious soaps on offer and then washing her hair, Candy dried herself on the towels and strolled back into the room. Yakami was already in the bed and threw the covers back to offer Candy a place.

Candy slid in, and the girl cuddled up to her. The feel of a warm smooth body shifting against her own was delicious, especially because it was so tender and accommodating.

"Tell me about the other side, Candy," asked Yakami, and she began to stroke Candy's hair and body.

Candy opened her mouth to speak and then stopped. She frowned as she realised the sheer difficulty of such a task. How could she describe her world to someone who had no idea of even its most basic structure? Cities with sky piercing towers made of impossibly valuable steel. People throwing away tin cans and old fridges, deserting cars that could have bought a mansion on this side because of their value. It would be like seeing someone carelessly tossing aside gold bricks. There were other concepts that would be equally abstract to Yakami, things such as television, countries, politics, computers, fashion, dogs, cats, planes, and especially freedom itself.

She started to ramble and express whatever came to the front of her mind as it arrived. Yakami did not seem to mind and just closed her eyes and listened to the deluge of information without questioning it.

A knock upon the door interrupted her. As Candy looked around and wondered what to do, Yakami jumped out of bed and opened it.

A tall Nubian girl was pushing a large cart, and she handed Yakami a pair of steaming rectangular trays. Yakami bowed and thanked her before closing the door and bringing Candy her meal. Candy was familiar with a bento, but the various compartments of this alien version had far different fare separated into each. The boiled rice was normal, but the vegetables were strangely coloured and had an odd texture and delicious flavour. She thought the battered and fried curls of seafood were shrimp, but they were longer and tasted more like oranges. The slivers of seasoned meat were juicy and succulent, defying comparison.

Once they had finished, they set the empty trays aside, and Yakami assisted Candy in getting ready. The woman helped her style her hair and manicure her nails, gave her some

cosmetic shades of the style the masters of the palace preferred, and gave her an outfit to match her own. After this,
they simply waited and talked, existing in a state of anticipation of being summoned.

CHAPTER EIGHT

Candy spent a couple of easy days in the room where all she had to do was rest, relax, and enjoy Yakami's company. Perhaps she was being given time to adjust and recover from her training.

Yakami took good care of her and told her about life in the palace. It was simple. When the priests or a Kami told her to do something, she was to comply and enjoy whatever it was they wanted. This could mean bondage, mundane chores such as fetching and carrying, or servicing them sexually, or even just posing for their visual pleasure. In the wardrobe, there were a number of outfits formed from lace, rubber, leather, silk, satin, and PVC to augment this last facet of their existence.

They were served food in the morning and in the afternoon. The door to the room was never locked, but they were expected to stay until called for or assigned a duty. The books were in the sacred language and were generally mythological or historical works concerning the Kami.

At around noon, a knock upon the door had Yakami rushing over to see who it was. A voice addressed her and as the messenger departed, she turned to Candy.

"We are required," she said with excitement and gestured for Candy to follow her.

Candy walked with the girl as they travelled deeper into the palace. They walked side by side, and Candy copied her partner when she bowed to those who passed them by. They were barely even noticed, but Candy was certain that if she failed to show them the expected reverence, its absence would be noticed, and the consequences would be swift and stern.

"Where are we going?" asked Candy.

"The play-quarters of Hafuri Oshin. He's very nice."

"What will he want from us?"

"He likes to have one of us bound and then he'll whip them to get him going, then the other will be there to pleasure him. If you're the one who gets tied up, he likes sounds of distress but not screaming. He hates that, and he'll gag you with pegs or something equally nasty if you offend his ears with wails."

Candy could barely believe what she was hearing. Yakami seemed almost jubilant at the prospect of attending this sadistic officer. She did not seem to care whether she was his lover or his bondage victim — she was just happy to be of use and to please. Candy started to gain some idea why her elevation from breeding stock was so rare, because those raised in the palace were dedicated to their superiors, and they were always ready to please and to take pleasure in that. It also made her wonder just why she had been spared the fate almost all other Earth women endured. Was it really just a matter of looks?

"Here we are. Oh, one last thing before we go in. Be respectful. He thinks he is on the verge of becoming Imbe, and he likes to be treated as such, but I heard from a girl who was serving as Nakatomi Gion's footstool that in truth he's pretty low on the list for promotion."

Yakami opened the door and they entered. Candy immediately mimicked her partner when she sank down onto her knees and placed her forehead to the floor. Candy caught a glimpse of the room before her eyes were staring at the bare flagstones — it was equipped for masochistic pursuits.

There was a large bed with a padded leather mattress and restraints set all around its dense wooden frame. The walls had cupboards and rows of hooks that bore weapons, bundles of colourful rope, toys, and other implements. Wooden beams crossed the ceiling and provided sparkling eyelets and there were other larger versions screwed into the floor. Candles ran along the base of the walls and cast their glow up across the various items to make them appear even more foreboding.

Oshin was sitting on the end of the bed in expectation of their arrival. He was a tall and very muscular man with short blonde hair that had been shaven away at the sides to leave a spiky crest. He had a strong jaw and dark ferocious eyes. Tattoos curled up his arms and reached up the sides of his neck and onto the sides of his head. Latex shorts clutched to his lower body and the legs of the garment reached almost to his knees.

The officer arose and paced around the two servile women, verifying their servility before heading away to start preparing his choice of restraint. Candy listened patiently as she heard him work and could not help but wonder whether she would be on the bed and ravished, or in this mysterious restraint and then whipped.

"Rise," commanded Oshin, and his words brought them both back onto their heels.

A circular wooden pole lay on the floor near a chain that ran from floor to ceiling anchors. The pole had two long metal strips set along either side, and one end terminated in a metal clip, while the other end had a leather collar attached to it. There was also a set of cuffs that had been linked by a coil of rope.

Oshin presented a small wooden disc. One side was painted black, the other white.

"In. Yo," he said, pointing to Candy and then to Yakami.

Oshin grinned and flicked the disc into the air. The two slaves watched it tumble and then bounce upon the ground. The disc rolled for a moment and then dropped with the black facing up.

"You, take off your underwear and come here," he said bluntly, directing his words to Candy.

With a tremble in her body, she obeyed and followed him to the site of her restraint. She tried to keep what Yakami said in the forefront of her thoughts, but her worries were hard to suppress.

The collar was buckled about her neck, and she was bent over with her rear facing towards the vertical chain. The officer nudged her legs apart and lifted the other end of the pole until it touched her pussy. He then applied the clip at the end of the strut to the rising strand of chain. This left Candy bent over at the middle with her neck connected to the chain by the pole beneath her. She swayed a little, and the cool metal on each side of the wooden strut tickled her pussy and inner thighs, and when she swayed more distinctly, it grazed her hanging breasts.

Candy felt him draw her arms behind her, whereupon he added the cuffs and threaded the rope through one of the higher links. He dragged in the slack and elevated her arms, bending her over a little more. He then paid out a length of insulated cable from the wall. The thin prong at the end was slotted into the rear of the pole near to the clip and Candy gave a yelp as the metal surfaces of the pole became charged with vicious current. The shock made her involuntarily arch up and this tugged the pole against her loins. The voltage gnawed on her pussy and with a cry she doubled over as best she could. The wrist cuffs stopped her getting any lower and left the pole loitering dangerously close to her skin. With her legs parted and her body hunched over, she quivered as she tried to maintain the static pose.

Candy shuffled a little to try to ease her position. It was awkward to stay on her heels, but as she moved, she caused the pole to brush her inner thigh. She gave a startled mew and gritted her teeth as her body bucked and accidentally brushed the pole to the other side to add more havoc. Her breasts swayed and then touched the upper reaches of the pole. This caused a sudden flash of mayhem through the flesh that again encouraged her to arch up and bury the pole between her legs. Candy frantically battled to overcome her responses and with her muscles tensed and her body shaking, she managed to get back into the pose that stopped the charged sides of the pole from touching her. Already her back was starting to ache from the position, and she was not sure how long she could accept it in silence.

Oshin patted her quaking rump and proceeded to the wall. Candy looked around and saw him take down an oval leather paddle. She gave a small whimper as she heard him slapping it into his palm, assessing its weight and verifying what it would do to her vulnerable rear.

The paddle clapped her right buttock, and the loud impact was met with a choked cry. The paddle had merely delivered a brief warmth to her rear, however, the impetus shuffled her forward away from the chain. The pole prevented her head from moving further forward, so the movement of her hindquarters caused her to slide onto the pole. Candy offered a bark of pain and tried to shuffle back, but then Oshin treated her other cheek to a hearty swat that again knocked her into the pole.

Candy leant back and changed her stance a little so she was more prepared for his actions. His hand reached out and stroked her rear, making her purr with pleasure as he caressed her skin. With a swift volley of sweeping assaults, he slapped the paddle from cheek to cheek. Candy gave gasping groans and abrupt pips of distress in answer to his strokes. The angry sensation welled in her rear and made the responses part pain, part secretive pleasure.

Her jaws opened wide, and she looked up a little to see Yakami standing by the door. The girl's body trembled with desire and her eyes sparkled with arousal. She was very obviously envious of Candy's position.

Candy looked back down and focused her mind on her ordeal. She latched only the effects of each slap and dragged them through her masochistic side to turn the sensation from a baleful thing into a treasure. Candy moaned and pulled at her cuffs as she started to process the paddling as something other than a crime against her. She elevated the volume of her protests and savoured each hearty swat of the device.

Candy gave a holler as he grabbed the pole and lifted the end to give her a momentary shock between her legs. Oshin laughed as she sobbed and quaked before him, then recommenced the paddling. The heat that was building in her rear was becoming harder to enjoy. The skin was getting raw, and each slap felt like it was becoming more virulent because of it.

"Mmmm, you suffer delightfully, slave," he commented, and added another swat to each buttock before hanging the weapon back on the wall.

He crouched down before her and ran his fingers over her breasts. She shook and then jerked to attention as he cupped the sides and drew them together. When he pressed the soft flesh to the pole, her head flashed up, and this drew the other end of the pole into her pussy. Her eyes screwed shut and her teeth were bared as she snorted and tried to endure his spiteful attention.

Oshin let go of her breasts and grabbed her elevated chin. He held her head up and prevented her from lowering and getting her loins off the pole. The flesh rippled with waves of pain as the charge caused the muscles to clench to a most energetic degree.

The officer held her tight as she battled to lower her chin and stop the ordeal. A hearty scream was gathering in her lungs and she could not stop it. She did not want to cry out. Not only did she not want any further horrors added to her sentence, but she wanted to be strong, to be obedient, to please the officer and not anger him. She was sure that Yakami could take this, and Candy wanted to be just as adept as her roommate. However, the officer was pushing her beyond her tolerances.

Candy's arms hauled at the cuffs and her neck strained against his strong hand as the pole sent crackling diabolic charges into her pussy.

The cry rolled up her throat and developed power like an avalanche. A tremulous murmur started to sound out and then her willpower snapped. Candy gave a full-throated yowl as she jerked and bucked from the terrible affliction. The officer instantly let go.

Candy sagged and the pole came free a moment before her wilting posture dropped her loins onto it again. She gave another yelp, straightened up, and mumbled curses at the device.

"Oh dear, and you were doing so well," he said.

Candy had failed to hold back her scream, but she managed to keep her words of begging firmly locked away. She had failed in her task and was now going to be punished for it. She did not want to compound her failure with even more disobedience.

Oshin grabbed a small wooden box and set it down before her. He opened the lid and drew free a wooden peg. He pinched her lips shut and then added the implement to them. The pincers instantly caused a crushed pain to roll through the delicate flesh. He added another on either side, and then another so that a row of five wooden jaws were clasping the whole length of her mouth. A steady cold pulse coursed through her lips as she sniffled and whimpered in dismay. She tried to pull free, but every attempt only caused the compressed flesh to suffer needlessly without having any effect on the devices.

Her thighs trembled and she fought to stay off the pole as her muscles grew weary and her spine started to flicker with aching riots from the warped position.

"Hmmm, we seem to have some left," he added jovially.

Oshin started to delve back into the box and each peg was swiftly snapped to a generous portion of Candy's breasts. Each application made her jerk and sob as each implement added more woe to her ordeal. Her hands clenched into fists and her whimpers flowed upon the five wooden mouths crushing her lips together.

He finished with the sternest additions to her pierced nipples. The wooden jaws pressed the tips to the rings, and this squeezing of the internal tunnel of flesh to the steel caused her to gurgle and sob as tears rolled down her cheeks.

"That's better," he said, and his hands started to wander over her body and relish the feel of her suffering.

Candy shivered and continued to try to stay still as his palms rose along the backs of her legs. They skimmed the smooth nylon before he groped her sore rear and rode his hands over her hips and back. His hands brushed the pegs to make the wooden toys rattle upon each other and add another degree to her dismay when they twisted their fleshy captive.

"Very nice. Now, you just stay here, slave," he said, and then turned so he might gesture to Yakami.

It was too difficult for Candy to see them, but what she could hear made her burn with envy. If only fate had let the disc land the other way up, then she could be on the bed, delighting in passionate sex instead of being here, in pain.

Yakami was groaning and gasping with ecstasy as the officer thrust into her nubile body, his focus no doubt locked on Candy's highly stimulating predicament. She could hear the energetic slap of hip to hip and the soft creak of the leather bed as they made love.

Several times, they paused so they might change position

and the lovers passed through several assorted positions until the officer found the one in which he wished to achieve climax. Yakami cried out with bliss as the officer roared with delight. Fresh trails of tears flowed down Candy's face as she heard the sounds of their pleasure and knew that it was one that she could not share. Riven with misery, she thrust her pussy back onto the pole and shocked herself in order to give herself a pain she could more easily process. The jealousy and anger in her heart was too hard to handle. She wanted something more physical to distract herself from it.

Candy jiggled and shook as the charge assaulted her. She sank lower and shifted to make her vulva part and let the pole slither into her deeper than ever.

Candy jumped off it with a jolt, but in moments, she was again giving in to the need to feel its awful effects. The bondage was driving her insane. The pegs were a terrible companion that she could not cast away, and the deep rhythmic throb in the crushed skin promised an ever more spiteful consequence when they were finally removed. The more powerful the pounding in the flesh grew, the more vicious the return of circulation would be.

Candy yearned to straighten up and ease her gnawing and incredibly frustrating discomfort, but she could not. The effects of the pole were almost a welcome distraction that erased her plight with episodes of scorching mayhem.

The couple dropped onto the sheets, and she heard them breathing deeply and steadily. Candy closed her eyes and tried to ignore the possibility that they would now sleep and leave her like this for hours. Fortunately, they were just gathering their breath while basking in the stupefying glow of sated carnal appetite.

"You can release your partner, slave," said Oshin.

Yakami climbed off the bed and trotted over to Candy. She quickly started to remove the breast pegs and dropped each one back into the box. Yakami hurried to clear them away as quickly as possible while Candy squealed onto her gag. Each release caused a flood of angry heat to course through the pinch and escalate her woe before it slowly trickled away as another gave her a fresh spike of dismal sensation.

The speed with which Yakami sought to attend her partner and alleviate her ordeal served to inspire the sadism of the officer. He was relishing Candy's steady subdued shriek in answer to the removal of the pegs and wanted to hear more of this enticing melody.

"Wait. First, yank that pole back between her legs a few times," he said as the nipple pegs came free and made Candy's jaws strain against the efforts of the clamping gag.

Candy's tear-saturated eyes widened with shock and she tried to pull free or to beg for Yakami to stop. Her lips strained against the pegs as the shaft was tugged up and suddenly assailed her crotch. Yakami let go and then repeated her motion. She gave Candy shock after shock, and each one made her legs flash to attention and every muscle clench as her muted howls battled the gag.

"Oh yes, keep going, slave!" he ordered, and Candy started to detect the sound of him masturbating.

"Harder! Longer!" he added.

Candy lost the sounds of his motions and words as she cried out and struggled within her bonds. Yakami would not disobey him. She was a trained slave of this palace and took pleasure in every facet of it. Candy felt resentment towards her for enjoying her work, but also jealousy that she herself was not yet so universally hedonistic.

"That's it. Now one long one. Make her *wail!*" he snorted as his hand became a blur of motion.

The orgasm of the officer was lost to Candy as she danced on the tips of her shoes and struggled valiantly to escape her roommate's abuses. The pegs kept her lips sealed and her snorting moans were long and full of desperation.

"That'll do," came the panting reprieve from Oshin.

Yakami quickly unfastened the restraints before the man could change his mind, and when her cuffs came free, Candy collapsed onto the floor. Yakami knelt beside her and in quick succession removed the lip pegs. Candy jerked and wriggled on the ground as they came free and then she held her pulsating lips in both hands while she whimpered and wept quietly to herself.

Yakami petted her gently, trying to console her as she recovered from the experience.

"So many tears," uttered Oshin as he saw the droplets arranged under where Candy had stood.

"Lick them up for her. Taste what you drew from her," he whimsically ordered.

Yakami slipped away from Candy and crouched on all fours so she could run her tongue upon the floor and steal Candy's pain riddled treasures.

"That was very entertaining. You both did very well, and you may go. I will get another slave to clear up everything else," he announced.

Yakami grabbed their thongs and helped Candy to her feet. Candy leaned to her for support and managed to amble from the room and back onto the corridors. She clutched to the girl for aid and for comfort, because she felt terribly ashamed and inadequate. She had been hoping to be a prize slave, something to cherish, and she was failing miserably. Candy knew that she was overreacting, but could not stop herself. The Kami Empire and indeed Pangaea itself was a realm of extremes with little or no tolerance, and no matter how well she done previous to this moment, a single failure had left her in mourning for her fate.

"I'm sorry I let you down. You warned me, I just couldn't take it," she uttered morosely.

"Nonsense, you did really well. That was a very harsh position. I doubt I could have taken it either," replied Yakami. "He must have been in a bad mood. Perhaps he found out the truth about his promotion."

"Don't patronize me," snarled Candy and tried to wipe the tears from her cheeks. Her arms failed her, so she just let them continue to sway beneath her as Yakami helped her onwards.

"I would never do that," replied the girl with a clearly hurt tone, and to help verify her words, she used the back of her gloved hand to remove the droplets that Candy could not.

"Oh you're just saying that."

"No, I mean it. You did really well to endure it as you did. Sometimes he can be quite benevolent, and sometimes, like today, he can be pretty vicious with us. You'll get used to it. It just takes time. I've been trained all my life for this."

"Thanks," Candy said succinctly.

She considered that this might be the reason behind her employment in the palace. Were the average slaves indoctrinated to relish every punishment, every pose, every act? If so, then perhaps the Kami wanted to see some genuine distress, to see someone endure their attentions who could not so easily delight in the mistreatment of her body. If this were the case, she was already doing well. This rationale helped soothe her concerns, because these were more of a bane than the lingering aches and pains of the session. The fact that Yakami was an honest soul was an additional balm to her psychological trauma. It was hard for Candy to trust anyone. On Earth, everyone had ulterior motives and could be a betrayer on a whim over a triviality. It seemed that Yakami just did not have such dishonest capacities within her, so Candy felt as though she could let her guard down in front of her. Did she actually have an ally now?

When they reached their quarters, they curled into bed without word and sought further solace in sleep. Their arms and bodies entangled, and soft breaths and heartbeats provided a lullaby.

CHAPTER NINE

For another day, Candy told Yakami more about her home and the person she had once been. It was becoming more like talking about another incarnation rather than any memory of her own, or retelling a story she had once read about in a book.

Yakami was always excited to hear more, and occasionally Candy thought that she was feigning this constant level of interest. Of course, Yakami was being exposed to a whole new world, one where slavery had largely been done away with, where crimes went unpunished, and where poverty and freewill existed side by side.

The oddest moments were when Yakami was completely flummoxed by a paradox, a contradiction of such magnitude that she just sat there dumfounded. The more Candy tried to explain and unravel the mystery, the more perplexed the girl became, and it caused Candy to realise just how absurd they were in the first place. Things she accepted and never considered were ridiculous notions here, and if there was one thing that bemused Yakami more than any other was the intricate and time intensive feat called *dating*. Yakami had tales to tell of positions, of experiences with the priests and slaves, of sexual escapades and accomplishments. When Candy told her of the lover she had been dating, one more adventurous than others she had encountered, and what they had done together, it took several fruitless hours to pause and try to explain this concept to her roommate.

It was a pleasant time of laughter and discussion, and

several times, they decided to take pleasure from each other's bodies as the whim took them. There was no discussion, no seduction, just a quick expressed notion to have one's breast kissed, be masturbated with finger or toe, spanked, or to be serviced, and then the other would happily comply.

The level of freedom in slavery was astonishing to Candy, and she doubted she could ever go back to the world she knew even if the chance presented itself. What would happen if at a company board meeting she just started to play with herself at the table because she was bored, or slid under to suck a corporate cock just because she thought the owner's face intriguing?

A knock came upon the door early the next day. When Yakami answered it, another of the slaves entered and surprisingly walked straight over to Candy as she sat brushing her hair.

"Lady Uzume desires you in the hall of the sun."

"I'll show her there," interjected Yakami.

The new arrival turned to her, nodded, and then sauntered majestically back out. The moment the door closed, Yakami danced about with glee.

"Wow, Lady Uzume! You must be *very* special. I've only ever been in her presence twice. Once when I was chained to the wall as decoration and once as a footstool. She's the Warlord's most trusted agent. I'm so envious! You get to try and please a real Kami!"

Yakami truly seemed to believe that these people were actually the gods and not the latest recipient of a hereditary title. Candy did not try to contradict this. The girl was lucky to have such beliefs. She imagined how ultimately fulfilling it must be to serve a deity, to just be in the presence of something regarded as truly divine, even if it were a lie.

"And her own Mikado. Mmmmm, what I wouldn't take to have *that* pinning me down and thrusting into me!" she purred, embracing her own body as she projected the feel of the Mikado ravishing her.

"So who is Mikado to the Warlord?"

"Sorry? Pardon?" she said, snapping from her alluring fantasy.

"Who's Mikado to Hachiman?"

"The Warlord and this palace are regulated by Mikado Ame-waka-hiko. He's the Warlord's most elevated general."

"The Mikado to Lady Uzume. Does he have a name?"

"Not that I've heard. Now come on, you shouldn't keep her waiting."

"Should I get dressed?" asked Candy.

"No, nude will be fine."

Candy swiftly finished brushing her hair, checked her make-up, and then walked with Yakami as she briskly escorted her into the upper reaches of the palace.

"Down that corridor and turn right. I'll see you back in our room. Make sure you remember everything. I can't wait to hear every little detail," she said with enchanted merriment.

Yakami gave her a quick peck on the cheek, then scampered off. Candy could guess that she would be back on their bed, masturbating as she imagined what Candy would be going through under the whim of those she revered so highly. The image brought a cheerful smile to her lips and she started to head towards her destination.

The door was tall and had a delicate golden lattice set over it. The curling ivy-like material sparkled with gemstones, and several glass panels allowed a small glimpse of the great and sunlit hall beyond.

Upon opening the doors, Candy found two large cabinets of pale wood on either side of her, and again the wood was carved with scenes and symbols of incredible detail. The huge circular hall had elegant marble pillars that rose up along the walls and arched out to support a vast glass dome. A delicate lattice held the diamond panes and allowed radiant beams of sun to stream down and fill the interior. The walls had a single line of heavy metal rings set along them and the floor was comprised of large marble slabs.

At the uppermost reaches of each pillar was an opening. From the stone aperture came forth a line of polished steel chain that reached out towards a ring in the roof before it passed through it and then dropped down towards the floor. Arranged in a wide circle, the eight festooned lines of steel connected to various items. There was a set of four heavily padded leather cuffs, a stout steel collar, a sling of leather, and a padded tabletop where the chain broke out into four individual lengths to attach to each corner. Another chain connected to the corners of a wooden panel that was shaped like a body with the distinct contours of hips, waist, torso, neck, and head. The surface was cushioned, and ringlets ran along the perimeter. Another chain connected to a cross of metal, and the dangling St Andrews cross was covered in dense leather shackles. There was also a small iron cage comprised of bars, and at the end of the last chain was a solid metal hood. It had been forged to outwardly present the elegant features of a beautiful woman with a most serene expression. Standing beside the helmet was the potent and alluring form of the Mikado to Lady Uzume.

The high priest wore tight leather trousers that had laces up the side and also at the crotch, where there was a most distinct bulge. It was no doubt inspired by the pleasure he was planning on taking from Candy.

The trousers dropped beneath tall and heavy boots that had red and yellow leather flame designs stitched up the sides. Tucked into his studded belt was a polished metal stave. The pommel was formed from a large ruby, with a ring of smaller rubies circling the top where a bushel of long leather thongs poured forth.

A woman stood a short distance from him, and it took a moment for Candy to identify her from her physique. Lady Uzume had donned a corset of pure white satin. The tight hourglass sheath just covered her nipples and drew in her already trim waist. It formed into dips along the bottom, and each ended in a suspender that in turn attached to white stockings with lace tops. A satin thong covered her loins, and she wore a set of matching ankle boots with a laced front and wicked heels. Without her veil, Candy could see that the woman was radiantly beautiful. She had pure Japanese features that were regal and sublime. Her eyes were dark, and her mane of jet hair was slicked back. Her skin was pale, her lips a striking red shade. In one fist she held a whip that matched that of the Mikado, save that hers had sapphire decorations. The other fist was clenched to the long vicious strands of leather pouring from the whip handle.

The Mikado lifted up the helmet and opened it at the neck. The hinges on top gave a soft squeal as the face and the back parted.

"Here, slave," he stated firmly.

Candy stepped into the sun, and the warm flagstones sent heat flowing into her bare soles. When she reached the Mikado, her breathing was quick and her body was tense.

Without another word, he engulfed her head within the metal shell and closed it. The interior was filled with padded rubber that squeezed her entire skull and left her breathing through a small tube that accessed a slit in the lips of the fake countenance.

There was a momentary grinding clatter, and the chain broke into life. Candy was hauled up so that she was left standing erect. She lifted her arms, grabbed the warm metal of the mask, and then slowly slid her hands down the impermeable visage when she was taken no higher.

Candy could not see and could not hear. The thick latex

interior and the dense steel hid all sound from her and left her feeling even more defenceless. She mulled over the image of the Mikado and Lady Uzume to help soothe her worries.

Her concentration was broken when long tongues of leather lapped across both cheeks of her rear. Candy jerked forward and grabbed her buttocks as she threw a cry down her breathing tube. As she hugged her cheeks, another flash of pain was painted across the fronts of her thighs. Keeping her left hand on her rear, she grabbed her burning thighs with her right. Another lash landed just below her breasts. Candy gave an even more energetic howl and both hands leapt to the most heinous spot of applied travail.

The two dominants paced around her and laid their mordant swipes to her body at will. Sometimes they skimmed down so that the tips grazed the tips of her rear and caused her to spasm wildly. Sometimes they placed their assault to a large area of her thighs or rear, or across the base of her back. The worst times were when they lapped at her breasts or flicked over or under a thigh to kiss her inner regions.

Candy danced and jumped, clutched at the pain when she could or clawed at the helmet as she sobbed and wailed within it. Skipping from foot to foot, she twirled and jumped, trying to find a way to shelter herself, but their whips always found a vulnerable area to attack. The endless crack of the infernal lines to her body continued as she howled and struggled to escape them, but confined as she was, she could do nothing save jolt and squeal in the sun. Rivulets of sweat were soon running down her body from her constant virulent efforts and from her distress.

Eventually she merely held to the chain above her head and clenched as tightly as she could. The whips continued their methodical and rhythmic assault. They made her chest thrust forward or dive back. Her thighs clenched together, and sometimes she hauled her feet from the ground in a bid to curl up and defend herself. This merely allowed them concentrate on her thighs and rear.

The lambasting suddenly stopped, and Candy stayed tense just in case it was merely a pause. No more strokes came, and she started to calm down. Dropping her hands to her sides, she hung from the chain and rasped down the tube. Her whole body was wet with sweat and throbbing from the punishing lick of the whips.

Strangely, in the wake of the whipping came a surging delight. The ordeal had been long and trying, and she felt overjoyed that she had survived it. She sobbed softly with elation and a glorious feeling of purification, of being used and in having pleased the sadistic wants of the pair. The heady cocktail of endorphins and adrenaline from her fight to escape continued to rush and her world of enforced darkness seemed to turn over while she was utterly intoxicated by the after-effects.

The whipping had been transformed in an instant. The relief from the pain made her surge with arousal and satisfaction. What she had hated and reviled moments earlier was now fondly embraced, and Candy almost wished the pair to continue. If she could have spoken clearly, she might have.

The helmet was opened, and Candy dropped onto her knees and grovelled before them, the light pouring through her eyelids. When she had accustomed to the light, the Mikado extended his weapon towards her, and she instantly grabbed it and lavished kisses to the base of the strands.

"How do you feel, slave?" he asked solemnly.

"Grateful, Mikado. Thank you," she blurted carelessly as she kissed the leather and relished the heat dwelling in her whipped skin.

"So you want more? You want to please your owners?"

"Oh yes, Mikado. More than anything."

"But say we want to amuse ourselves with your

suffering?"

"Anything to please you. *Anything*," she hissed

Candy's libido had taken over. Heedless of the consequences to her body, she needed more.

The Mikado let his gaze wander across the various hanging sites of bondage and then jerked it back to the floating leather-covered bed. He turned on his boots, and with the gentle creak of leather moving upon his stern physique, he strolled to the cabinets, gathered rope, and proceeded to the device.

"Here, slave."

Candy sprang to her feet and humbly rushed over as Lady Uzume walked to the cabinets to begin selecting what she wanted to use on her subject.

"Up onto it. Lie face down."

Candy climbed up onto the soft surface and stretched her fingers and toes into each corner. Her extremities brushed the chain, and as the table swayed slightly from her ascent onto it, the Lady dropped some items between Candy's splayed legs. She kept her face down to the leather and drew in its scent as she trembled with anticipation.

The couple began to work the rope upon her. The Mikado captured her hands, sealed them to the chain, and then started to create a detailed weave over her torso.

The net of expertly engineered rope started to tighten and haul her body down and into the padding. He pulled harder, and Candy gave a quivering sigh of delectation as she was ruthlessly crushed into immobility. Her fingers pawed gently at the chain as she felt herself growing wet with fresh desire.

Lady Uzume busied herself with the capture of Candy's feet and then stood back to watch her priest at work.

Every time a finger or hand brushed Candy's skin, she surged against her bonds. The rope slithered and stretched upon her, increasing by degrees until she was fully controlled and served to their appetites. The Mikado finished with loops around her upper thighs that caught other strands, drew her hindquarters down, and fiercely pressed them to the leather.

The hand of Lady Uzume reached across and wandered up and down Candy's stretched legs. The passage of the Lady's silken skin upon her own was glorious. She felt so privileged and even more open to surrendering to their whims.

"First, a warmup," she decreed, and handed an item to the Mikado that saw immediate use.

The heavy flogger each of them now bore had thick leather strands that issued from their stout leather-encased handle. The impacts of the weapons resounded through the hall and echoed back upon themselves as the Mikado and the Lady stood on either side of her and flogged her exposed body.

The thrashing made Candy jerk with each swipe as the strands fell without warning on her thighs, shins, rear, or across her rope-cocooned back. The strokes started to warm her skin, tenderising her and cultivating her submission. The hesitant discomfort they gave allowed her to get used to such sensations, to gradually build her tolerance and make her amenable to the harsher play she knew would come.

The flogging paused, and Candy sagged into her cocoon as she heard the bright snap of surgical gloves being drawn into place. There came a soft squirt, and suddenly lubricated fingers were working themselves into her anus. Candy gave a sultry moan as she felt herself being opened by the exploring wet digits.

"That's it, slave. Let my fingers in. Other things are going to be replacing them soon," purred the soft, seductive voice of the Lady.

The paired digits acquired a third that stretched her a little more. The trio plunged as deep as they could and then slid back out.

"Mmmm, such an inviting rear. Don't you agree Mikado?"

"It dances as well for penetration as it did for the lash, my

Lady," he answered.

"Well, let us see what else it can take. Are you ready, slave?" she asked while stretching Candy with a fourth finger that again extended her elasticity.

"Oh yes, Lady Uzume," she moaned.

A round orb followed the fingers. The anal bead pressed to her sphincter and started to widen her. Candy groaned as she reached the widest point of the toy and then gave a bark as a flogger dropped across her back. The sudden sound of the stroke made her clench involuntarily and the ball shot into her. Candy strained against her ropes with a gasp as she felt the sphere rocket into her body and leave her sphincter gnawing on the string that attached it to the next one. Her canals were being kept spread upon the inserted sphere, and it was a sensation as eerie as it was wonderfully debauched.

"There, that wasn't so bad, and that was just the first, slave," attested Lady Uzume.

The next bead touched her rear and was pushed forward. Candy easily cleared the broadest part, but the bearer took the string and held it. Her convulsing opening clenched to the ball and tried to draw it in, but it was not moving.

"No, not yet, you greedy slave. You have to wait."

The bead was pulled free, and this made Candy whimper from the odd and titillating sensations. The flogger dropped onto her back twice more, and the stinging swats made her churn with passion. She was an amusing experiment to these people, a toy as easily controlled and used as the beads that were being deployed on her. Candy felt intoxicated by this level of subjugation.

The orb was tried again, and again she was teased before the flogger struck to make her instinctively flinch and ravenously devour the ball. Candy whimpered and slithered against the ropes as she felt it nuzzle up against the first.

A third was introduced, and then a fourth, and finally a

fifth. Candy's insides were choked with a distinct presence that seemed to fuel her trance of masochism. Writhing in the ropes, she moaned and panted, rolling the muscles of her rear to feel the orbs shift and move.

"There, all installed. My, look at you wriggle. It is fortunate that my Mikado tied you down nice and tight, slave, or you'd be squirming all over the palace otherwise," said the woman as she stroked Candy's quavering buttocks.

"Although I think her bonds can contain more," offered the Mikado.

"We shall see," was the perky response.

A soft humming tune reached her ears, and a vibrator slipped beneath Candy. The wet toy slid between the leather and her body to stretch along her pussy and nudge her clitoris. Candy quaked with rapture as the machine filled her pussy with intense vibrations. Coupled with the bondage, the beads, and her complete vulnerability, she was in heaven.

"There, now let's see what else we can do to liven her up," announced the woman.

The pleasure was taken to new levels as the string of the beads was taken and pulled. The last orb started to emerge, opening her anus, and causing her to murmur with delight.

"Here it comes. Now give me back my bead, slave," she said.

The vibrator pressed to her a little more forcefully and a bead was popped out. Candy clutched the chain for help in weathering this bizarre and overwhelmingly seductive treatment.

"And the others," said Lady Uzume, and another bead was drawn out to plague her with contradictory input.

"Actually, I've changed my mind. Back in they go," capriciously stated the regal woman.

Candy shivered in delighted turmoil as the exposed pair were quickly pushed back into her. The sensuous play was swiftly dragging her up towards climax, and Candy buried her face into the padding while readying to smother her scream in the dangling bed.

"She's almost there, my Lady," commented the Mikado.

"Well, we can't have that. She has not earned such a privilege just yet," decreed Lady Uzume.

The string was grabbed, and a steady and relentless pull drew them from her as a charging train of brutal sensation. Her sphincter rode the backs of the escaping toys and stretched upon one before dropping to the string and then being hauled open again in rapid succession.

Candy's head jerked up to the limits of her neck, and her screech of erotic response reverberated through the hall. The last bead jumped from her, and she slapped her cheek to the padding. Gasping for breath, she trembled and sobbed. Her senses were reeling from the acute and bizarre feelings that she was experiencing.

"All out. But I think this little hole is still hungry."

She heard the sound of more lubricant, and then a bead touched her rear. She almost regretted their return, because she had barely managed to handle the last session of their use. A repeat performance might be too much for her to handle.

She gave a gasp of shock and fright as the bead moved forward and proved to be of a far larger variety. The broad circumference swiftly stretched her wider than she could accept and caused her breath to race and jaw to clench.

"Come on, slave. Take it! Take my bead! Show me your devotion!" sternly announced Lady Uzume, who then chose to press harder rather than grant a reprieve.

The muscular ring suddenly filled with an angry rending fire. Candy gave a squawk of distress that caused the bead to retreat. Her punished rear closed and recovered for a moment before the behemoth returned. This time it managed to gain a little more entry before she gave a similar protest and brought another retreat.

"You're *going* to take this, slave. I have decided that you will. So relax and endure."

Candy tried to stifle her protests as the ball sought to slither into her again. When her body gave a pained twitch, the bead retreated.

Lady Uzume was making sure that each attempted insertion gained a fraction more ground before giving her a moment to recover.

"Almost there. Just a little more and it will be in, slave. You are doing well," said the woman.

Her rear was ruthlessly taught to accommodate the huge trespassers, and then she finally cleared the broadest region. Her sphincter was throbbing with intense fires that made her shudder and whimper.

"There we are, in it goes. All the way."

The Lady pushed it with her sheathed digits, and the bead thundered into Candy and suddenly swelled her insides. Her tracts had not been tutored in housing the ball, only her sphincter had been shown how to accept it. The bloated presence was painful and frightening.

"Oh God! Take it out! It's too much! I . . . I . . . Pleeeease!" she cried.

"No, slave! Endure it! You'll get used to it in a moment!" said the woman with a harsh yet passionate tone.

Candy shook and sobbed as her insides were riven with anguish. She fought to spit it out, to regurgitate it if only for a moment. Candy flexed her tracts and fought to excrete the monster. Her insides could not handle this crash course; they needed education like her opening. The fingers of the Lady did not move from keeping it installed, and Candy's anus did not have the strength to defeat her.

"It's not coming out, slave. Not until you've calmed down!" she warned.

"Pleeeese! I can't . . . Oh the pain! It hurts so much! Please! Stop!"

"Silence, or I'll stuff another in you right now!" snarled the woman.

The virulence of the woman's words held a powerful authority that Candy could not question. Sobbing to herself, she pressed her face to the padding and fought to endure.

Her insides begrudgingly started to grow used to the invader, and the keen distress started to fade away to leave her feeling even more swollen than ever before. As the drastic sensations faded, she noticed the more subtle varieties present within her. It was then that Candy began to discern that a string was emerging from her rear.

"There we are. Good, slave. Now you hold onto that for a moment," gently offered Lady Uzume, finally taking her fingers out.

Candy gave a whimper of dismay as she felt another bead touching her opening. The orb quickly moved forward and started to plough into her.

"You can take another, slave. And you will, for me!"

The bead started to demand entry, and her rear started to pulsate with distress once more. It was a faint echo of the previous torment, because her rear was getting used to such insertions. The bead slipped through her, and her rear closed to the string. Candy gave a gurgled croak when her rear was bloated with another intruder that cosily pressed up to the first.

"You think she can take a third, Mikado?"

"Definitely, my Lady."

"I concur. Here comes another one, slave."

"Oh please, Lady, No! No! Not yet!" she protested.

Candy's body was still trying to acclimatise to the insane plundering of her rear. It felt like she needed to go to the toilet more than ever in her life. Her body was being tricked and was in turmoil—she needed time to get used to it.

"Yes, slave! And don't argue. You belong to us, and we want to fill you up with beads," staidly decreed the woman.

Candy gave a long drawn mewl as she was again stretched upon the dimensions of an anal bead. Without mercy, it was pushed through her rear and shoved into her canals. The bead pushed the others deeper and added immeasurably to the feeling of having her rear choked from within. Shuddering in her restraint, she felt the woman's fingers withdraw.

"You may begin, Mikado," she said and strolled around to Candy's head.

The woman stepped back and folded her arms across her corseted chest.

"You are going to take ten strokes of the cane, slave."

Candy had a brief moment to contemplate the words before there was a subtle whistle of displaced air and a stern hack delivered the bamboo strut across both of her cheeks. There was a loud thwack and an instant of minor anguish before her entire rear seemed to expand and explode with pain. Candy's neck strained forward, and she screamed at the limit of her lungs. When her howl ebbed, she dropped her face to the table and sobbed uncontrollably. The first withering slice had been unendurable. Candy swore that she could not face nine more, she just couldn't.

"Give her the next, Mikado."

"With pleasure, Lady Uzume."

"No, wait, I c-"

Candy's petition was turned into another screech as the cane slammed across her rear. The skill and strength with which the Mikado applied it were too terrible to tolerate and Candy's agonised howl roared around the hall before she collapsed into her bonds. She twitched and wept freely as the pain devoured her world and left her unaware of anything but its searing might.

"Please, no . . . no more," she uttered dejectedly when her senses finally started to settle.

"Number three, Mikado," said the woman.

"Of course, my Lady. Here comes your third, slave."

The sceptre lashed into her buttocks and Candy wailed. She struggled against her ropes, she hauled and tugged, trying to get free and escape any more applications.

"And now, the fourth, Mikado."

The weapon attacked her again just as she was about to start recovering from the previous strike. The pain cast her to new plateaus and temporarily froze her. Her howl consumed all her breath, and the pain kept her paralysed while she lay tensed and rigid. Her jaws were stretched wide, but her scream was being deprived of fuel. When the misery had faded a little, she sank into the cushioned top and panted for breath. Her senses tumbled over and tears rushed down her face. She could not take any more. The need to find relief from her duress encouraged her to remove at least one of the afflictions to her body, so she flexed her muscles and started to try to eject the beads.

"A fifth, if you please, Mikado."

The attempt to spit out an orb was thwarted when the cane swung around and landed at the tops of her thighs. The region erupted with anguish, and Candy's howl explained it in full. The moment the stroke started to lose its potency, her hidden quest was given a massive boost. She squeezed, and with a soft pained mew, she felt her rear open and a ball pop free. The spike of discomfort that regurgitation brought was nothing compared to the cane and was barely even noticed.

"Ah, we have a problem, Lady Uzume," announced the Mikado.

"And what is that?"

"An anal escapee."

"Oh dear, how very disappointing, and she was doing so

well up until now."

The Lady moved closer and leant down onto the table. She folded her arms before Candy's flushed features and rested her chin on them. The woman's face was just a few inches from her own but was still distorted because of the veil of tears clinging to her eyelashes.

Candy's terrible pain quickly evaporated. Her body was mass-producing endorphins to counter the torture of the cane, and now that it had stopped, her system was being flooded with them. Her masochism was devouring her soul, and suddenly she was in the most diabolic ecstasy.

"Such a pity," said Lady Uzume, and gently traced the contours of Candy's slack face. "You were quite a sight, slave. But you are new to this lot, and I should go easy on you. I woudn't want to damage my Warlord's prize before he gets home."

Candy managed to lift her head up and regard the beautiful features of the Lady through bleary tear-filled eyes. Her libido pushed words from her mouth that she could barely even comprehend.

"I'm sorry, Lady. Give me the full ten. Right from the start."

The woman's elegant features did not move, and Candy wondered if she had spoken in the wrong language or had just hallucinated the insane request. Then the alluring face acquired an elated grin that only served to make Candy even more proud of her dedication to their sadistic desires.

"Mikado. I think we have a real gem here. Proceed from the very first! Again, Mikado. All ten strokes. And shove that bead back into her while you are at it!"

Candy gave a whimper as the wet orb was pushed back inside her. The Lady stayed where she was so she could assess Candy's travail in full. Candy moaned as she was stuffed, and the woman gave a mild titter of amusement.

"And if it starts to come out, give her an extra stroke to

make it return."

The cane swished down and sank into the soft flesh of her rear. Candy jolted to attention and wailed.

"Again, Mikado! Now! Quickly!"

The weapon struck again and elevated Candy's cry. Why had she demanded this abuse? What had she done? Candy's regret was lost as the cane assailed her again.

"Harder, Mikado!" she demanded.

The arm of the man employed more brawn, and Candy's yowls became even more enthusiastic. She wanted to beg them to stop, to retract her foolish solicitation of this abuse, but all she could do was to holler as the cane thrashed her again and again. The woman's face was a picture of delight as she watched Candy suffer unspeakably. Lady Uzume was drinking in Candy's nightmare ordeal as though it was the most succulent fare imaginable.

The last stroke fell, and Candy flopped her head down. While she rasped for breath, the hand of the Lady again reached out to trace lines in the sweat and tears that now decorated her visage.

Candy was trembling uncontrollably. Her whole backside was thundering with a swell of residual pain that was promising to take weeks to fade.

"Please, Lady Uzume. Please, don't let him stop. Please!" she panted.

Candy's heart was aching for more. She was addicted to the intensity of her pain. It was a narcotic potion, and one that she was hopeless to deny. The last few strokes had taken her to heights of deranged bliss the likes of which she had not even thought possible.

"You want more, slave? You want to please me?" she whispered softly.

"Yes! Yes! Please! Cane me!" sobbed Candy.

"Candy wants the cane, Mikado. I suggest you give it to

her!"

The Mikado needed no further permission. He could assail her with blows and watch her delightful form flick and wriggle, buck and shudder all he wanted. The cane visited Candy with regular precision. Each heinous swipe was of such strength that it almost stole her mind before the anguish retreated to expose wicked ecstasy, and then came another hack.

Candy's screeches and yelps flowed around the hall with the timed thwack of the cane. As the caning continued, her screams began to fade and soon she was taking her punishment in near silence. Her eyes were wide and fixed to Lady Uzume. Her body was rigid, and she was possessed by the sensations. She had no idea how many strokes she had received. Everything was lost in a tempest of the most powerful forms of alternating excruciating pleasure and sublime pain. The Lady held up her hand to pause her servant.

"Oh, you look so gorgeous, slave. Writhing and moaning. Suffering for my amusement. You are quite the beauty when you are in such pain," she said with a licentious edge to her voice.

Candy could not believe that she wanted more. She just could not resist the lure of continuing this most delicious of torments. She did not want it to end.

"Then please, have him give me more. But gentler, please. Not so hard, I can't handle such severity."

"As my slave desires," said the woman, and then she again gestured to the Mikado.

Candy's request was not for mercy. She had to ask for a decline for another reason. The hardest of his strokes were too seductive. She was afraid of what would happen if he continued with such virulent dispensing of discipline. Her mind wanted it. Her psyche yearned for him to thrash her with every ounce of muscle he could muster. Her masochist side was alive within her and was ruling her every thought. She was aching for more, but she was fearful that her body might not be able to take it. If she did not try to control herself, to put some reins on her masochistic urges, she might never leave the table alive. However, she could not just stop, either. She needed to work her way down from the levels she was at, to wean herself off the alluring agony, because she had no idea of the consequence of rash withdrawal.

The cane continued its onslaught. Candy jumped against her ropes with each stroke, and her body convulsed as she was again submerged in her deranged bliss. The Lady stood up and started to clamber onto the table. Candy was so delirious that she could barely register the actions.

"Oh slave, this is turning me on sooooo much," she practically growled.

She grabbed Candy's head and lifted it up. With her legs spread wide ,she shifted forward and pressed Candy's face into the front of her thong. She squeezed her thighs to the sides of Candy's head and nudged her flanks with her heels.

"Do you smell my enjoyment of your pain, slave?" she asked.

Candy drew in a breath, and the scent of the woman's obvious arousal was undeniable. The perfume rolled through her senses and snatched her mind. Her body seemed to fill with new vigour, and her mind was drenched in sudden arousal. Candy's libido had leapt at the scent and was more potent than ever before.

"Cane me, Lady Uzume! Please! Punish me!" she cried as she buried her face into the woman's pussy for reassurance and commitment to her ultimate desire.

"Mikado! Give me that cane! Hurry!" she barked. Lady Uzume's passion was blatantly inflamed to intolerable degrees.

The noblewoman snatched the cane and started to rain the

most potent swipes down into Candy's quaking rear. Her crotch rubbed against Candy's features, and the scent of her grew as she extracted her own thrills. Candy's whole world seemed to enter a euphoric state. She was in a depraved nirvana to know that her owner was taking sexual pleasure in doing this, and suddenly she could not even feel the cane. Candy was aware that she was being thrashed, but all she could feel was something akin to pleasure. It was more consuming and infinitely darker and more powerful than anything she had ever known before.

"Mikado! Yank those beads out and take her!" bellowed the woman as she held even tighter and increased the speed of her attack.

Candy felt the beads thunder from her a moment later. Her rear had grown used to being closed and in not giving way to giant orbs, so it erupted with new dismay at being forced to do so again. The cane descended with greater wrath and fed the leviathan of her pain-charged libido before it turned even this torment into a glorious treat. The balls stormed free, and the motion brought Candy into a realm that resembled orgasm. She knew what a climax felt like and indeed, it was some sort of relation to this, but this was a far different beast.

The table rocked, and the Mikado leapt up and buried his raging cock into her throbbing rear. Candy was still in shock. The caning had stopped, but she was still lost in the giddy heights of rhapsody. The numerous contusions in her rear and the ferocious pain they were unleashing was ensuring that she did not sink out of the malevolent clutches of her bliss.

The Mikado's cock was as impressive as his physique, and it was matched with his skill at wielding it. He churned her anus and ravished her with gusto.

The Lady reached forward and dragged her nails against exposed areas of flesh. As she continued to claw at Candy with impassioned glee, she also continued to stroke her thong against Candy's face.

"Oh sweet Sun-Goddess! I . . . I . . ." she gasped.

The woman's hands crushed Candy's head within a powerful hold as her thighs pressed in and smothered Candy's breath. The Lady screamed with elation and her body jerked and convulsed. The Mikado bellowed and filled the hall with a long animal bray as Candy felt him come within her. They stole their delight from her tortured bound body and announced their passion in deafening clarity.

Once sated, the pair settled and slowly managed to extract themselves from their slave.

Candy lay still and rested in her ropes. Her eyes were unblinking and fixed forward. She looked and felt as though she had been lobotomised. Her mind and sanity had been washed away on a tidal wave of sensation.

Candy breathed in uneven fits and twitched on occasion as her startled nerves tried to find way in which to operate successfully and coherently.

"What a performance," gasped Lady Uzume as she held to one of the support chains to help her stay upright.

"I don't believe I've ever seen its equal in at least a century," panted the Mikado.

"And how is our precious, slave?" she asked, leaning in towards Candy's stolid features.

"F . . . fine . . . Lady . . . U . . . Uzume," she stammered.

Candy's throat was having trouble forming anything else other than the screams and cries it had so fixated upon for so long. "Thank you. Oh thank you, so much."

"A true pleasure, slave. Now I think you may need some rest."

Scarcely conscious, Candy hardly felt the ropes moving or the hands that scooped her up and started to take her away.

CHAPTER TEN

"Oh, Candy!"

Candy initially thought that Yakami was expressing horror or concern.

The girl was looking over Candy's body as she lay face down on the bed. Having barely been aware of being set free and carried by slaves back to her room, only now did she fully process that she was not longer in the hall of the sun.

"Just look how much pleasure the Kami took from you!" she exclaimed.

Candy stirred and gave a whinny of irritation as she felt a delicate finger brush some of her move vibrant weals. Even the lightest brush made the skin scowl with resentment.

"And, mmmmm, I smell the cock of the Mikado on you," she commented, and Candy felt savouring snorts around her rear and then some soft kisses. Yakami shivered with passion as her lips vicariously tasted the area that a deity's manhood had pounded. The girl wandered up towards Candy's face and she suddenly froze.

"Oh, oh my! Can it be!"

Yakami sniffed hesitantly at Candy's features and then choked back a sigh of utter relish.

"Oh Candy, Candy, please, please let me kiss you!"

When she did not reject the offer, the girl ducked in and started to kiss and smell of Candy's nose, cheeks, and mouth. She muttered half formed words of envy and adoration, utterly entranced by what she was coming into contact with.

"The pussy of Lady Uzume! I've never ever been this close

before! Oh I smell how much pleasure you gave her, oh Candy, I'm dying of jealousy."

Her attention again wandered back down to Candy's buttocks, and a passionate kiss made her yelp and stiffen. Yakami apologised and calmed herself. Her lust for the Kami was overwhelming her and bringing discomfort to her roommate when she really needed a more considerate hand.

"Here, let me get some salve. It will help heal you."

The girl went to the drawers and returned to the bed with a glass jar. She removed the large cork and started to scoop out a thick purple gel. Candy gave a sob and her fingers clenched to her pillow as Yakami started to ease the cool substance over her bruises. The gel robbed them of a great deal of heat and the distress seemed to fade away after just a few seconds.

Yakami's assistance was interrupted when there came another knock upon the door. Yakami wiped the gel off her hand and answered the door. Candy ignored the conversation and just prayed that she not be required again just yet. She needed time for her body and her mind to heal from the ravages of the insane session with the Kami.

When Yakami came back, she gently touched Candy's shoulder to gain her attention.

"Oshin wants me. You just rest and recuperate. Let the salve do its work."

Without further work, Yakami dashed from the room and left her alone. Candy laid her head back down and closed her eyes. The salve was stripping all the havoc from her rear, and she slipped into a sleep that was interrupted when the door opened again.

She turned and was surprised to see the Mikado of Lady Uzume wandering casually towards the bed.

"Good morning, slave."

Candy started to rise, but he stopped her with a dismissive

wave. She was surprised to learn that she had slept through an entire night and not noticed.

"Do not bother rising, slave. I am just here for a brief visit," he stated.

Candy slumped back onto the covers and trembled with excitement as he perched himself on the side of the bed and let his hand travel upon the curve of her back. He made sure not to touch her welts and continued to enjoy the velvet texture of her skin as he spoke.

"You were exceptional yesterday, slave. Lady Uzume is quite taken with you, as am I. Is there anything you require?" he asked.

She considered everything that she could ever wish for. Freedom was no longer even in her mind. The Empire had opened a sealed and decadent vessel within her soul, and she was now a hopeless and loyal subject to them. The idea of beseeching sex with the magnificent high priest sitting beside her was tempting, as was another session of bondage to enhance its pleasures, but her body was raw and battered and she would need more time to recover before she indulged her masochism again. A thought slipped onto her lips before she had even really considered it, but it stalled and remained unspoken as she pondered whether it would be taken seriously.

"Well, there is one thing. I'm afraid to ask though."

"Tell me, slave. I may be of a disposition to grant you a favour after the show you put on for us."

"The woman who shares my room, Yakami. She . . ."

"Yes? You do not wish to share your room? You want someone else instead?

"No, no, nothing like that. Could you, well, would you take her?"

"Where?"

Candy looked up at him with a knowing smile. Yakami had been so accommodating and helpful, and Candy wanted to repay her.

"Ah. I see, How very generous of you, slave. You continue to evade all hint of predictability, and that is not so easily done, especially after five centuries. Any particular reason for this?"

"She was very nice to me when I arrived," answered Candy, and it was only then that the strange nature of his words permeated the image of Yakami screaming in ecstasy as the Mikado thrust into her pert and delightfully tempting rear.

"Then soon she will know what it is to be my plaything," he said with conviction and arose from the bed. "I have duties for now, but when I have time to spend freely, I will spend it on Yakami."

"Thank you, Mikado," humbly offered Candy.

The Mikado looked down at her and gave a broad grin.

"Perhaps you could try thanking me properly?" he added.

It took a few seconds for Candy's mind to see where his intentions were, and she immediately hauled her weary form from the bed. She settled onto her knees and leaned down to kiss his boots. The leather tang upon her tongue fired her libido, igniting it like furnace. The flames rose higher, and so did she. She arched upward, then drew him from his voluminous trousers. His cock swelled immediately against her hand. She held it reverently and offered minor and delicate movements of her fist to further excite him.

His hands folded across his chest, and she could feel his domineering glower upon her as she stared at his shaft. She teased him for a moment longer, and then opened her mouth to tickle her tongue to his tip. She offered small circles around his head and then several long laps that poured the broadest part of her tongue upon him. Her grip shifted back towards his balls and thighs, and she slid her maw along him until he was sheathed as deeply as she could comfortably accept. She pushed on a little further to entice her masochism, and then with a small gurgle she started to thrust her head back and forth.

With her lips locked to him, she danced her tongue within the sealed cavern, and her hands adored his physique with lust.

The Mikado watched her with almost impassive detachment, and only when she felt his cock starting to swell with the final moments before ejaculation did a reaction manifest on his features. His eyes drifted half shut and rolled as his muscles rippled with a series of flexes. He gave a murmuring purr and then a long hiss of endurance as she coaxed forth his seed and ravenously consumed it.

Candy offered a few more drives of her head for his satisfaction, then settled back. Again, she deliberately laid her rear onto her ankles to revive her welts and make her body quake with dark ecstasy.

"Gratitude accepted," he said calmly, and after restoring himself within his trousers, he turned and marched from the chamber without another word.

Candy released a nefarious giggle and shuffled back under the covers. She gained another brief period of sleep before Yakami came back to the room.

"How was it?" enquired Candy.

"Oh, nothing out of the ordinary. Tied down and orally servicing him, then a night restrained next to him in bed as a tight bundle. He whipped me this morning, but was due out on patrol and did not have time for anything more elaborate," she answered wistfully, as though she had been hoping for something more.

Candy decided not to mention the Mikado's visit so that it would be all the more potent a surprise when he turned up at their door and demanded Yakami's body. Instead, she decided to investigate what he had said.

"I have heard the Kami make mention that they believe, I mean, that they are old," she said.

"Yes," stated Yakami and went to their wardrobe.

"Well, what does that mean?"

"Warlord Hachiman is over nine hundred years old. Lady Uzume is a little younger. I think she is about six hundred and fifty," she absently commented while sifting through the clothing on offer. "Ooh, a new skirt. Nice."

"Surely you can't be serious? I mean, they can't be immortal."

"Of course not. It is the work of House Sukuna-bikona. In ages past, the Kami found a strange cavern filled with a fungus that they had never seen before. It is called Lingzhi, and it rejuvenates and revitalises the body and soul,"

Yakami was speaking as though this was fact, but such a thing just could not be true. The girl took out a latex kimono and held it against her body to see how it would look. The black shimmering folds rippled in the light, and the red spiralling pattern gave it an eerie, almost lifelike quality. The garment itself was cut to be very revealing. The slits at the side rose high onto the hip, and an opening on the chest offered a tantalizing open view of the wearer's cleavage.

"But that's absurd," retorted Candy.

"You have told me of many things that I had never even heard of, and they all exist in your world and defy my comprehension. However, in your jungles and forests, there are things that might cure all manner of ailments that have yet to be stumbled upon. Here, the Kami have found Lingzhi. It is unique to our world and is more precious than any amount of metal."

"Very Arrakis."

"Pardon?"

"Nothing. Sorry. An *other side* reference. So all they do is eat this fungus and that's it?"

"Not quite. When prepared properly, it makes you Kami for a whole new lifespan. When the Kami of a Great House partake of it, there is a great festival in their land. Gifts are given out and celebrations held. Such events occur every century or so, and I do hope I will get to see one."

"So they don't age?"

"It heals the body and charges the flesh. When the effects start to wear off, they begin to rapidly assume their true age, and that is when they return to the cavern to partake of the gift."

"Only the Kami go there?"

"Lingzhi grows very, very slowly and only in that one sacred place. So it is very precious. Sometimes, a priest who has done some great service to the Empire may be permitted a chance to partake of it. They are then made young and have a century of youth before the power fades. They age in a day and pass from this realm happy and content."

"Sometimes I feel as though I am lost in a dream," uttered Candy, and Yakami gave an amused laugh as her only response.

The girl put the dress back in the wardrobe and walked to the shower. Candy heard the water start to run and suddenly she slipped from the bed and started to saunter towards the source of the noise. She watched Yakami's naked form in the deluge for a few seconds. The girl was quite exquisite. She had a glorious body, and she moved with a sublime elegance. Like some sort of nymph, she lurked amidst the steam and slithered within the flow of water, her smooth curves sparkling in the light as her hands drifted all over them. Candy continued to arouse her passion with the voyeuristic show before she chose to act.

Candy opened the door and moved in. When Yakami noticed her arrival, she gave a jerk of shock and flung her back to the wall. When she realised what was happening, she eased her pose and extended her arms to bring Candy closer.

Candy gave a shiver of pleasure as the warm jets of water tickled her skin and her lips nuzzled against the slender woman's neck. She kissed the wet skin as rushing flows of sparkling water continued to cascade down over them both. Yakami's hands cupped Candy's shoulders and started to caress them as the kisses began to lower.

Candy stretched out her tongue and started to circle each breast and then gradually spiral up towards the nipple. When she arrived, each was stiff and hard against her. She played them with a tongue and a hand, alternating regularly as Yakami leant back against the wall and gave long sighs of joy. The girl cupped her assets at the base and offered them up for easier attention, but it was not long before she could not stop herself from massaging them.

Candy started to head lower, and her hands ran over the girl's slick hips before she squeezed her rear. Yakami's thighs trembled with anticipation, and she revealed herself as much a devotee of masochistic indulgence as Candy when her hands started to focus on her teats with some pulls and pinches that rolled them between her fingers. Each self-inflicted attack made her flex and quake with new degrees of prurience.

Candy let a waggling tongue and lavish kisses decorate her partner's thighs for a short time as her hair hung to her head in sodden strands and partially obscured her view. On a whim, she pulled back. With one hand, she swept her hair back, and the other she lifted between Yakami's thighs. Candy extended a finger that immediately started to worm its way into the girl's rear. The water was an adequate lubricant, but it still took effort to gain access, especially because Yakami kept clenching in lewd fits.

When her digit was through, she eagerly wiggled it about and pawed at the girl's inner channel. Candy hooked her partner's sphincter and gave small pulls that caused the girl to croak with delectation. The sounds rushed out as a shrill snort when Candy ducked back in and pushed her tongue up into her roommate.

After tasting the girl along the full length of her tongue, Candy retreated and began to tickle her clit with more focused attention. Water flowed into her mouth, and Candy swallowed regularly as she continued to dance her tongue upon the jiggling girl. Yakami's fingers reached into Candy's hair and began to comb through the strands as she was serviced. Candy continued her attention until she felt Yakami's quivers grow more distinct.

The girl's hands fled her scalp and slapped to the wall. Yakami clawed at the tiles as she buried her chin into her chest and gave soft barks of rapture. Her eyes were screwed shut, and her mouth was parted into a most alluring O of delight.

The sight of Yakami being encompassed by such radical bliss took Candy's desire and gave it an unexpected twist. Before she knew what she was doing, she hauled her finger free, leapt up, and grabbed Yakami's wet tresses. The girl was pliant to her will and did not fight as she was forced to the floor.

Candy lifted Yakami's arms out and then straddled her upper body. Her shins pressed forcefully into the girl's biceps, and she gave a vague murmur as Candy applied more of her body weight to keep them trapped.

"Worship me," ordered Candy.

Yakami's eyes sparkled with rapture as she was subjugated by another slave. She started to crane her neck up, but Candy started to hoist her hindquarters away. Yakami tried harder, and Candy placed her hands on her hips as she swayed and made the girl struggle to access her. The sight of their bodies as they flowed with warm translucent sheets of water was highly titillating, but Candy wanted to play some more before she let the girl attain her goal.

Candy's chest was running with water, and this caused a small waterfall to pour from between her legs. The excess pattered Yakami's face as she got closer, and just as her lips brushed Candy's pussy, she gave the girl a light slap to each cheek. Yakami recoiled with an abashed expression.

"I didn't say you could worship me there!" she hissed with a wide and libidinous grin.

Yakami looked startled for a moment, and Candy wondered if she gone too far. Then Yakami echoed the smile and started to adore Candy's inner thighs with sultry licks and dithering kisses.

"Muuuuch better," said Candy.

She sank her fingers into Yakami's hair to help support her while she worked, although because of her forced lifestyle, Candy knew that Yakami's neck muscles had to be capable of much more than this.

Candy savoured the humble attention for a time and then decided that she wanted a more distinct form of fulfilment. She used the reins of the girl's hair to pull her back. Their eyes met, and Yakami froze as she anticipated a command. Candy held off on her response as she studied the yearning in Yakami's features. The girl's eyes were glazed and alive with lust. She would do anything for her.

"Now you may serve me," she stated, then regally lifted her head up as she let go of the girl.

Yakami trembled beneath her with dissolute wantonness, and Candy's back arched as a deft tongue started to ravage her loins. Again, she found that Yakami's skill was unparalleled, and Candy was rapidly marched into orgasm by her educated ministrations.

Once she had taken all she could from the flitting oral fiend, Candy pushed her back with a palm placed to her forehead and stood up. Yakami floundered on the wet floor and stared at the towering nude form before her.

"Shave me," said Candy and leant back against the wall as the shower continued to pelt her exposed torso.

Yakami quickly grabbed a razor and curled around Candy's feet. She then started to attend her legs with the most reverent devotion, moving slowly and ensuring she covered every millimetre.

It felt good to have a shade of control again, to take a moment to step back from her submission and just play at being the mistress for once. The inclination was fleeting, and it felt as though she was indulging it not only as further thanks to Yakami, but also to provide a more distinct contrast for the next time when the ruling Kami elite again subdued her.

Yakami's own submissive nature was constant and all-powerful in her mind. When she was ordered to submit, no matter to whom, she did so with utter elation, and this was brazenly revealed with the sheer pious adoration being shown to Candy's legs. Every sweep of the razor was conducted as though she was attending the most vaulted Kami, and her face was a picture of sated glee.

Candy watched her trim each of her legs and then clear away the emerging stubble at her pussy before she set the implement aside and again settled her face between Candy's legs. After having watched the slow and meticulous chore, Candy was as ready to enjoy the girl's tongue again as Yakami was to offer it.

She held to the wall and steered her breasts under the jets of water to stimulate them as Yakami again served her up to another long and succulent climax.

Weary from their lengthy erotic shower, they emerged in silence, dried themselves, and climbed onto the bed. Tangled within each other's arms they found ready escape into sleep, and as Candy felt herself drifting away, she knew then that a similar fate was befalling her former persona.

Each day in this realm was causing her to sink further away

from the person she had been. She was becoming more open to experience, more willing to lose herself to anything the Kami Empire offered. Perhaps the view of submerging into this fate was not correct, because it implied a loss, a form of degradation. Perhaps she should look on it as rising higher, floating upward and sloughing off the shackles and burdens of a lost psyche and a distanced reality, because the utter fulfilment she was finding here was most definitely not something to regret or fear anymore. Candy was being set free of Candice, and the process was sheer ecstasy.

CHAPTER ELEVEN

Candy had spent a couple days recovering from her session. The salve greatly speeded the healing of her treasured bruises, and in some ways she regretted this, because every time she felt them, or saw them, she was reminded of her session with Lady Uzume and the Mikado, and that brought forth all the intensity of that encounter. They were also a medal, an award that she had earned through her devotion to them in that wondrous hall.

Candy was then summoned again and escorted by the messenger. Dressed solely in stockings and elbow length gloves, she walked into the designated area and found an arena of unearthly erotic excess.

The hall had a low domed ceiling, and the walls had numerous golden fixtures spaced along them. Each was formed to resemble a human female who was crying out in distress. Each figurine's tongue was extended from its maw, and upon the golden effigy rested a tall white candle. The wax had red veins wandering through it, and the candles each released a heady perfume into the air.

The floor had numerous large cushions thrown across it to create a soft yielding carpet of velvet and silk. Sprawled upon these were the forms of the Kami.

Lady Uzume was reclining on one of the large cushions as the naked form of Mae studiously devoured her pussy. A large metal collar had been set around Mae's neck, and Uzume held a leash to it. Uzume was clad in fishnet stockings and knee-high leather boots. A wispy leather belt embraced her waist and held the stockings up with several thick suspenders. Her breasts were free and exposed, and her elegant arms were covered with tight fitting gloves.

There were several other women present, but they were not fully human. Each of them was tall and lithe with ranks of dense and compact muscles. Their skin had the hint of scales to it, and along their necks and back were reptilian patterns of purple, blue, and red. Each of the women had a long slender tail that was clearly prehensile as it curled and flexed amidst the soft pillows. They had no hair at all, and their brows were heavy, their teeth slightly pointed, and their ears were merely recessed pits. Their eyes had a distinct yellow shade and contained slit shaped pupils. Despite their inhuman qualities, they were still highly alluring.

They prowled around the cushions, moving with a serpentine grace that made them seem only semi-corporeal. There were trussed human forms amidst the room, and the Wani hybrids were digging around for them and then playing with those that took their fancy. Some forced the slaves between their legs, teased them, nibbled at them, tightened their bondage, or warped it into new and distressing configurations. The faint mews of the slave made the women hiss and ripple with relish.

There were only two males present. The Mikado was naked and sat with Nakatomi Jemma and Ammalia kneeling beside him. Both women were clad only in a pair of tight vinyl shorts.

The other male was a powerful form that was sprawled casually upon a large pillow. He had the same reptilian traits as the women and had vibrant purple markings over his chest and up his arms. He regarded his fellow women with an amused interest as he drank from a large golden goblet.

Candy barely had time to take in the sight when she felt

something cool and smooth slither around her shins. The hold tightened, and the tail yanked her feet from under her. She collapsed onto a pillow and gave a gasp as one of the women jumped up and pinned her down. The woman's strong fingers clamped to Candy's wrists and her body slithered over to straddle her.

Candy stared up with awe at the strange form and the exceptionally attractive breasts hanging just before her.

The woman grinned and gave a purring hiss. Her tongue poured over her teeth, and the lengthy organ emerged to trace a path up Candy's neck. Candy shook and gave a wanton groan as she imagined what this preternatural organ would feel like inside her.

"A new arrival. How very sweet of you to attend, my dear. Are you late? Or were you summoned?" whispered the woman with long and sibilant tones.

"I was summoned," said Candy as the tongue curled around the back of her neck and tickled the opposite earlobe.

The tongue flashed away, and the woman brought Candy's hands together over her head, pinning them down together with one hand. The other hand gave a light slap to her cheek. The stinging flick cast Candy's head aside, and the woman leaned in again so she could whisper directly into her exposed ear.

"You call me *Mistress*, slave. Forget it again and I'll make you regret it."

"Sorry, Mistress. I meant no offence," gasped Candy.

"How is it that a concubine trained from birth to respect her betters fails to do so? Is House Temmangu becoming slack in their duties? Do I have to punish them, as well as you?"

"I'm from Earth, Mistress. I've only been here for a short time."

"Oh, so you're the Kami-tsu-ko that they call Candy?"

"Yes, Mistress."

"Superb."

Candy arched her spine and gave a whimper of pleasure as she felt the agile tail of the woman reach between her legs and start to brush her pussy. The woman leant in and lapped at her neck again. The organ was cool and slick, with little moisture to it.

"You like that, slave?"

"Oh yes, Mistress."

The tail reached in and tickled her clit for a moment before it poured into her and wriggled to create surges of bizarre sensation. The woman's tongue lowered and began to embrace Candy's breasts. It circled around the base and tightened to make them swell so that the tip might then dance upon the raised nipple. Candy was overwhelmed by the alien experience and shuddered beneath the writhing, sultry form.

"How about . . . now!"

The tail dropped down and exploited Candy's own wetness to lubricate entry into her rear. The smooth scales rolled through her sphincter and charged onward. Candy jerked as she felt the invasion and saw that the woman's eyes were half closed as she concentrated on manoeuvring her dextrous extremity. By touch alone, she negotiated her way deeper into Candy.

Candy bucked and struggled. The feeling was simply too absurd to withstand. She could feel the appendage working its way deeper into her, following the twists and turns of her body. Her opening was starting to hurt as the width of the tail started to force it open to new levels.

Gurgling and sobbing, Candy pulled against the woman's grip and tried to shuffle free. The power of the creature's thighs and her hand easily overcame her. The reptilian woman's muscles were like iron.

"You're not going anywhere, slave. You're going to feel me deeper than you've ever felt anyone before," she attested, and gave a little scowl as she pushed on even further.

The extra jolt made Candy cry out as her anus was stretched more than she could accept in silence, and she felt the tail flex and reveal its entire route within her. Only a fragment of her resulting shout escaped, because the woman dove in and smothered her with a kiss. The lips of the woman sealed her maw, and the tongue thrust in to curl within her mouth. Candy's eyes bulged as the full measure of the organ folded and curled within her. It kept her jaws wide and made her cheeks bulge and ripple with the internal motions. Her own tongue was squashed into the base of her mouth as the strange woman gagged her.

Her eyes stared into the inhuman slits of the woman's, and tears began to well as she felt the tail starting a methodical dance. Parts of it sought to straighten and made her insides flicker with distress. The feeling was like nothing she had ever encountered, and it was terrifying because of it.

The woman savoured Candy's angst while she was ravished. The tail started to ride and rock within her. The most acute of penetrations had a distinct ecstasy to it, but the power and monstrous severity of it was too frightening.

The unearthly sodomy continued for long minutes, and then the tail started to draw free of her. Its flight made Candy vibrate and screw her eyes shut as the feel of the lengthy appendage sliding free of her anus tore through her psyche. It eventually came free, and the woman recalled her tongue.

The woman sat up and put her hands on her hips as Candy shook and embraced her own torso. The echo of the feeling was still haunting her rear and she was in shock from the event.

"Did you enjoy that, slave?"

"I . . . I don't know, Mistress," truthfully answered Candy. She was not sure whether she could process it as pleasurable, but it was not really quantifiable as painful either.

"Well, off you go then," chuckled the woman and lifted her thigh so that Candy rolled out from beneath her.

Candy flopped onto a pillow and tried to gather some semblance of sanity. As she opened her eyes, she gave a surprised squeak as she found herself staring into the imploring wide eyes of a bound slave. The woman had been sealed within a rubber cocoon, and straps had been set all over it to compress her into a single stalk. She was massively gagged, and her stare was wild. Candy looked down and saw that one of the hybrids was pressed to her rear, and her monstrous tongue was busily thrashing into the girl's anus.

Candy smiled as she looked into the woman's eyes and kissed her smothered mouth before climbing onto hands and knees and heading off.

"Ah, there you are, Candy," announced the Mikado.

Lady Uzume turned round and panned her stare across the sea of bound women and predatory hybrids to see her slave approaching.

"Come here, slave. I want you to meet Warlord Toyotama-hiko. I have told him and his daughters all about you," said Lady Uzume.

Candy quickly scuttled over between them and stayed on her knees with her head lowered.

"Hmmm, I've never had a female from the other side," commented the Warlord.

"Well, I think it's about time that we rectified that," lightly stated Lady Uzume.

Leaning over, Uzume gestured to Jemma and then to Candy. Jemma arose and grabbed some leather cuffs from between some pillows. She moved behind Candy and started to apply them to her body. Candy did not move—she just sat there and let herself be contained.

Sets of thick leather cuffs were buckled to her ankles, her wrists, and then above her elbows. Two short chains were used to connect them, and this forced her arms together behind her. With her chest thrust out, the strong woman then easily picked her up, and cradled in her arms, Candy was delivered to the Warlord.

Candy was set down so that she was facing up with her legs drawn apart. Rings in the floor accepted the cuffs and kept her forcibly open.

The Warlord shifted forward and slid beneath her hindquarters. His skin was cold and slick as his tail reached up and curled around her body, exploring her as he positioned himself.

Candy gave a jerk and cry as his manhood thrust into her. With her body splayed upon his lap, the Warlord lay back and casually launched up into her body to push to the limits of what she could accommodate with his huge cock. The skin was slightly rough, and this created ridges that made her pussy shudder and bounced her clitoris upon them. His dimensions and his texture were shockingly delightful.

Candy gasped and gave a twitch each time he fired upward, his actions making her tense as she fought to accommodate him and process the sensation.

His hands joined in and started to draw across her torso and breasts. Candy responded by arching back and offered him the full plate of her body.

The Warlord's fingers had slight curved talons, and these thick fingernails left light scratches upon her. The minor discomfort was a definite added treat and Candy gave whimpering mewls of debauched delight as she was ravished by the Wani hybrid. She steered her hindquarters and took as much of him as she could while flexing her muscles to add extra stimulation.

"How is she?" asked Lady Uzume.

In the corner of her eye, she saw the Mikado thrusting into Mae as she continued to try to pleasure her owner. The

Nakatomi had found similar employment, and Jemma had her face between the thighs of a hybrid as another of the alien women busily worked her hand into her pussy and slowly sought significant access for her extremity. Ammalia was kissing one of the women and the two of them were locked in a tight clinch, their bodies pressed together so that the tail of her partner could flick between their connected loins and stimulate them both simultaneously.

"Admirable. A lot less frantic than most concubines."

"So we can say our House has helped you attain another first?" she suggested.

"Ah, but there are firsts, and there are *firsts*, Lady Uzume. Yourself for instance."

"What do you mean?" she replied coyly.

"You have never visited my palace. I have treats there even you would appreciate," he offered slyly.

"The Warlord keeps me busy," came Uzume's dismissive reply.

"I'm sure I could arrange something with Hachiman. Besides, do you never desire to become a reigning Kami rather than a subordinate?"

"I am loyal to my House and my ruler."

"I am not questioning that. Your loyalty has been proven to be irreproachable and without equal. But surely you must want to elevate your standing? You have most certainly earned it."

"And what would you suggest, Warlord?"

"Come to my palace. Consent to be my equal. We could rule the Wani together and establish a distinct and separate force," he purred as he plundered Candy's body.

"Warlord Hachiman would not be pleased," Uzume replied softly.

"The Sun-Goddess and Moon-God could be persuaded to permit it. They already think Hachiman has too much power over the Houses of Fire. The Mitama, the Wani, me, you. Perhaps command of the armies should be divided for the good of the Empire."

"And why would you not seek this . . . pardon me a moment, Warlord." She flashed her attention to her oral devotee.

"Slower, Mae!"

Lady Uzume harshly slapped the girl's cheeks several times and then reached under to crush a breast in a fist. Mae smothered her wail into her owner's crotch as the Mikado slammed himself deep, punishing her insides. His pounding manhood was inspiring Mae's lust and making her tongue work faster than the Lady wanted. To correct this, after the chastisement, he hauled free and threaded himself into her rear. Mae shuddered violently as she was pierced, and Lady Uzume returned her attention to her guest. Clearly, Mae's rear was not as easily accepting of the Mikado's phallus as her pussy was.

"Why do you not seek this post alone, Warlord?"

"I am Wani. It is unlikely that they will charge me with the rule of my own kind. However, if a Kami of noble blood and birth were to share this responsibility with me, equally . . ."

"But what is there to do with this post? The Kami Empire is stable, secure, and invulnerable."

"A time comes where the Houses of Fire are to embark on a great crusade. The Sun-Goddess and Moon-God must wonder about leaving all of this matter to Hachiman alone. That is too much power for one man. I think they would be receptive to at least breaking away a small portion of it."

"You must have links to Amatsu mika hoshi and his spies to know of this."

"Not really, but the Wani know conquest, and I catch its heady scent on my tongue with ever increasing potency."

"I will dwell on your words, Warlord, but for now, let us dismiss talk of such politics and enjoy our comforts."

"As you wish," said the Warlord with a hint of irritation.

His irked nature manifested as spite towards his restrained lover. The Wani moved forward to stretch Candy's legs against their bonds, and keen aches flickered along the tendons and swelled in the joints as he started to rack her. His tail curled around the chain that connected her wrists and pulled her back towards him. This arched Candy up into an uncomfortable bow. He pulled a little harder, and Candy offered him a whimper of protest. The sound only encouraged him further. The Warlord's claws slid across her body and opened small grazes as he thrust deep and hard.

Candy grunted and gasped with each drive. She felt the manhood of the vicious Warlord flick with new passion, and it seemed to grow even larger within her. Candy sobbed as he continued to ravish her and finally had to cry out from the stress of having him jab deeper than ever before. She felt him come within her and continue his thrusts, savouring her dismay as she tried to endure his spiteful lust.

"Not bad. Not bad at all," he commented.

Shifting back along the large cushion, he simply deserted Candy's body. She dropped down and lay sprawled before him, her legs wide, her loins twitching as she gasped for breath. Candy could still feel the long scratches all over her chest like hot rewards for her submission to him.

It was clear that Toyotama-hiko was very enamoured with Lady Uzume. He wanted her, very badly, even to the point of sharing power with her. The fact that she was steadfastly keeping him at a distance only seemed to make him more anxious to acquire her.

"Lady Uzume. A herald has arrived. Warlord Hachiman will be here in two hours!"

The woman cast her plaything aside and leapt to her feet. She clapped her hands to gain the attention of everyone in the room.

"Nakatomi! Mikado! To work! And apologies to our honoured guests, but we have preparations to make."

"I completely understand, Lady Uzume. Your dedication to your master is, as always, impressive."

Candy was quickly untied, and Nakatomi Jemma told her to return to her room and clean herself up. Other members of the priesthood entered and started to carry out the more restrictively bound females, but a few were stopped when one of the Wani women decided that they wanted to continue playing with the cocooned and defenceless slave a little while longer. Groans of distress emerged from the tight sheaths and abundance of tight straps that hid away a struggling female.

Candy entered her quarters and found them empty. Yakami had no doubt been taken so that she could be prepared for the Mikado. She strolled over to the bed and ran her hands along the vacant area. She smiled and patted the covers, wondering what the Mikado would do to her friend.

She showered and tended her hair and makeup, then started to hear a distant and steady rumble, like that of endless thunder. Intrigued, she looked out of her windows and saw a large force heading across the fields towards the palace. Far below in the courtyard and in the grounds, teams of priests and slaves were being herded around and established in new bondage furniture. A line of bound serviles was set along the final stretch of road to the palace, creating a decorative avenue for the forces to progress down. Candy stared with longing at the contorted forms that were strapped and bound into immobility, and she contemplated the sensations she would experience in some of the more potently alluring ones.

Her hand wandered across her own skin and started to proceed lower. As she glared with unbridled lust at the visions of containment, her finger started to slowly brush her sex.

The ruler of the Great House rode a black-skinned Tyrannosaur amidst a dozen other such beasts. They were all armour plated and had magnificent banners fluttering in the breeze.

The procession moved down into the stables, where a view was less easy to obtain, so Candy returned her lewd gaze to the slaves and continued her masturbation. She stopped as she heard the door open.

Candy turned to see Nakatomi Jemma enter alone and shut the door behind her. The woman held strange metal devices in her hands that looked like a steel thong and matching collar.

"You are to be prepared to meet Warlord Hachiman," she said firmly.

Candy stepped away from the window and watched in silence as the woman attended her. The item was separated into two pieces and a band of steel was closed about her waist. The hoop was hinged at the side and the other end bore a covert lock. The Nakatomi made her suck in her stomach as much as she could, and even then, she had to pull and drag at her skin so she could properly close the device. The fierce grip held over her hips and created a significant crimp.

Then the other item was taken up. The semicircle of metal had an inner surface that had two thick and spongy plugs emerging from a similar cushion of absorbent padding. Each end of the steel section had a barbed arrow-like fixture jutting from it that would slip into the waistband and lock to it.

The Nakatomi bent her over and spread her legs to ease the application of the device. The plugs nestled against her pussy and rear, and with a shove the band leaned itself heavily to her crotch. The two upper regions slid into two slots in the waistband, and an internal locking mechanism took hold and refused to let go.

Candy was now rendered utterly chaste. The Nakatomi

tested the implement by trying to wiggle a finger under the crotch band, then to pull open the steel, but everything had been engineered with precision, and her attempts were completely ineffective.

Candy felt very strange to have access to her own body removed. She had been bound tightly and deprived before, but this item allowed her freedom to move and act but left her without the capacity to touch herself. In some ways, she preferred the more comprehensive forms of restraint, because they left her with no options. This item left her able to move but frustrated her with denial.

The collar was closed around her neck and the similar lock was engaged. The Nakatomi took up a lead and clipped it to the ring that had been welded to the front of the plain polished band.

"Come with me, slave," ordered the woman.

Candy did not speak and merely obediently followed her guide while her mind raced with fantasies of what the Warlord would want from her. Would he be more cruel than his subordinates, or would his savagery have been tempered with age? Jemma drew Candy up through the higher levels of the palace and to a large antechamber. Three fully armoured human warriors stood against the walls on either side of her. They stood to stern attention and held assault rifles with grenade launchers. They had a pair of ornate katana upon their backs, and their features were lost behind fierce masks that even hid their eyes behind one-way silver panes.

The large double doors at the other end of the room had the emblem of the Mitama formed from embedded jewels, and a large jade oval was set in the floor immediately before them.

Standing in the centre of the room was Lady Uzume. The woman looked devastatingly powerful in her military garments. A close-fitting leather catsuit also bore the sections of armour Candy had seen on the warriors. Paired katana crossed her back as automatic pistols dwelt at her hips. She had donned fierce makeup and tied her hair back into a stern bun that was pierced by three silver stilettos.

The Nakatomi reverently handed Lady Uzume the leash and then retreated with a bowed head.

Lady Uzume took a deep breath and stepped forward towards the doors. When they stepped onto the jade section, Candy felt it sink a little. There was a click, and the portal parted before them. There were some distant, muted whimpers, and then Candy was being drawn in.

The doors closed and Candy looked back to see what had caused the subtle noise. She saw that two women had been sealed within leather suits and bound horizontally to serve as living mechanisms. Their bodies were held in a broad harness of leather that kept their backs along the door, while their legs extended out onto the walls. By straining up, they opened the doors, and by arching back, they closed them. Their legs were splayed wide, and she could see hidden wires entering their crotches. Stepping on the jade plate no doubt activated some sort of command that assailed them with pain or pleasure to make the living pistons comply.

Candy turned to face the rest of the chamber, which was formed as a regal throne room. The circular hall had plain walls with iron sconces that each released a flickering column of flame. A set of six stone steps rose up to a large and highly ornate throne. The iron chair had riveted plates and deep velvet cushions. Sitting in this chair was the Warlord himself.

He was of average height, and his body was slender and lean. His muscles were very defined, and he bore several scars that crossed his arms and chest. His face was passive, with glittering jet-black eyes. His black hair was worn short, and he had several golden earrings. Strangely, he was not tattooed, and he wore only some weathered and scuffed leather trousers, heavy boots that had seen much use, and a metal bracer on each forearm.

Lady Uzume marched proudly to the base of the steps and bowed deeply. Candy sank to her knees and placed her forehead to the ground.

"Welcome home, Warlord. How was your voyage?" she asked cordially.

"Tedious. Tsuki-yomi is not easy to negotiate with."

"Were you successful though, Warlord?"

"Candy is now ours. And at no small price, I may add. There were several other Houses making significant bids for her."

Candy could not believe that she had been auctioned yet again, this time without her knowledge.

"We will have to show some gratitude to those more directly responsible, but I am sure that particular debt can be handled with ease. Now, let me see her."

Lady Uzume rose and pulled on the leash to bring Candy back onto her feet. The Warlord arose from his throne and slowly marched down the steps. The man had an almost tangible power to him. He radiated authority and command, and Candy felt her legs going weak beneath her as his implacable stare rolled across her form.

"A powerful woman from the other side. A leader. With wealth, influence, and might. Feared, respected, envied. Now she is mine. A concubine to do with as I wish," he said, and walked around behind her to assess her rear view.

Candy could now see why she had been so eagerly vied for, and why so much effort had been made on her behalf. They wanted a trophy, someone from Earth of significance. She had been a force. That much was true. Her face might not have graced front pages, posters, or televisions, but her decisions and choices could affect the fate of nations. By owning such a person, would a Kami not show just how powerful they were?

"Not bad at all," he commented. "But speaking of gratitude. I have heard that Toyotama-hiko is here."

"Yes, Warlord. I have been keeping him entertained. His visit was unexpected."

"And no doubt occurred because of my absence. Did he seduce you away, Lady Uzume? His eye strays to you often," asked the Warlord with a jovial tone to his bold voice.

"No, Warlord. I am eternally pledged to you and your House," was Lady Uzume's soft reply.

"As I have heard. Slaves make very comprehensive informants. Your loyalty deserves a reward," he stated.

"If my Warlord wishes."

"He does. So, you have enjoyed this slave's body?" he asked, and moved out in front of the woman.

"Yes, Warlord."

"You would like to again?" he said.

There was a strange tone to his voice. The Warlord was insinuating something else.

"Oh yes, Warlord!" exclaimed Lady Uzume, her fervour showing that she had some idea what he was proposing.

"Then strip for me, and we will see to it," he announced.

Lady Uzume's hands were frantic as they started to unbuckle her armour and extricate herself from her weapons and attire. The Warlord walked back up to his throne and took up a bag from behind it. As he came back down, he removed a bundle of rope from within.

He took hold of Candy's hands and brought them before her. Rope encircled her wrists and crossed up to her elbows. He formed some swift knots, then tugged the coils about her waist. Her arms were pulled to her belly, and he pushed her back down onto her knees. Tilting her head back, he took out a funnel and pushed the end of it into her maw. The funnel was already fixed into a dense rubber strap that was quickly buckled around her head and tightened into place. The rubber pressed to her face and helped create a near airtight seal.

"Stay still, slave," he ordered.

Candy froze and stared up at the ceiling as she heard Lady Uzume strip off the last of her attire. His words seemed to have petrified her muscles. The Warlord spoke with a voice that tolerated no dissention or even questioning of his will. The might in each syllable could control her body more than her own mind ever could.

The Warlord reached into the bag, and then Lady Uzume was handed a chastity belt to match Candy's. With eager hands, she willingly donned the item and settled down on her knees beside Candy.

"And now for the elixir," he said softly, and presented an ornate glass phial. Inside was a pale substance that looked a little like body oil. He removed the silver stopper and took hold of Candy's chin. She stared at the strange bottle and watched as he slowly tilted it and caused a steady trickle to emerge. It dropped into the funnel, and Candy felt the slightly warm substance trickling down the back of her throat. When he had finished, he unbuckled the funnel and set it aside.

Lady Uzume was fed a dose that she eagerly accepted before the Warlord set the emptied vial aside and took up Candy's leash. She was towed up to the throne as Lady Uzume followed closely behind her, her eyes fixated with the wiggle of Candy's hindquarters.

"You have proven that your wish is still for you to remain under my rule. I think you should do so, literally, while I hold court in this room and see to the matters of the House."

The Warlord touched an area of the throne, and with a sudden lurch it scraped aside and exposed a sturdy metal hatch. He reached down and hauled the trapdoor up to expose a metal shaft.

"In you go, slaves. My Mikado will be here soon, and I have

much to ready and process."

Lady Uzume immediately moved over and sat on the lip before lowering herself within. There was a metallic tone as she dropped down and landed deep inside the pit. The Warlord unfastened Candy's ropes and removed the leash.

Candy looked inside and saw that the shaft dropped down about three yards. Lady Uzume was standing upright and was reaching up to help Candy get in. About a yard up from the bottom was a heavy barred grill. It was hinged against the interior wall, and the exposed upward end had three holes in it, no doubt placed there to accept bolts from the other wall that would lock it into position when it was shut.

Candy stared at the shaft with unease. Such close confinement, the blackness, the metal fencing her in on all sides. She felt claustrophobia taking hold, but one look at the sultry naked form of Lady Uzume banished her fright and she started to climb down. Lady Uzume took hold of her and brought her down into the lowest portion of the pit. She grabbed the hatch and lowered it to leave the two of them huddled and pressed together.

"Have fun, slaves," said the Warlord.

Hachiman touched the same secret control, and the throne ground back into place. Candy and Uzume looked up and watched the image of their owner vanishing as the base of the chair closed. There was also the soft scrape of metal against metal from the hatch as the same machine that was closing their pit slid heavy bolts into the barred internal hatch. There was a split second to act before the grill was sealed to keep them in a tight box. Neither of them acted, and they were suddenly plunged into darkness.

Uzume let a hand travel around Candy as they were compressed together in the void. Candy did not know how to respond. This was a ruling Kami. Now she was confined and locked up with her. They were both held in chastity, had both been fed some mysterious brew, and were destined to linger in tight isolation for as long as the Warlord wished.

Uzume's lips started to kiss and lick at Candy's skin, and the faint sensations started to quickly gather in potency. There was a strength to her reactions, one that was far more acute than normal. Candy's loins swelled with hunger, her skin tingled, and her mind throbbed with a wanton lustful desire.

"Wh . . . what's happening to me?" she said with concern.

"You are succumbing to the effects of a Yakushin brew. It sharpens the touch, stimulates the mind and . . . other regions," she purred.

Uzume was clearly experienced and comfortable with the effects. She might be a dreaded force and a ruling Kami, but it seemed that she found delight in being a subjugated plaything to her Warlord.

"Why did you choose this?" asked Candy.

"Hachiman is my master. I am his willing slave. He alone can do this to me, and I relish every opportunity. I am his, just as you are mine. But here, in this cell, we are equal for now. Enjoy it while it lasts, Candy."

Their hands flowed on capricious whims to stroke and fondle, to squeeze, to grope with abandon. Every touch was glorious as their skin was charged with input that made them quiver and moan. They rubbed their breasts upon the flesh of their partner, and their lips trailed along limbs, face, and torso. Their tongues lapped and their lips sucked on nipples and fingers. The chastity belts were both a bane and a blessing. They each so fervently wanted to indulge their carnal appetites, so the frustration of being deprived was maddening, but the level of bliss being so freely conjured by a mere touch might well make cunnilingus a fatal event.

Candy stretched her arms up through the bars and pawed at the cool metal wall beyond as she felt Uzume nibbling on the cheeks of her rear. Hands reached around and tickled the underside of her breasts before they focused more devotedly on her nipples. The interior was hot, and the metal was now slick with sweat. Their bodies ached even as they were pleasured. Their contortion and inability to straighten up cultivated severe distress, but it was a discomfort that could be countered through committed licentious play.

Candy slid back down and shuffled around to draw Uzume against her. The stiff points of their breasts brushed one another, and they began a lethargic and passionate oral exchange. They suckled upon each other's tongues and lips, let the tips roll up and down their necks and skip from nipples as their hands freely cruised over their own body and that of their lover. They traced the defiant walls of their sexual prisons and found that although they could squeak a finger along the front, the ample padding maliciously absorbed all the vibrations, and nothing reached their starved and ravenous pussys.

Candy's mind was being carried on waves of libidinous frenzy. Her entire world was devoted to filling every inch of her skin with tactile rhapsody. Her head swam in the darkness and her thoughts were locked solely on touch and sensation. Time had no meaning in their ecstatic tomb, and all the while, they had the knowledge that their Warlord was sat above them dispensing orders as they languished deep beneath him.

After what could have been days of heated passion, there was a shrill metallic squeal, and then a column of impossibly bright light suddenly dazzled them. The throne slid aside, and they shielded their eyes until they had adjusted to feeble light of the throne room. The bolts to the hatch sprang back, and Lady Uzume stretched upward to open it. She climbed out from the pit and extended a hand back down to her partner.

Squinting against the silhouette of the woman, Candy took

her hand and was pulled up from their damp erotic sarcophagus.

They stood up and stretched their long-folded bodies. They both took a moment to exercise their weary and sweat-sodden limbs, and the aching presence in their joints and muscles swiftly vanished. The sheen of perspiration that was coating their skin evaporated just as quickly, and the exercise helped keep them warm as it tried to steal their body heat.

The Warlord stepped forward and applied a small key to their belts, and finally the infernal chastity devices came away. The cool air that rushed over the concealed areas made them both sway and gasp with pleasure. Their hairs stood on end and goose bumps arose over their arms and legs. The Warlord set the belts aside and returned to his throne.

"Kneel side by side," he announced.

Candy and Uzume quickly took their positions before him. The Warlord settled back into the comfortable and imposing seat. His hands clasped the armrests and tensed as he gave his order.

"Take hold of your nipples, slaves."

Uzume's hands leapt up and applied pinches to her teats. It was clear that the moment the Warlord chose to take control of Lady Uzume, she became a compliant and anxious toy to his desire. The change was radical, swift, and remarkable. The woman had been an implacable dominatrix since they had first encountered one another—now she was as loyal a submissive concubine as Yakami or any other slave in the palace.

Candy's hands crept up more slowly and she took hold of her teats. She stared up the steps and to their owner for reassurance. His eyes bored into them both and were full of grim relish in seeing his property obey him.

"Now squeeze," he ordered.

Uzume gave a gasp as she applied a most forceful compression. Candy was less able to instantly traumatise her nipples and her pinch was much less fierce.

"Harder," he said with a broadening grin.

Uzume trembled as her tendons rose against her hands. She started to hunch over, her mouth dropped open, and she panted with strain. Inspired by the woman's dedication, Candy instantly increased her strength. She gave a croak of pain as the nuggets throbbed and sent struggling waves of distress through her breasts.

"Harder!" he snapped.

Uzume gave a cry as she pushed herself to the limits. Her fingers were trembling with strain as she panted and whimpered from the pain. Her eyes remained adoringly locked to the Warlord, and tears were coursing from them. Candy strove to try harder, and as she squashed her nipples in the most virulent pinch she could muster, she too felt watery trails trickling down her cheeks.

Candy stared up at their oppressor and found that they were tears of happiness and contentment. Warlord Hachiman ruled and owned them so completely that he could command such acts from them, and they would be done with full commitment and utter loyalty.

The notion to beg for mercy did not even rise, and the longer they shivered in travail before him, punishing their own bodies for his amusement, the more lost they became to his reign.

"Enough," he finally decreed.

Uzume let go and dropped onto all fours. Her head stayed low and her back remained arched while she gasped for breath. Candy released her own teats and dropped back onto her haunches. She cradled the abused nuggets and gave soft whimpers as the effects of compression gave way to a terrible storm of returning circulation and distressed sensation.

"Very good, slaves. You may come up here," he said, and beckoned with one crooked finger.

Uzume started to crawl up the steps and Candy chose to adopt a similar method of travel. The two of them ascended and then knelt down before him.

"Kneel upright."

They complied immediately. They knelt to rigid attention, as though they were on parade. Pride and a commitment to impressing and pleasing their master was paramount.

"Now, I want to watch you both come."

Uzume's hand was again the swiftest, and her fingers instantly dropped onto her sex and started to caress it. She obeyed instantly and with verve to every command of her Warlord.

Candy felt a momentary pang of embarrassment, but the need to finally quench her sexual thirst was too demanding to deny. She fixed her stare to him and started to caress her loins. The pleasure that rushed through her was all the more potent because of all they had done in the pit, also because of the level of dominance being applied to them. Hachiman had shown that he controlled them completely. He did not even need to involve himself with their torment. If they did not amuse him, or if it just suited his mood, he could make them discipline themselves.

The Warlord lay back and smiled contentedly as his two servants each stroked their clitoris and whimpered with pleasure. Candy had a concern that he would make them stop before orgasm. After the mind-bending sexual frustration of the pit, she questioned her ability to comply should he demand such abstinence. However, if she betrayed the rule of the Warlord, she was sure that his fiendish imagination would make her bitterly regret her weakness with a most diabolic form of punishment. If he were indeed as old as Yakami had said, then with centuries of life amongst the bondage displays and slaves to contort and make wail with misery on a whim, he would be a master of breaking the spirit of a recalcitrant female.

Her fears proved groundless when Uzume was the first to climax. She was at home with such actions, and her absolute love of the Warlord had charged her with intense arousal that needed very little stimulation to bring to fruition.

The sound of Uzume rasping and groaning with rapture was an auditory aphrodisiac that quickly elevated Candy to a similar state. With eyes filled with the image of the Warlord, she twitched and moaned as she indulged herself with a long and highly satisfying orgasm.

"Good, slaves. You may rest at my feet for a time."

Lady Uzume and Candy curled up around his booted feet as the Warlord sat and contemplated whatever it was that he had been told while they lurked beneath his throne. It was a satisfying position in which to dwell, and Candy felt utterly at ease with her lot. Uzume closed her eyes and held lightly to his boots. It was obvious that Lady Uzume enjoyed having slaves to bind and use to serve her sadistic tendencies, but at heart, she was a submissive creature through and through.

The hall was quiet and peaceful, and Candy found a tranquil peace. Finally, he came to some unspoken decisions and stood up.

"Come, slaves. Enough of work, it is time for play," he broadcast and immediately strode towards the wall.

A section gave several deep resonant clanks and slid back. The secret door exposed a dark chamber where flickering torches and iron braziers with glowing coals bathed the shadowy interior in a hesitant amber twilight.

The naked forms of Lady Uzume and Candy leapt to their feet and gave chase as he vanished into the darkness. As soon as they entered, the door slid shut and locked behind them.

The interior was almost medieval in its construction and style. The dense ragged bricks had large iron rings set in them, and many had lines of chain swinging from one to another.

Anonymous sites of heavy restraint dwelt in the deeper pools of shadow and their contours were hinted at by the refraction of light upon them. The ambiance was both treacherous and alluring.

"Stand here," ordered the Warlord.

Candy and Lady Uzume took places near to each other and found that they were situated beneath heavy metal rings that hung directly above them. The Warlord vanished into the shadows, and Candy took the opportunity to quickly look around. She saw Lady Uzume's garb piled neatly in the corner along with her weapons. She looked to their owner who met her gaze and offered a wicked and knowing smirk that exposed her knowledge of what was going to happen next.

Warlord Hachiman appeared with a length of thin silvery chain that hung in long coils from his fist. He reached up and slipped one end through the ring above Lady Uzume, and left it dangling. He passed the rest through the ring above Candy and then vanished again.

This time, he returned with two leather sheaths. He dropped one on the floor and started to apply the other to Candy. Her arms were drawn behind her and slotted into the triangular sheath. She found that the single mitten at the end was less tight than usual, but this was compensated for with interior ranks of wicked spines. The vicious little fangs pressed to her skin and caused sharp flickers of dismay whenever she tried to move them. The laces tightened to make her thrust her chest out, and straps encompassed her chest and crossed in her cleavage. Then another belt was taken up from the tip of the mitten and brought between her legs. Hachiman hauled it up so that her arms were pressed to her back, then clipped the end to the front of her collar. The belt was now being tugged forcefully against her pussy and rear to create a compressing strain that she could not defeat. The arm sheath wanted her to arch back, but the belt to her collar fought this influence.

As she tried to adjust to the demands of the position, War-lord Hachiman applied a similar arm sheath to Lady Uzume. Ball gags were acquired, and each was pushed into their maws before it was buckled firmly about their heads.

The two captives stared at each other's distorted face, their full lips sucking on the large dark rubber orbs. Then the reason for their containment and gagging appeared in the hands of the Warlord.

A slim chain linked the clover clamps, and there was a clip in the centre of it. This was summarily attached to each of the strands of metal dangling above them.

The Warlord held the evil implements in one hand and leant in to kiss Candy's nipples. She knew his intention but was powerless to resist as his nibbles and flashing tongue caused each point to rise up and present itself to the jaws of the clamps.

Candy ground her teeth to the ball gag and whimpered as each teat was snatched and held by the toys. The throbbing presence started to gather its usual secret potency, and she stared at the whitening nuggets with escalating dismay.

The Warlord went to Lady Uzume and applied the clamps to make the woman shiver and sob. He then took the hanging chain and started to pull on it. The chain rattled against the rings and Candy gave a mortified squawk as her clamps were drawn upward. She lifted onto tiptoe and danced from foot to foot while the struggling havoc in her nipples was massively enhanced by the haul.

He lifted Lady Uzume's clamps in his other hand and when she was sufficiently elevated, he clipped them to the chain.

"Now, while I think on what else to do and then prepare it, you two can stand there. Don't go anywhere," he said with a diabolic chuckle, then wandered off to begin searching through the various sites and implements to find something to his fancy.

Candy stared at Lady Uzume as they both swayed and strained against the leather sheaths. Every movement translated as another pull that only piqued the mayhem being inflicted on their stretched nipples. The small fleshy stalagmites retracted and lengthened as the two of them sought a pose that might be a little easier than any other.

Cramps started to wring the soles of Candy's feet and she tottered back. Lady Uzume gave a squeak of pain as the retreat punished her. She glared at Candy and endured the distress before committing herself to a similar retreat. Candy replied with a holler of her own when she was pulled back and then raised onto the very tips of her feet. Lady Uzume then showed a degree of mercy and moved back again.

Chastened for her lack of balance, Candy sobbed and watched her partner in duel nipple suspension. Tears were in both their eyes as they listened to the Warlord prowling around. They flexed and strained against the sheaths and gained nibbling chastisement from the numerous spines. It was a maddening form of confinement, because any movement they made only made it worse for themselves and for their partner. Candy tried to lift one leg while perching on the other. She sought to exercise the raised limb as quickly as possible and try to banish the agonising cramps. However, by placing all her weight on the other leg, she only made her situation worse. Her efforts were quickly abandoned when she lost her balance and caused a stern haul to both their nipples that made her cry out against her gag and Lady Uzume to arch upward with a chagrined wail.

Hachiman appeared suddenly, and the clamps fled from Candy before she even knew he was there. She dropped back with a yowl as her teats detonated with suffering.

Candy swayed her torso from side to side and danced

around in circles as the terrible affliction rose to new heights and then tardily started to vanish. She crouched down as best she could and pressed her nipples to her thighs to try to comfort them.

A frightened mewl from Lady Uzume drew Candy's gaze up from the stone floor, and she saw the Warlord adding a weight to the vacated end of the chain. He let go and the dangling burden ensured that Uzume not only found no relief from the demands of the ordeal but also had to endure its increase.

Candy's sheath and the gag were removed, and the Warlord wasted no more time as he approached Candy with another selection of rope. She had her arms drawn behind her and the wrists crossed at the small of her back. Rope curled around the joints and forged a series of figure of eight loops. The bonds then created a weave just below her shoulder blades that sent paired lengths over her biceps and around her chest. The two strands crossed between her breasts, and when they were tightened, they created a slight bite to the root of her assets. Candy's arms were now hugged to her sides and a final circle was made around her waist to haul it in and keep the entire web in place.

Sitting on her knees, she felt a hand enter her hair and hold tight as the other delivered a bright red penis gag to her lips. Candy accepted the stubby replica phallus and gave a weak struggle as it was buckled tightly about her head. As soon as it was installed, the Warlord used her hair as reins to draw her down onto the ground. Candy lay flat before him, her arms bound behind her, her mouth filled with a wide artificial penis. Lines of dribble started to escape over her lips and form small puddles on the ground as she patiently awaited his next action.

The Warlord walked to the wall and held a large red candle up to one of the torches. He turned and watched the flame rise from the wick and illuminate his iniquitous glower.

Hachiman strolled casually around Candy's subdued form and waited as the molten pool of wax grew. Anxiety started to rise as she anticipated her punishment.

Candy gave a whinny and jerked as she felt splashes drop across the peaks of her rear. A moment later the heat of the wax poured into the skin. The Warlord continued to circle her, and trailed another brief line across her buttocks. Candy gave another cry of shock and jerked her rear into the air. She struggled against the ropes, and as the heat started to subside, she calmed and settled back onto the floor.

A trail was deposited across the back of her left thigh. The leg jolted up and out, stretching as though it could flee the effects of the scorching rain. Candy pressed her face to the floor and mewled as the effects faded.

The other thigh was treated to a line, and another quick motion drooled more into the cleft of her rear. Candy's chest lifted up and her head jerked back. She clenched her teeth to the gag and cried out as burning fluid attacked her hindquarters. The spike of havoc eased, and as the fires faded, her body wilted back onto the floor.

She had the ability to flee, to roll onto her feet and rush off and avoid his assault, but she knew that he would catch her, and bind her, and she would be helpless to this abuse. The ordeal of having to stay still and tolerate his attention made it all the more enjoyable. She was proving her loyalty and devotion to him and her own masochistic nature. Her arms had been kept out of the way, but she could still run away, but she was being made to stay put and accept her torment.

The candle tilted less distinctly and started to spit single droplets down onto her body. The steady rhythmic rain began to drip onto her thighs and then migrated across her rear. The candle lowered a little, and the effects of each landing grew in intensity. Candy gave a spasm and an abrupt bark of dismay with each touch. Drop after drop fell upon her. They made her wriggle and mewl as she strove to stay in place and continue to acquiesce to his wishes.

She felt his foot nudging her legs apart, making her splay herself before him and open herself to the worst of the candle's ravages. The ardent drops started to fall upon her inner thighs and long dribbles rolled down the skin as she jiggled upon the floor and guttered ululating dirges between her brief cries.

Every fibre of her being demanded that she flee, that she dart away and get out from under this incendiary monsoon, but her desire to please and to excel overrode her animal instincts and against all reason she remained where she was.

A long pour ran up one thigh, crossed the cleft of her rear, and moved down the other thigh. The pain reached a new zenith as the red trickles rolled into her crotch and reached her pussy. Candy flashed to attention and howled as her arms strained against the ropes. Her legs stretched out as far as they could, and the crust of hardened wax cracked as her muscles flicked to attention.

The candle moved away, and she dropped back down, sobbing softly as she tried to weather the squall. The heat between her legs slowly faded, and she cuddled her distress. She embraced it and transformed it, making it a pleasure rather than a form of pain. Candy suddenly gave a purr of contentment as she mulled over the last mordant chapter in her treatment. It had been hellish to endure, but now she was flying again on a cloud of debauched relish. The pain was still significant, but with it was the delight that she had come to nurture and cherish during her various trials.

The candle resumed its steady dripping attack, and the spots started to coat the length of her legs. Her shins were slowly covered, and then severe applications commenced with the slow coating of her feet. Her exposed soles were incredibly pained by the wax, and her howls grew to new and enthusiastic levels as he dripped the molten drops onto them. Her leg started to twitch and move, but the fledgling signs of rebellion were crushed when he merely put his foot to the limb and pinned it down. Candy jerked and hollered as he started to pour a significant amount of the reservoir onto her foot. The spattering cascade swiftly covered the skin and filled the delicate flesh with ferocious agony.

The wax began to dribble between her toes as they clawed at the air, and only when the whole extremity had been liberally coated did he move to the other. The process had not allowed her to take the second coating any easier, and again he had to step onto her limb to keep in place.

The Warlord stepped free and blew out the candle. Candy stayed spread upon the floor. She stared blankly forward as she panted and wafted on a haze of depraved delectation. Her skin was raw and aching, but her mind was adrift and soaked in dark bliss.

The Warlord chose to take up a heavy flogger and combed his fingers through the thick strands. Candy smiled against the gag as she readied to feel the sultry lick of the leather across her body.

The Warlord employed the weapon to strip away the wax, and the heavy pounding shattered the crust and dragged it away with ease. The snap of it to her body made Candy squirm. Her skin had been left sensitive, and the flogger gave her steady doses of travail. It was easily withstood, and the mild scourging only served to facilitate her prurient mood. The swats to her soles were harder to take, and the handful of swipes he delivered between her legs pushed her tolerances to the limit, but still, Candy managed to endure.

"There. All gone, and since I cleaned your feet, you may now reciprocate and clean my boots, slave," he announced impassively.

He unbuckled the back of the gag, and Candy let it slip from her mouth and drop to the floor. She struggled to get her legs under her and then she shuffled forward on her knees. Bending over, she began to lap at the leather of his footwear. The dust that had been caught in the scrapes and scuffs left a strange acrid taste on her tongue as she devoted herself to the Warlord.

"The Wasteland is such an arid place, as you no doubt found when you arrived here. It takes such a toll on my uniforms, but you're doing a good job of rectifying that," he said wistfully.

Standing to attention, he seemed completely indifferent to her as she scuttled around and polished every inch with a fawning tongue. Her arousal was now burning within her. The derogating act of abasement wove a sultry spell, and as she licked, she pulled at her ropes and yearned to rise higher. Candy ached to feast on his cock or have it invade her, and clamping her thighs together, she swayed and squirmed with licentious passion.

"You're having quite a lot of fun down there aren't you, slave?" he asked.

"Oh yes, Warlord. Thank you."

"Good, then you may pleasure me, slave," he said, as though it were the most minor triviality.

Lady Uzume gave a protesting and envious moan as she continued to suffer because of her pose and because she was going to have to watch that which she was going to be denied.

Candy could predict that the woman would make her suffer for this boon, and the fact that her next session of torture under the woman's rule would be motivated by such jealousy would only make it all the sweeter.

The Warlord gave a pull to area section of the ropes, and they started to open their knots and tumble from her. He then unwound them from her arms, and she was given freedom once more. The Warlord then seemed to ignore her and concentrated instead on forming the weave back into a meticulously neat bundle.

Candy snapped to attention and reached to his trousers. She unfastened the laces at the front and gently reached in to draw him free. He was only semi-erect, because her attentions were nothing too out of the ordinary. For a moment, she considered taking him in her mouth, but then another idea came to her.

Candy held the root of his member and began a slow shuffle of her clenched hand. As she did so, she leaned in and let the tip of her tongue curl around his head. She lapped and felt the organ swelling with appreciation. She took long licks up the length and then stretched herself up.

Taking her breasts, she closed them to his cock and started to stretch her torso up and then retreat a little. Candy quickened her rate to masturbate him between the valley of her assets. She held her flesh tightly to his manhood and watched the end emerge and vanish as she bounced under his gaze.

Candy felt his cock twitch, and the Warlord gave a growling purr of pleasure. Splashes of his seed spattered her neck and breasts. She continued her motions to ensure she fully satisfied him, then slowly sank back down onto the floor. She enveloped him with her mouth and her tongue lavished him with attention as he wilted within her maw, but Warlord Hachiman was not so easily sated. He had other stimulations that rivalled fellatio.

He drew himself from her and slotted himself back into his trousers. Then, and after putting the rope away, he quickly captured her collar with a chain link leash.

"Hmmm. I think I want to have you on display in the garden. There was a new display stand that I wanted ready by the time I returned, and I wish to see if my engineers succeeded."

The Warlord drew Candy away and towards the door, which again parted at his approach. She gave a final look to the deserted form of the sweating and tormented Lady Uzume and saw a savage grin appear against her gag. Uzume knew what Candy was in for, and was visibly relieved that she had not been the one chosen to pleasure her master and thereby earn such a fate. The view was cut off as the door sealed in his wake.

Concerned as to what was in the garden, Candy was shown out through the halls and watched as every priest and slave bowed deeply to their lord.

"This item should be most pleasing to the eye, and also, if you can manage it, you might even be able to earn yourself some pleasure of your own."

Candy tried to think on what might be waiting for her. Images of all the various creations that she had seen swallowing up and bending hapless concubines rushed around in her mind's eye.

The cool and humid winds of the Kami Empire enveloped her as they entered the main courtyard, and she was swiftly shown into the sprawling gardens of pulchritude and bondage.

They came to a small clearing, wherein there arose a small wooden stage. The circular plinth had four small braziers spaced around the perimeter. They were made of cast iron, and the small pile of coals within them was unlit. Three small steps rose to access the display stand, and there was a metal lever rising from one side.

To one side was a section of stage that was clearly cut out from the rest. The disc was obviously designed to rotate and alternate between the two items on offer. One side of the disc had a curved metal beam that bore a wheel at the top whose outer surface was armed with a queue of small rubber tendrils. She could see that when activated, the wheel would spin and lash the air with the small and vicious tongues.

The other side of the disc had a stout wooden post rising from a hole in the floor. Strapped firmly to this post was a female form, and she was kept on her knees by a plethora of leather straps. Her ankles were fixed to the rear of the pole, and her arms were folded up and behind it. She was completely sealed within a sheer catsuit that made her body shimmer as the gossamer fabric accentuated her curves. Her head was pinned back to the pole, and she had been blindfolded by the application of a wide leather strap over her eyes. The interior of the strap was lined with fur that ensured she had no way to even sneak a vague look at what awaited her.

The rotating section of the stage was placed before a wooden frame. The site was shaped like an inverted Y that reclined back and which had numerous straps riveted to it. At the end of the stage opposite to the disc was a small hole from which emerged a length of chain that ended in a large clip and lying beneath the frame was a single leather sleeve. The triangular item had red laces and was adorned with strange curling decorations that were all etched with red stitching.

Candy was delivered to the frame and laid back against it. The Warlord fixed belts across her chest in a cross formation and hauled on them so that she was pressed into the smooth, varnished timbers. Another was drawn across her forehead to leave her staring up at the overhanging branches of the clearing and the patch of sky visible through them.

The Warlord drew her legs apart upon the wide *V* section of the frame, and her ankles were bound. Straps ran above and below her knees, over her thighs, and then another tight embrace was pulled over her inner thigh and to each hip. These last straps hauled her hindquarters to the pole as another cross section was dragged over her stomach and tightened to an exceedingly intense degree. Utterly immobilised, Candy felt him take her arms and draw them straight down.

He pulled the sleeve onto them and forced her hands into the single ball at the end. The laces were hauled in to ensure her limbs were pushed together, and the overlaying buckles were applied to further add to her security. The sleeve was held in place by two straps that reached up to grab the underside of the frame and prevent her sloughing it off.

Candy gave a whimper of pain as he took the clip that resided at the pointed end of the sleeve and started to drag it away. The contortion made her shoulders flare with havoc, and the twist to her arms made her strain against the numerous straps. The waiting chain was attached to the end of her glove, and she was left with her arms bent back to a highly uncomfortable degree.

"Wh . . . what's going to happen to me, Warlord?"

"No more words, slave. This is a place of silent condemnation," he reported, and from the side of the beam he lifted another strap. The leather strip was pulled over her maw, and a large stout phallus was revealed on the inside. The rubber affair was stumpy and spread her jaws wide before it plunged in and was fixed firmly into irrevocable place.

"I'll leave you now, slave, and you can try and figure out the dynamics of this little display all by yourself."

Candy heard him pull the lever back, and from within the depths of the stage came several cranking grinds and some soft switching sounds. The wheel started to whirl, and she heard the soft whistle of its many small whips hurtling through the air between her legs. The disc between her extended feet started to turn, but she could not see which way or how far.

Puzzled, Candy focused on the pain in her arms. It was starting to make them flicker with more stress than she could easily accept. She pulled on the chain and found that it moved. She pulled harder, and it moved a little more. Straining with effort, Candy combated the anonymous weight that was attached to the chain and sought alleviate the stress on her arms.

Candy unexpectedly felt a warm breath against her inner thighs, and she gave a gasp before her arms went slack from shock. The weight yanked them back into position and created a painful wrench to her shoulders. She cried out against the gag and struggled to draw her arms back down again.

Candy kept her efforts going until she felt the breath of the girl again. She closed her eyes and gave a quick prayer that the eventuality that she was hoping for would manifest. Candy then pulled a little more.

The girl's lips touched her pussy, and instantly the slave was spilling her eager tongue into Candy. The girl assailed her with diligent kisses and a suckling attention that made her mewl and arch against her bonds. The muscles in her arms started to heat from strenuous exertion. The chain was connected somehow to the submerged area of the girl's post. When the girl was facing her loins, pulling on the chain would pivot her over and into her pussy.

Candy's limbs were soon burning, but the glorious feel of the girl lapping at her sex was too deliriously pleasant to let go of. Beads of sweat appeared on her face as she snorted and fought to hold her in position for as long as she could. With an angry snort, she finally had to give up. The chain drew her arms back, and the woman was towed out of position.

The stage made some more covert noises, and after a few moments to again gather her strength, Candy started to pull. It was a terrible torment to have to fight so hard to gain the girl's tongue and then to be made to endure the monstrous efforts to keep it there, but if she could show the strength, she could earn the pleasure. The Warlord had indeed created an admirable site of fiendish torment for her.

Candy gave a squeal as she felt the whirling rubber strands lick between her legs. She instantly relaxed her arms, and they were jerked back into position, but the wheel did not retreat, and to her horror, it actually clicked a little closer. Candy jolted and strained against her bonds, trying to find some way in which to move her crotch out of its infernal range. The wheel spun unevenly, tilting from side to side so that it distributed the stinging swats across her inner thighs as well as against her sex. Hollering against the gag, Candy suffered a prolonged scourging before the stage gave a deep clunk and the wheel retreated.

Gasping for breath and with her senses reeling, she tried to recover from the awful experience. She now knew the full measure of her ordeal. She could languish in her confinement and endure the bondage. On the other hand, she could pull on her sleeve, exercise her arms, and draw something between her legs. The girl would pleasure her for as long as she could hold her there, but the disc randomly changed, and she might end up pulling the whips in. If that happened, she would have to endure a prescribed duration of their abuse.

The whipping had been harsh enough that she initially chose to refuse the offered effects of the stage, so Candy lay in the firm arms of the frame and stared blankly at the sky. Her arms were again aching, and she lifted them back just a little to ease their suffering. She made sure not to draw anything too close between her legs, and after a few stretches she let them relax again.

She managed to fight off temptation for a time, but the boredom of the position soon started to set in. She was used to input, and although she feared the whips, she desperately wanted the attention. Lingering on the frame, all she had to pass the time was dwelling on her memories. The time in the pit with Lady Uzume, the Warlord, the many pleasures and wonders she had seen and experienced in the Kami Empire. Eventually she could tolerate no more, and with a resigned sigh at her lack of willpower, she gingerly started to pull on the chain.

Candy stared down as best she could and tried to gain even the most fleeting clue as to what was coming towards her proffered pudenda. If she could get just a glimpse, she might be able to find out what was scheduled for her and perhaps avoid it by letting it go before the stage committed to a setting.

With her arms flexed, she gradually pulled in small increments, hoping that if she felt the whips, she might be able to let them retreat before she activated the process that drew them in and locked them in position.

She felt a steady brush of air against her pussy and instantly let go. It was too late. The mechanism engaged and drew the whips in as Candy hollered and tried to stop them. She lurched against the bonds, and the leather straps creaked with strain as she felt the awful swipes slapping against her thighs and sex. There was nothing that she could do to affect her plight, and she was left to endure the terrible punishment.

The whips retreated, and Candy sagged within the straps. She could feel the tickle of sweat as it trickled down her form. She shivered and recovered her breath, and despite the distress the whips imparted, the feeling of abandonment to this dreadful machine was highly titillating. She had the option of just accepting the bondage, but if she wanted more, she had to risk the consequences. She was served to a fate that she herself brought down, and each session of pussy flogging was engineered by her own wanton urges. It felt just, it felt proper, it felt divine.

She pulled on the glove and almost hoped for another session of the whip. There was now a resonating heat between her legs, and it was making her libido unfurl.

Candy shuddered as a warm wet organ tunnelled into her body and then retreated to tickle her clit. She tensed instinctively, and this pushed the mouth even more firmly between her legs. Candy held the girl there so she could let her explore her with her tongue while Candy herself moaned with ecstasy against her gag.

The girl continued with alacrity and drove Candy towards orgasm. Her long session of bondage and fantasy had stirred her arousal, and the flogging between her legs had greatly bolstered it. The problem was that she was almost out of strength. Her arms were torn with strain, and she was having to fight for every second of enforced oral servitude. Her face was flushed with tension, and she clenched her jaws to the gag to try to find the energy. All she needed was a few more moments, but the stress was keeping orgasm at bay. Her fight to keep the girl in place was eating at her pleasure and making it harder to acquire. Climax was only seconds away but the harder she fought the more slowly it approached. Eventually she felt a muscle flash with a sudden flick of pain, and she was forced to relax. She yelled her fury against the gag as her arms were tugged back and the girl vanished. Snapping her limbs against the bonds, she cursed her deprivation. Her loins were churning with rhapsody. A few licks, a single long stroke of her clit, even a kiss, and she would be there.

Candy tried to move her hips, to try to bring herself to orgasm through willpower alone. It was a foolish dream, but she was so frustrated she had no option but to try.

Candy let her arms rest for a while. If she managed to acquire the woman again, she wanted to ensure she snatched climax before she became exhausted. When she felt more confident, she started to pull on the chain.

She gave a huff of relief as the girl graced her pussy with her tongue and began to attend her with every portion of skill and effort she could muster. They were both slaves, and when they had the chance, they tried to do everything they could to pleasure one another. Candy was grateful for the girl's diligence and would have dearly loved to return the favour. If they encountered one another again, perhaps she could, but for now, she was the subject and the girl was the sex toy.

Candy thought she heard footsteps, and then she darted her eyes to her side as she saw two figures appear. The two men looked over her bound body with intrigue and amusement. She stared at them with longing, hoping that they might help her. One of them was tall and dark skinned. His head was shaved, and he had a brawny physique. He wore a studded chest harness and dense leather gauntlets on his forearms. The other was a slim individual who had accentuated the paleness of his skin with a black leather waistcoat. His long brown hair was formed into a tight plait with several barbed decorations set along it to help keep the mane under control.

"So this is the one from the other side?" asked the pale warrior.

"Everyone seems to have her name on their lips. Lady Uzume and her Mikado seem highly taken with her. I wonder why? She doesn't look like anything special."

"But she got to play with the Wani daughters, so one must wonder what Ame-waka-hiko thinks of her."

"The Warlord has been keeping his Mikado too busy. If the plan goes ahead, he'll have to be ready."

"If the plan goes ahead, there'll be plenty more like her to sample. Then they won't be quite so precious."

"It'll never happen. It's just an experiment to see who is loyal and who is anxious to advance. Those who are content will continue as normal, those with ambition will start to jockey for more power, new commands. Amatsu mika hoshi is probably just testing the Kami."

"Well, if it's a dream, it's one I shall indulge."

"Speaking of indulgence, shall we have some fun with her?"

"You believe it's permitted?"

"If she's supposed to be kept private, they shouldn't have

put her out here on display."

Candy watched with wide eyes as they started to strip. The sun was starting to set, and priests could be glimpsed lighting braziers and torches. As stout columns of flame spread a warm radiance through the gardens, Candy tensed against her bonds and readied for what was no doubt going to be a very long night.

Her thoughts momentarily turned to Yakami, but they did not linger. People drifted in and out of her life so quickly now. They were fleeting presences that contributed to her experiences and then vanished. Now that she was with Warlord Hachiman, would she see Yakami again? Or Oshin? Had they joined the Slavemaster, her Captain, and Lei, in a forsaken past?

The Kami Empire had consumed her, and there was still so much more to explore and learn of this wondrous place. Somehow, she knew that her questions could not even vaguely encompass the number of hidden answers.

The two officers closed in, chuckling with merriment as the bound form of Candy lay captive before their desire. Candy stared up at the sky and smiled contently against her gag.

Candy's adventures in the Kami Empire and the secrets she finds continue in
Dragon Candy 2.

GLOSSARY FOR THE KAMI EMPIRE

Izanagi and *Izanami*: The creator deities, the names of the two forces whose interplay create and move the vortex between Earth and Pangaea.

The Kami: the various deities of earth and heaven. The lords and manifestations of thought, deed, and substance.

Mitama: The essence or emanation of god or spirit. The name given to the Imperial Army that enforces the will of the Kami and marches under the banner of *A-Katsu* (I conquer).

Shintai: The God body, the earth form, or symbol of a deity.

The Primary Powers of the Kami Empire

Yatakagami: The Sun Goddess. Supreme Ruler of the land who is always accompanied by her sacred crow — *Yatagarusa*.

Musubi: Lord of growth. He is the tactician, the planner, and chief advisor to the Sun Goddess.

Tsuki-yomi: The Moon God. The lord of darkness. He is the keeper of time, and his House plots the path of the vortex on Earth. His House alone is not subject to the rule of the Sun Goddess.

Amatsu mika hoshi (Dread star of heaven): He knows all, but cannot leave his shrine. He controls a vast and highly secretive spy network that watches the Empire, the lands about them, and trains the operatives that go across to Earth to send ships and planes into the vortex. He is the chief advisor to the Moon God.

The Kami of Water

Toyo-tama-hiko (Rich jewel prince): Supreme Warlord of the Water.

Naka-tsu-wata-dzu-mi (Middle sea body): His House conducts submerged patrols in the ocean waters. His troops ride aquatic Dinosaurs such as the seventeen-metre long Kronosaurus.

Uha-tsu-wata-dzu-mi (Upper sea body): His House provides surface vessels and reptilian steeds to protect and patrol the ocean traffic.

Soko-tsu-wata-dzu-mi (Bottom sea body): Warlord of the deep. His House oversees seabed construction and harvesting, along with ocean bed mining for valuable minerals.

Midzu-chi (Water-father): Warlord of the Rivers. His House conducts river patrols to maintain security and order either by boat, or on trained fifteen-metre-long Phobosuchus (Horror crocodile).

Midzuha no me (Water-female): The concubines of the Great Houses of Water.

The Kami of Air

Ame no minaka-nushi: Supreme Warlord of the air

Shinatsu-hiko: Lord of the Wind. His House is responsible for the sending of all radio communication.

Shinatobe: Lady of the Wind. Her House is responsible for the receiving of all radio communication.

Hayachi (Swift father): The Messenger. His House handles all overland messages and items of import, and sees to their safe delivery.

The Kami of Fire

Take-mika-dzuchi (Brave-dread-father): The master of thunder, Warlord of the artillery regiments.

Hachiman: the Warlord who commands the Mitama.

Ame-waka-hiko (heaven-young-prince): His Mikado and highest-ranking general.

Uzume (Dread female): His most feared and ruthless agent.

Ashua: Guardian Warlord of the courtyard, protector of the inner lands. His House is the police force of the Empire.

Toyotama-hiko: the Dragon Warlord. He is part Wani and second in command to Warlord Hachiman.

Wani (Dragon): Eggs of the Dinosaur tribes were taken centuries ago, and the offspring raised as Wani. From the best of these warriors were bred more until an army was created. They are now fanatically loyal warriors. They are fierce, fearless, and serve as the backbone of the Mitama.

The Kami of Earth

Kagu-tsuchi (Radiant father): The fire god. Lord of power and energy, his House runs the nuclear plants.

Kamado no Kami: The furnace deity. Lord of the furnaces of wood, oil, coal, and hydroelectricity.

Inari: The Lord of the rice fields. His House sees to the feeding of the general population.

Susa no wo: The Lord of rain. His House oversees all plumbing and irrigation.

Oho-toshi (Great harvest): The lord of gathering. His House sees to the harvest and the safe storing of all food.

Uka no mitama: Lord of the food spirit. His House ensures good crops and plentiful harvests. They provide knowledge, equipment, and expertise to guarantee growth. They breed and raise the best herds for slaughter. They also train humans to fulfil the role of beasts.

Ho no Susori: Lord of the fishermen. His House builds boats, provides equipment, and sees to the smooth running of the fishing fleet.

Hohodemi: Lord of the hunt. His House hunts Dinosaurs to replenish the stock. They also see to the breeding and training of new steeds and herd animals for domestic use. They also train human ponies.

Sukuna-bikona: (Little prince): A House of dwarves that see to the brewing of wines and other drink. They also produce many medicinal remedies and maintain a large medicinal thermal springs. It is in his underground palace that the sacred spring of longevity is located.

Temmangu: The Lord of learning and calligraphy. They are the teachers of the young and old, and indoctrinate and educate new slaves.

Ishikoridome: The stonecutter Lord. His House is one of architecture and building.

Toyo-tama: (Rich jewel): His House are jewellers, and makers of finery.

Ohonamochi: Lord of physicians. His House tends the injured, the sick, and the many slaves of the Empire to ensure their health and survival.

Yama tsu mi (Mountain-body): Lord of the trees. His House is responsible for tree-cutting, lumber, timber, and the maintaining of forests.

The ranks of the Kami Priesthood

Mikado: Chief Priests of a Kami. They see to the running of the House and its affairs and responsibilities.

Nakatomi: Mediators between the priests and the Kami. They regulate and assign the slaves of a House as the Kami or Mikado decree.

Imbe: The preparers. They ensure that the lower ranks see to the preparation, cleanliness, and order of slaves, equipment, and chambers.

Hafuri: Inferior grade priests that see to the basic tasks of the House and its responsibilities.

Negi: The lowest priestly rank that is responsible for the most mundane functions of the House.

Kamube: A slave who has earned freedom through

exemplary conduct and service and now tends the House as the priest's dictate while still holding authority over other *Kami-tsu-ko*.

Kami-tsu-ko: A slave dedicated to a House.

The Underworld of the Kami Empire

Yomi: The land of darkness where slaves and criminals are banished. Once sent to Yomi, one may never return unless via personal pardon from both Sun Goddess and Moon God.

Bimbo-gami: The Lord of poverty. The Kami of sexual frustration, teasing, and enforced chastity.

Naki-sahame: The Lady of weeping. The feared sadistic dominatrix of Yomi.

Ashiki kami: The rulers of Yomi.

Oni: The inhabitants of Yomi. Many are former *Hafuri-tsu-mono* and have been elevated from that caste to assist in the running of the realm.

Hafuri-tsu-mono (flung away things): Those sent to Yomi.

About the Author

Born and raised in San Francisco, Talia Skye spent part of her early career living and working in Japan where she discovered her passion for writing, scifi, and BDSM. She currently lives in London, and continues to explore those worlds.